Ember

ECHOES OF ASHES
BOOK ONE

J. E. SCHMIDT

ILLUSTRATED BY HOLLY HILLMAN

Owl Griffin
Press

Copyright 2018 J. E. Schmidt
Echoes of Ashes: Ember – Book One
By J. E. Schmidt

ISBN-13: 978-0692985434
ISBN-10: 0692985433
LCCN: 2017917896

Published by Owl Griffin Press

Illustrator: Holly Hillman
Cover Artist: Jennifer Munswami

Rogena Mitchell-Jones, Literary Editor
RMJ Manuscript Service LLC
www.rogenamitchell.com

Owl Griffin

─── Press ───

FOR MY MOM

TABLE OF CONTENTS

Shields may break, crossbows snap, swords rust in their sheath.
Fear not, young pup, if this doth pass, you'll always have your
teeth.

—Stanza from a canid lullaby

Look at him! Look at his ears! Such demonic features; tempting
our women, soiling our society with vicious mockery! No longer!
He shall taint us no longer! For it is the will of the Goddess that
we must eliminate this evil from the eyes of our children and our
elders!

—Naviar Soloth, priest of Lisia,
Crucifixion of the Elves, 524 P.A.

Fear is not something that holds us back. I dare say it is the
greatest motivator of them all.

—King Hadvark, Rokswing, 1015 P.A.

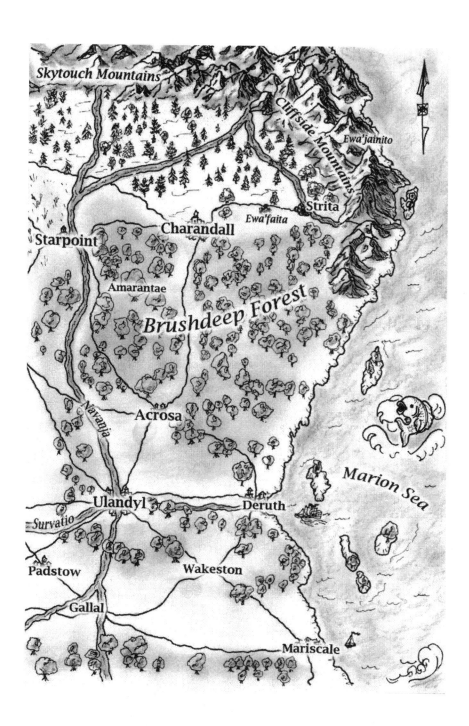

PROLOGUE

LIGHTNING FORKED ACROSS the sky, electric tendrils grasping at clouds and spreading like embers over a fire. Its flash in the night illuminated the forest below... if only for a moment, casting stark shadows on the faces of the bloodhungry canidae stalking through the woods. They had been hunting for days, relentless in the pursuit of their prey. Their leader, a gray canid called Karkos, lifted his nose and inhaled deeply, nostrils fanning and absorbing the scents in the air.

Canidae are the anthropomorphic wolf people of the Far Land, coming in all varieties of colors and breeds. These canidae, however, were quite unusual. They were bloodhungry, having consumed the flesh of another sentient creature, and thus were corrupted, preferring the blood of that race of creature to all else. This made them excellent bounty hunters and often cold-blooded killers. And, though bloodhungry hardly ever worked together, these canidae were for a specific purpose. A mission—one they must not fail.

The rain was delaying their progress, muting the scents

around them. It was making it even more difficult to track the elf girl, and Karkos's small pack was getting frustrated. He could hear them muttering and whispering behind him as they walked, clearly disgruntled with hunting this late at night and in the rain. Their pelts were dripping, their armor soaked, and they smelled vividly of wet dog.

"Quiet," Karkos growled, baring his teeth slightly and angling his head to look at them. They fell silent as he eyed them. His ruby irises glinted as lightning flashed once more. "We are too close to give up now. It could be another *month* before we find her again, like last time. I don't think any of us want that." His gaze never wavered, settling on them each in turn. After a moment, he turned forward again, gesturing. "Fan out. I thought I smelled her directly ahead."

They spread out in a wide formation, combing through the woods with their noses in the air. Thunder cracked right above them, the earth under their feet vibrating from the sound. Several canidae had already drawn their swords, as they were more fearful than the others were. On high alert, their ears perked up and swiveled to capture the quietest of sounds, even through the pounding rain. These nervous canidae were the oldest recruits, having tracked the elf girl from the very beginning. They had seen what she could do, and they would not be caught off guard.

Their search dragged on through the night as the girl's scent fluctuated from strong to weak every few minutes. They appeared to be making little progress. It seemed hopeless once again, and they began to worry they would have to start from scratch to find her. The rain was relentless, each droplet that struck them lowering their morale.

Suddenly, a glimmer of hope. "Here!" howled one of the canidae far to the left. The others howled in response, blood pumping through their veins in anticipation of the hunt to come. They turned to close in on their comrade's location, sprinting through the mud. Lightning flashed again, and thunder, like

2

cannon fire, sounded soon after.

Without warning, right in front of them, a new light flashed. Several of the experienced bloodhungry stopped in their tracks, whining in fear, for they already knew what had happened.

"You cowards!" snarled Karkos, in the lead, continuing his pursuit. He came to a small clearing, though it was not natural. The trees blasted away by something powerful, their trunks smoking and cracked. Those closest to the center of the blast were nearly disintegrated—and lying on the forest floor at the apex of the blast site was a canid.

Karkos came to a stop when he reached the scene, feeling grim. The other canidae came out of the woods, in turn, each coming to a halt when they realized what had happened. After a moment, Karkos approached the body of his pack member, kneeling beside him and pulling his eyes shut with his clawed fingers. One of the bloodhungry behind him howled as the others soon joined into a mournful chorus. The eerie sound could be heard for miles, and even the clap of thunder could not silence them.

"At least he fed one last time," lamented Karkos, noting the blood around the dead canid's muzzle. His bloodhungry instinct tempted him to lick the blood from the dead body, but he resisted, keeping his composure regardless of how intoxicating the elf blood smelled. He turned, instead, to his fearful pack members, who looked to him for inspiration, though fear filled their red eyes.

"We are closer than ever before!" Karkos barked. "Our fallen comrade was able to weaken our prey before taking his last breath. He tasted her flesh!" The tails of the other canidae began to wag, several of them opening their jaws to pant with anticipation, drool collecting at the corners of their mouths. "Know this: once we catch her, we will be rewarded with more elves than we can possibly eat!" His tone fell dark as he looked each of them in their scarlet eyes in turn. "But we must

3

remember, should we fail, our fates will be worse than death."

He turned around toward her scent, which was now much stronger than before. He pointed toward the treeline with his sword. "Now go! Find her!" he howled. The others howled back in return, and they took off into the woods, renewed resolve consuming their every breath.

CHAPTER 1

IN A WOODED land of old, a bustling river town lay dotted within the trees. This crossroads was the permanent home of few, but the temporary lodging of many. Those permanent residents were nearly all of the race of mortal creatures called felidae, who built the town centuries ago to reap the location's potential for trade—for this town of Ulandyl was positioned very deliberately at the meeting place of not only two large rivers but two main roads as well.

The felidae, or cat folk, known to be both clever and quiet, often deal with money and trade, and with their sly tongues, they are often able to secure the most fruitful bargains. A handsome species, they come in many colors and breeds. Their tails vary in length, their ears and muzzles as well, and altogether, simply appearing to be bipedal cats, but with the ability to spin the smoothest of tales and tell the most convincing, wicked lies.

They are the people of Ulandyl, making their living off the travelers, be it through trade and barter or thievery and deception. Nevertheless, Ulandyl was filled with kind people who always had a story to tell and a job to offer, and this was one of the reasons Laderic often found himself passing through, and even staying perhaps a day or so longer than necessary.

On one particular day, seated in a small, local tavern, he picked up on some information that would change his life forever.

Bang! Through the old tavern door burst a pair of worn-out men, whispering amongst themselves. The rain tapped on the wooden roof as the swollen river had risen more than a few feet, thundering on its course without delay. The two men were sopping wet, dripping from their coats, and wetting the dirty, wooden floor. It was several hours past midnight, and they caught Laderic's attention. He sat alone, his own pint hardly touched. His eyes drifted over to them, but his face remained stoic.

"I'm telling you, there were at least six of them," said one of the men to his comrade. The felid barkeep angled his head toward the men, who were speaking as if they didn't care who was listening. However, with most of the tavern's residents already asleep at this hour, there were hardly any people around who might overhear.

"I'm sure you were only seeing things," scoffed the other, flipping off his hood. His hair was black and shaggy, and a thick mustache crowned his mouth. "Bloodhungry hardly ever travel in groups. Why, they hardly travel in pairs!"

The other man flipped his hood off, as well. His eyes were wide, fearful, his hair lighter in color with a clean-shaven face. "I am telling you what I saw," he said, quieter this time. "And these were working together, tracking something."

Laderic sat up a bit straighter at his table, lifting his pint and taking a drink. The two men seemed to notice him then, tilting their heads toward him, and pausing for a second. "What were they tracking?" Laderic asked nonchalantly, sounding bored and vaguely skeptical. He inspected his tankard closely as if it were bothering him.

The man who appeared scared looked at his friend, and then back at Laderic. "I–I couldn't see in the dark. It was raining, and I couldn't see anything but someone running in a cloak. That was it," he said.

The other man shook his head again. "You're just tired, Harlan. And it's raining. It was probably just a couple of *regular* canidae, chasing a deer or something."

"No, it *wasn't*," countered Harlan. He wrung his hands. "I know a bloodhungry when I see one. Besides, canidae aren't usually this close to Ulandyl unless they have to be." He turned to look at Laderic. "You believe me, right?"

An unconscious man at a nearby table snorted, shifting a bit in his drunken state. There was a long silence in the room except for the constant rapping of the rain.

Laderic stared back at the man, pondering for a while before shaking his head. "Your friend is right," he said. "It's dark, raining, and late. You might have just got scared and seen things your mind fabricated in the darkness."

"No, I know what I saw!" He slammed his fist down on the table. "Just you wait. I'll find *someone* who believes me." With that, he stood, whirling around toward the stairs. His coat flared out behind him, flinging droplets of water onto the floor. He marched toward the felid barkeep, shoving a few coins into his paw, and heading up the stairs.

The other man sighed, standing up, and glancing at Laderic. "Sorry about that. He isn't very fond of the dark. Especially by himself."

"Who is?" remarked Laderic. "Especially in these times."

The man nodded. "Ay. The name is Yasser. My brother is Harlan. Sorry to have caused you any grief tonight." That last part he addressed to both Laderic and the barkeep. He smiled grimly. "Enjoy your drink." He turned, walking toward the stairs as he looked at the bartender. The cat man nodded, gesturing up for him to continue, for Harlan had paid enough for them both.

Before he made it to the third step, Laderic made his decision. "Yasser," he called. The man turned his head.

"Yes?" he asked, hesitantly.

"Where did your brother say he saw this pack of canidae?" Laderic asked curiously. He raised one of his arms above his head, stretching a bit to shake off his stiffness.

"Only a few miles south of here, just below the river crossing, in the Weald. He said they were running through the woods when he saw them, just before he crossed the bridge." He turned completely around, facing Laderic once more. "Why do you ask?"

Laderic shrugged. "No reason. Just curious about which area I should think about avoiding the next few days." He locked eyes with Yasser, unblinking. The man stared back, thinking.

Finally, he shrugged. "I guess... if you put any stock into this story of his." He turned back around and headed up the stairs. "You have a good night."

"You too..." muttered Laderic, too quiet for him to hear. He stared at his cup, turning it between his hands. He had hardly touched the alcohol inside. He wasn't even quite sure why he had bought it, not being much of a drinker himself. More out of boredom, if anything, he supposed. *What else is a mercenary to do on a jobless night?*

But now... it appeared as if he had received a stroke of luck with Harlan's story. What better to do than rescue a poor soul from a pack of bloodhungry canidae? In exchange, of course, for a reward.

He shivered at the thought of it, however. Canidae were not his favorite species to... well, *take care of.* Like felidae, canidae are animalistic-looking folk, with the most basic difference being they take after wolves instead of cats. Aside from that, the two are different in nearly every way. While felids are very tactful and good with their words, canidae prefer to fight first, ask

8

questions later. Those Laderic had had dealings with were kind, yet blunt and loyal as ever. However, they were fierce warriors with nearly unlimited stamina and a pack mentality to their core.

Combine that with being bloodhungry and... Laderic shuddered once more as he stood from his table. He had dealt with only a few bloodhungry in his day. One was canidae, and it was by far the nastiest to deal with, but even though it had been a canid, it had still traveled alone.

Bloodhungry is the common term used for any canid or felid that had tasted the blood of one of the sentient creatures of the Far Land. By nature... once tasting the blood of another sentient being, they begin to prefer that blood to all else, going out of their way to murder the innocent to feed their hunger. They remain sentient themselves, though transformed into beasts with an uncontrollable urge to hunt and consume members of their chosen species—be it dwarves, humans, or even other canidae and felidae.

However beastly and inhumane their actions, their preference for a certain type of blood makes them excellent bounty hunters—if you don't mind overlooking the innocent people that would be murdered by them in the process to sate their hunger. Some have no limits on what they would do to fulfill their personal desires, no matter the cost—regardless of who it is they have to hire to get the job done.

Bloodhungry are outcasts, feared by society, and therefore, work and exist in solitude. Their peers shun even the ones who try to control their urges, the sight of their piercing red eyes being too much for most to bear. Laderic sighed as he reached toward the ground and grabbed his leather bag, slinging it over his shoulders on top of his coat.

"Rismak," Laderic said, addressing the barkeep. The russet colored felid swiveled his ears in his direction. "Do you happen to know if Midiga still lives in that same house, up a couple blocks near the market?"

9

This task would require more than just himself, and if Laderic could trust anyone to back him up in Ulandyl, it was Midiga.

Rismak padded over toward the corner of the bar where Laderic stood. "As far as I know, she still does," he confirmed with a purr. "You aren't actually going south of the river at this time of night, are you?" he asked, concerned. Rismak had known Laderic for many years, having grown quite fond of both him and his consistent business. "You aren't a felid. You cannot see in the dark."

"Ah, Rismak, that is what torches are for," said the mercenary with a grin as he started toward the door. "Keep the pay for my room tonight, in case I return alive." He was joking, but the cat took him seriously.

"Don't do anything risky," warned the felid ominously as Laderic opened the door.

"It's me. I'll be fine," he assured. He pulled his hood over his head and walked out into the rain.

CHAPTER 2

THE DOWNPOUR WAS relentless as Laderic walked the dark streets of Ulandyl. Felids, with the natural ability to see in the dark, had never quite got around to lighting their roads with torches or lanterns. In their mind, if you cannot see in the dark, don't go out in the dark. It was very simple.

Yeah, right, Laderic thought, trudging through the mud, ducking his head into his coat to keep some of the rain off his face. The city of Ulandyl was quite spread out, covering all corners of the crossing where the rivers met. Six bridges spanned the rivers, connecting each of the four quadrants of the city. Four of them made a square atop the waters, and the other two connected diagonally above where the rivers met, forming an X shape. In the middle of the X was a tall lighthouse, the beacon shining at all times.

Throughout the water, around the network of bridges, were houses and hotels on stilts, providing space for travelers to stay for more than reasonable rates at all times of the year. If you could overlook the fact that you were suspended above the rushing river and pointed boulders that peeked their heads through the black water every now and then, they were quite worth the bargain.

The rivers that met were called Navanja and Servatio, running north to south and east to west, respectively. Where they met in the center of Ulandyl, the water constantly raged. As each river fought with the other to flow in their desired direction, neither gained an advantage. Choppy water and rough waves made it nearly impossible for boats to cross through the city, so the docks were spaced along its perimeter. If goods needed to be transferred downriver, they would first need to be unloaded to shore and carted across the bridges to the other docks.

The wide bridges that created an *X* above the crossing were an extension of two major roads that intersected just where the rivers met. The road that led to the northwest was named Laborem. The road that led to the northeast was referred to as The Walk. These two paths were some of the most traveled roads in the Far Land, and thus, Ulandyl was quite prosperous.

The Savage Lion Inn—the tavern Laderic had just left—was in the northeastern section of the city with the rivers to the west and south. Laderic, however, headed north toward some of the more permanent houses, where most of the felid residents lived. The streets were empty. Felidae generally out during the night were instead holed up in their houses out of the deluge. The rain poured, and as he walked, miniature rivers of mud ran around his boots as they squelched down the road. But he was close. Up another hill and around the corner, he came to a line of older houses in one of the more established parts of the city.

Midiga's home was a small, wooden place with one door, two windows, and a chimney. Laderic knocked on the door, huddled in his coat. "Midiga!" he called. No answer. The rain was relentless. He knocked again, harder this time. "Midiga, I know for a fact that half of your race is nocturnal. I know you happen to belong to that half. Please, open up! It's cold!" Still no answer. "And wet!" Nothing. Laderic sighed. "If this is about that time in Padstow, for the fiftieth time, I'm sorry!" There was more silence, and Laderic was about to give up until he heard the sound of several locks being undone. The door swung open, and Laderic stormed inside, out of the rain. "Gods, Midiga, I hate water just as much as you do!"

"Well, you shouldn't have pulled that stunt in Padstow then, hmm?" purred a feminine voice. From the shadows of the room paced the elegant feline. Her fur was a sleek blue-gray color, like a deep colored smoke. She was nearly indistinguishable from the darkness around them, and without the dim light from the coals in the fireplace, Laderic wouldn't have been able to see her at all, save for her sparkling amber eyes and a patch of white fur on her forearm shaped like a crescent moon.

"It was one time. And it wasn't my fault... Can you light a torch?" he asked, looking around, frustrated. "Not all of us can see in the dark, you know."

Midiga chuckled, removing a torch from its sconce and lighting it with the coals. "Better?" she asked, mounting the torch again. Her long tail swept from side to side with her hips as she walked. "Do you have that money you owe me?" she asked, raising her eyebrow.

"Uh, well, not exactly," Laderic stammered, having completely forgotten he owed her anything in the first place. He looked around, trying to change the subject. "I see you've been doing well," he said, gesturing around the room. The house was quaint and cozy. Animal pelts hung on the walls with large metal hooks. In the corner was a mat on the floor, plush and filled with down. There was one chest, a small table, and a single chair. The rest of the room was bare.

"I like to think so," she chittered, looking around as well, purring warmly. She smiled, pointed ivories showing. "I don't need much."

She demonstrated this even in her clothing. She wore simple cotton clothes, neutral in color, and as minimal as she could get away with. Felids never wore shoes.

"What brings you to my den?" she asked. Laderic took a seat in her chair, laying his coat on the floor beside the fire to dry. He ran his fingers through his hair, shaking the water out of it. Despite his best efforts, he was still damp as ever. He sighed, resigning himself, before turning to face Midiga.

"I got a tip a little bit ago that I figured might interest you," he began. He then relayed the story of the two men entering the tavern and their own story of the bloodhungry canidae. The cat listened intently, both ears swiveled in his direction. "He said there were at least six," he finished, leaning back.

"Impossible, bloodhungry hardly ever work together, not even in pairs," she hissed, ears flattening against her skull. Her claws sheathed and unsheathed with anxiety.

Laderic shrugged. "Maybe. That's what I was thinking too, but there has to be *some* truth to his story, and even if it's just two traveling together running down some poor wretch, we still might get some kind of reward out of it." He crossed his arms, waiting for her verdict.

Midiga growled under her breath. "If it gives me a chance to kill some dogs, I'm in," she decided. Felidae are naturally nervous around canidae, even if they aren't bloodhungry. Midiga, having grown up in Ulandyl where canidae were quite uncommon, scarcely tried to disguise her racism, and since she'd had quite a few bad experiences with them in the past, she believed her negative disposition was more than justified.

Laderic nodded. "We can loot their things and see what payment the victim might provide... if they're still alive. Maybe there will be enough to cover what I owe you, and we might get some leads on where others might be. I don't like bloodhungry any more than the next man—"

"Or cat," Midiga interjected with a grin. She didn't like to admit it, but she was excited at the idea of chasing a lead. She had been dying to get out of Ulandyl recently. It had been over a year since she had last had any excitement. Much too long in her own opinion. She was a wanderer at heart and had been sedentary for too long. She hated not having anything to do. It gave her too much time to think, to drown in her own thoughts.

Midiga looked Laderic over once again, ears tilting in his direction as she changed her tone. "Where have you been, Laderic? It's been a long time since your last stop through Ulandyl." Her eyes scanned him, and she furrowed her brow, worried. "Hopefully, not getting into too much trouble."

Laderic's mind flashed through his escapades of the last year. He glanced at his bag on the floor behind him. "Nothing too rough, just the same as always. Steal from the rich, give to the needy, keep whatever's leftover—you know the drill." He swallowed, glancing at his bag and back at Midiga. "Well... actually... gods, I don't know if I should even show you."

"What is it?" she questioned, ears perking up. Her tail flicked left and right with anticipation.

Laderic sighed, pulling his pack off and rifling through it. He pulled out a small pouch, one that fit in his palm. Midiga watching, he gently pulled the strings to open it, revealing a sparkling stone that had its own sort of light, shining with a brilliant ruby color.

"A spectral stone!" The felid recognized what it was immediately, eyes wide in awe. Subconsciously, her hand drifted toward the gem, as if drawn by an unseen force. She flattened her ears slightly, looking back up at him. "Why haven't you sold this? You could get quite the price for this one. You'd have enough to repay me three times over!"

"Yeah, or take the chance that someone would rat me out for having it," he replied, putting it back in the pouch. "The goblins that had the stone didn't know what it was, or so they claimed before I killed them." He put the pouch back in his bag. "You

16

know how it is. Getting caught with one of these can get you thrown in jail, or worse, sent to deal with the spectral it belongs to. I'd rather try to return it to them. It's the only way I can see myself getting any kind of reward out of it." He grimaced, imagining himself being caught and forced to face the spectral it was stolen from. "It's the safest way, anyhow."

Spectrals are beings born with an affinity for the truest kind of natural magic. Human in appearance, they are consumed by an element before birth. Once this element comes to fruition, they are trained as powerful sorcerers, remaining aloof from the rest of the world to practice the art of magic. Once trained, they select a stone to become their spectral stone, which they meditate with each day for the rest of their lives. It focuses their power, and they are able to store energy for later use. After years of meditation, the stones become wells of energy, able to be accessed at a moment's notice to allow the spectrals to perform amazing magical feats.

Most spectral stones are worn as pendants or found in staves or crowns. However, the one Laderic had in his possession was the naked stone on its own. A fire-dancer stone at that. If the spectral that lost their stone were to discover Laderic had tried to pawn it, he would be hunted and likely burned to a crisp. It is extremely frowned upon, even amongst thieves, to take a spectral stone, due to the extreme consequences. Laderic was putting his own life in danger just by carrying the stone on his person.

"I don't know who originally stole it, but somehow, those goblins had one, along with the rest of the loot that I may or may not have taken." He finished his story, reaching into his bag again. "I had enough to get my pack enchanted with an expanding charm to make room for my things. And enough to buy these." From his belt, he drew two long daggers, each encased in thick black leather. He carefully removed one from its sheath to reveal a peculiar blade. It was sleek and iridescent,

17

seeming to shine with all colors of the rainbow. It captured and reflected every ray of light with dazzling beauty. "I still keep my sword on me, but these are nice in certain situations." He held it out to Midiga, letting her feel its balance.

To test their sharpness, the felid pulled a whisker from her muzzle and held it above the shimmering blade. She dropped it and watched as it sliced the whisker clean in half as soon as it touched the strange metal. "Very nice," she said, leaning back again. "Those are extremely sharp... Dwarven made?" she questioned.

"I don't know that much, but I know a good blade when I see one," he said, sheathing it and hooking both of them back on his belt. He glanced out the window. The sun was already starting to rise, twilight peeking over the horizon. "If we are going to save this poor, hunted traveler, we should probably get moving soon."

She nodded, her shadow flickering in the firelight. "Right. Let me grab my things." From the wall, she retrieved a set of thin leather armor, the heaviest armor she could be bothered to wear. Then she padded over to the wooden chest on the floor, kneeling and opening the heavy oak lid. From within, she drew a curved, polished bow and a quiver loaded with arrows fletched with black feathers. She bared her teeth in a wicked smile, feeling alive once again.

"Let's go."

CHAPTER 3

THE LIGHT OF dawn was just beginning to show, and the rain calmed as the two headed out toward the southeastern section of the town. Just past the last dock to the south, the dark forest loomed. This was the northernmost section of the Weald, which spanned most of the southern part of the continent, becoming thick jungle as it neared the equator. These woods south of Ulandyl were notorious for being thick and inhospitable. The trees extended far to the south, making up the territories of several traditional felidae kingdoms, and almost completely surrounding the closer, coastal human city of Mariscale to the southeast.

Midiga and Laderic made good time, reaching the edge of the Weald just before sunrise. It was still early morning, only a few hours since Laderic had heard Harlan's tale in the Savage Lion Inn. Quietly, they exited the city and darted into the woods.

Moving with the swift grace of a hunter, Midiga wasted no time searching for tracks in the mud or signs of a disturbance. Deeper into the forest they traveled, keeping their eyes peeled, not only for clues but for signs of the dark creatures that cared to reside in the woods, as well. Laderic could handle many kinds of unforgiving creatures, including bloodhungry, quite well in his own opinion, but that didn't mean he would welcome any unexpected surprises.

After nearly an hour of searching, they came upon a lead. "Here," breathed Midiga, waving Laderic toward a tree with her paw. "Look." He walked over, feet sinking into the muddy forest floor.

In the bark of the young tree was a prominent claw mark. The mark carved was deep in the trunk, revealing a green-tinted interior.

"It's fresh," Laderic murmured, running his fingertips over the mark. "Otherwise, the exposed flesh would have died and turned brown already."

"You're telling me this as if I don't already know," chided Midiga softly. Her whiskers twitched, sensing the delicate changes of the air currents. "The angle of the mark suggests they went... this way," she concluded, gesturing east. Laderic nodded, and they continued their search.

Though the sun was making its ascent, the woods remained dark as ever, the canopy of thick, green leaves shielding the ground from sunlight. A small red fox darted through the pines, disturbing the stillness of the brush. Birds were beginning to sing their morning song. Large water droplets fell from the leaves, occasionally splashing on the scalp of Laderic or Midiga. The droplets were huge and cold, soon chilling Laderic's head, at his own annoyance.

"I hate rain," he muttered, lifting his leg and stepping over a fallen tree. "Especially cold rain in the spring."

"Quiet," shushed Midiga, ears swiveling in every direction, listening.

"I mean, isn't spring rain supposed to be kind of warm?" he mused, marching through the mud. It squelched loudly beneath his boots. A branch snapped up when he lifted his foot, and, like a whip, sliced clean through his pants, cutting his leg. He cursed, frustrated.

"I said quiet!" Midiga said with a snarl. Laderic looked at her, taken aback. She was standing completely still, on high alert. Her muzzle was raised, teeth bared. Her nostrils flared, ears aimed directly ahead. "I hear something."

"What is it?" Laderic breathed, barely audible. Midiga kept her head trained due east, silent. Her tail twitched. She stood motionless, hardly breathing, daring not to make a sound.

In the distance, she could hear the shuffling of bodies through the underbrush. "I hear... at least five individuals. Moving fast." She huffed finally, looking around them, eying the canopy of leaves. "Normally, I would climb a tree to get a good view, but these woods are so thick... it would be pointless." She raised her nose in the air, inhaling deeply. The wind was blowing toward them, masking their own scent, but bringing with it a wealth of information to Midiga. She could smell heavily the disgusting smell that was wet canid, and also... a smell she was unfamiliar with. With that, she started moving again, faster than before, in the direction of the disruption. The thrill of the hunt was beginning to grip her, and the excitement caused her breathing to quicken.

Laderic followed, and the two carried on for another couple of miles or so when a bone-chilling howl pierced the still quiet of the morning. This was not a lonely howl from a sad hound dog. No... this was a hunter's call. A signal that prey had been sighted. They froze for the duration, an eerie few seconds of ominous tension. It sounded like it was coming from right in front of them.

"We might be too late." Laderic grimaced, starting to move once more and taking the lead. The ground had elevated to an incline, and they were nearing the top of a steep hill, and at its crest, a shocking scene revealed itself.

From their position at the hilltop, Midiga and Laderic spotted six canidae moving through sparser trees in formation, closing in on a rocky cliffside to their left. A small waterfall no more than four stories tall cascaded over the wall and crashed to the forest floor below where a smaller river raged, swollen with the recent rain. The waterfall formed from a small fork in the Servatio River to the north. The forest floor below met the rocky wall, perfect for cornering unsuspecting prey. The canidae were on the same side of the river as Laderic and Midiga, but the blanket of trees below hid their target from sight.

"Let's go!" urged Laderic, running down the hill toward the pack of canidae. Few trees grew on the steep decline, and his feet moved so fast that he felt nearly out of control. He could sense Midiga's presence beside him as he ran. Several of the canidae that had been moving in formation paused, snapping their heads around, intrigued by the new scents moving closer to them. They fell out of formation in confusion, now turning their attention to the west where Laderic and Midiga emerged.

A high-pitched scream pierced the early morning, coming from the rock face, and most of the canidae turned back around to continue pursuing their prey. Three of them stopped and squared up to Midiga and Laderic, teeth bared in hateful snarls. Behind them, the river roared without pause. The area in which the two groups met was only dotted with trees as the forest thinned out along the river, favoring tall grass instead in the clearing.

"Oh look, a stray," one canid spoke with a snarl. It was gray in color with its red eyes standing out against its fur. Red eyes—the mark of a bloodhungry. The other two growled deeply in their chests, gripping short swords and holding them at the ready. All three of them wore crude tan leather armor. The gray one also wore a helmet, embellished with a golden coin that looked hastily glued onto its surface. A crude symbol of leadership. He addressed Midiga directly, brandishing his own sword toward her menacingly. "You should mind your own business, cat!" With that, he barked in the canid language, and the others lunged forward to attack.

"Hey!" yelled Laderic at the gray canid. "I'm right here, you know." He huffed, a little offended that the gray bloodhungry hadn't even acknowledged him. He dodged a sloppy swing from a sword. canidae were clumsier when it came to combat than most, less agile than felidae or even humans. What they lacked in dexterity, though, they made up for with brute strength and stamina.

"This is not a good time, idiot," Midiga snapped, backing up. The other two canidae had teamed up on her. Due to their instinctual dislike of each other, the gray canid had decided she was their primary target. "I could use a hand," the felid hinted, keeping her eyes on her attackers.

Laderic nodded, continuing to watch his own attacker, gauging his every move. The rust-colored canid stalking toward him had yet to take his eyes off Laderic's throat. The wolf man swung once again, and Laderic sidestepped, dodging the attack easily.

Canidae might not have the best technique, but often times they didn't need to. Their strategy for taking down prey was to tire it out, as their stamina was virtually unlimited. Once their attacker would grow weary and inevitably make a mistake, they go in for the kill. For the throat. And even without weapons, their claws are still deadly sharp—almost as much as felids, though they aren't able to retract them like the cat folk.

Midiga was attempting to back up and get a bit of range to fire her bow, but her attackers weren't giving her a chance. As soon as she would reach for an arrow, one of the canidae would snap at her arm or swing their sword at her head. Only protected by her unsheathed claws, she held them at the ready.

"Mrow!" she cried in her own language, lashing out at a canid that had lunged for her again. He was slow and clumsy, and she made him pay for it. She landed a slice across his nose, and he whimpered in pain.

Laderic had removed his own weapons, the twin daggers, and was holding them at the ready. They shone in the new morning sunlight, dazzling and colorful. One, he held facing forward in his right hand, toward his enemy as he might hold a sword. The other he held hilt first, the blade pointing behind him. With a blade pointing in each direction, the pose allowed for more freedom of movement, allowing him to either attack or defend, even with his back turned.

Wasting no time, knowing he would tire out before the canid even started to pant, he decided to make his move. He lunged forward, feigning an attack with his right-handed blade. The canid dodged left, and Laderic rotated his body in response, spinning away, and jerking his left arm backward. It all happened in seconds. The blade buried itself deep in the canid's side, and he yipped in pain. Laderic continued twisting, then pulled the blade out, whirling around to face his opponent once more. There was a large gash in the canid's left side, and it was bleeding profusely. He dropped his crude sword to the ground, holding his side in pain. His red eyes burned holes into Laderic, murder written in his gaze.

When Laderic's canid had snarled in agony, the two closing in on Midiga had become distracted just long enough for her to draw an arrow. She fired it point-blank at the black canid to her right, landing the shot between its eyes, killing it instantly. Now, it was only her and the gray one that had spoken the first time, the one who appeared to be the leader. He flinched slightly when she shot his companion. Newfound hatred for the felid consumed his mind, and he growled deep in his throat.

"I *said* you should mind your own business," he barked, moving closer to Midiga so she couldn't draw again without opening a weak spot. She took a few steps back, and her tail bumped into a tree. The canid's fur was standing on end, and his

EMBER — ECHOES OF ASHES — BOOK ONE

body quivered with anticipation. "Or at least to stay out of mine. I am Karkos, I am thirst!" He howled, snapping at her arm and grazing her skin, drawing blood. His pupils contracted in euphoria as he licked her blood from his chops. Midiga watched, horrified.

A high-pitched howl pierced the forest then, coming from the cliffside. Karkos's ears twitched. He bared his teeth in a vicious snarl, taking a step back from Midiga. "Unfortunately, your blood is not that which we crave, but I assure you, my brethren aren't picky!" Suddenly, he yipped something in his own language. The wounded canid, which had been focused on Laderic, pivoted and lunged at Midiga. His sudden retreat caught Laderic off guard, and he looked on, helpless.

"Watch out!" Laderic yelled, knowing it was too late, but still turning to give chase. Midiga's reflexes were inhuman, and her feline ears had caught the canid switching positions. She rounded to face him just in time, and he tackled her to the ground. The gray canid turned and ran back toward where the other canidae had gone before.

"Don't let him escape!" Midiga yowled, shoving the injured canid off her body. Laderic turned to give chase, but humans were much slower than the wolf people were. Nevertheless, he followed Karkos into the trees, toward the rocky wall where he guessed they had cornered their prey.

Midiga rolled over onto the injured canid, pinning him to the ground and dodging a snap at her neck. She wrenched another arrow from her quiver, arcing it over her head. "Bad dog," she said with a hiss, before stabbing the arrow into his eye socket like a dagger. He let loose an unintelligible scream before his body went limp, and he fell into darkness.

She wasted no time removing her arrow from his face, standing and then giving chase to Laderic. It took her only moments to catch up to him. The muddy ground was hard for Laderic to maneuver through, as his shoes sinking deeper into the mud as they neared the river. Midiga wasn't restricted, going shoeless as all felidae did. She was light-footed, and her strides seemed to glide across the ground. She pulled ahead of Laderic, hoping she wasn't too late.

Without warning, from up ahead, a bright white light followed by a thunderous boom shook the forest. Hundreds of birds took off from the trees, cawing and screeching as they flew away from the explosion. Laderic stumbled and fell. Even Midiga was nearly shaken off her feet. The light had come from the cliffside, but she pressed on, undeterred. The trees were sparse, but not enough for her to get a decent view of what had happened.

She rounded a tree to a shocking sight. In a clearing, against the foot of the cliff, three canidae were dead, the earth below them indented in the shape of their bodies as if they had been blasted into the ground. Trees were smoking and blackened, and the rocky wall itself was charred and fractured. On her right, she spotted Karkos, swimming across the river away from the clearing with a couple of other canidae. He looked injured, but still mobile. She turned to follow them, groaning at the idea of having to swim. Then a strange sound stopped her in her tracks. A high-pitched whimper was coming from a smoldering hole in the rocky wall. The indentation was smoking and fresh.

Laderic had finally caught up, noticing that Midiga had paused in her chase and was going to inspect a hole in the wall that had mist rising from it. As she approached, a young woman stepped out from the hole. She wore tattered brown clothing and a green cloak and hood that covered her hair and ears. She limped out of the wall, scanning the clearing, a single dagger in her right hand held at the ready. Then, she looked at Midiga, golden eyes narrowed, worried.

"They are dead, I hope?" she asked, almost uncertain. Her voice was soft and smooth, though she was breathing quite hard. Midiga nodded, brow furrowed. The woman sighed, exhaustion and relief emanating from her. "They had been chasing me for days. I cannot thank you enough—*oh...*" As she spoke, she sank toward the ground, landing first on her knees before falling to the ground.

Midiga jumped forward, not quite fast enough to catch her before she hit the mud. "Laderic!" she cried, holding the woman's face just above the ground. He was already running to her side. He turned the fainted woman over and felt her neck for a pulse.

"She's alive," he said, out of breath. Cradling her head, he continued, "But her pulse is weak. We should take her back with us." Midiga nodded, reaching her hand-paw under the woman's shoulder and lifting her with Laderic's assistance. The mystery woman was several inches shorter than Laderic, very light and easy to lift. Together, the two made their way back to Ulandyl as fast as they could, worried for the life of the one between them.

CHAPTER 4

THE SUN WAS high in the sky when they arrived at Midiga's place once again. Carrying the woman several miles, as they did, tired them both out, and they were relieved when they closed themselves in the house. Gently, they placed her on Midiga's down-filled mat and stood to look her over.

Her hood had fallen off while they were walking, but they had quickly put it back on her once they realized its purpose. Her ears were elongated and pointed at the tip, clearly marking her as an elf. Now, they removed it once more, getting a better look at her features. She had long, wavy, chocolate-brown hair, knotted and unkempt, looking like it hadn't been washed for days. Cresting her forehead was a beautiful chain of amber and bronze. Her skin was porcelain and flawless. Her hands appeared delicate with long fingers ending in mud-encrusted fingernails. The pants on her left leg were torn—blood coating them—yet no visible injury found. Covered in bruises and cuts, she was emaciated and gaunt, but through all of this, she had a natural beauty unlike any the two had ever seen.

"I've never seen an elf before," Midiga remarked, staring wide-eyed at the young woman. In the Far Land, elves are very secretive beings, keeping to themselves, hidden deep in the north. Once, elves were great protectors of the whole continent, but now, and for over a thousand years, they have remained closed off and secluded from the world. It is said there is not a mortal alive that knows the location of the last elvish city, and some people are even naïve enough to believe that elves are purely a myth, when, in reality, they have simply disappeared into the ice.

"I have, though it was years ago," said Laderic. "A friend of mine is married to a renegade elf. That's probably what she is." He scratched his beard, looking the elf over once again. He narrowed his eyes. "But why is she being hunted?"

Renegade elves were elves that had grown to dislike the secretive nature of their people and chose to leave the elvish capital to live amongst the other races, where the laws and rules of living are much less strict. Elves were not punished for leaving and becoming renegades but were also not allowed to live amongst elves ever again. To keep them from returning and bringing the culture and ideas of outsiders with them, all of their memories of elvish culture—and the location of their hidden capital—were wiped from their minds.

He bent down, reaching toward the woman to rummage through her pockets. Midiga slapped his hand away. "What are you doing?" she hissed. He reached back down into her pockets again, as if she hadn't just stopped him.

"We saved her life, and now she is in your house," he explained, his face stoic. "I want to know what sort of weapons or magic this little lady has on her. If she's in here with us where we're vulnerable, we need to know what to expect."

"She was running from bloodhungry hunters!" Midiga quipped in protest. "Anything she has on her is probably for her own protection."

Laderic looked up at his friend. "Ask yourself this—why is she being hunted?" he demanded. Midiga froze with her mouth open. "Renegade elves are *never* hunted for deserting—that is unless they've committed some sort of crime. She killed three bloodhungry canidae pretty easily." He looked back down at the girl. "And why are they tracking an elf anyway? I've never heard of even one bloodhungry seeking elf blood, let alone a whole pack of them. Where did they even taste elf blood in the first place?" He narrowed his eyes, filled with mistrust. "She *must* be dangerous if someone wants her dead that badly. Those canidae weren't hunting her at random—she is being tracked. What if she kills us in our sleep? I would rather not take that chance."

He reached toward her belt line and grabbed the holster for a blade. At this, the elf's eyes popped wide open, and she sat up fast as lightning, in the same motion, pulling the dagger from her belt and pointing it at Laderic. Taken aback and startled, he lost his balance, falling onto the floor. "What are you doing," she accused. Her voice was cold, laced with the desperation of a cornered animal. She stared into his eyes, her own eyes blood red in color, captivating and terrifying at the same time.

"I… we… we were just…" He looked at Midiga for help.

Midiga sighed, taking a step in front of Laderic. The elf looked up at her from her spot on the bed. "I am Midiga, and this is Laderic," said the felid, holding her paws up to show they were empty. "We mean you no harm."

"You are the one who saved me," breathed the elf, relieved. She lowered her blade. At this, her eyes changed colors back to golden yellow. "At least, you are. *He* is not." Laderic raised his eyebrows and opened his mouth to argue.

"He helped," Midiga interjected before Laderic could protest. "And I only helped, as well. Something else must have saved you. There was a bright white light right before we reached you. Do you remember what happened?"

"I made that light," said the girl. "I was cornered, and they were closing in on me, so I used my magic to... make them go away." She stated this as a fact, her voice flat and commanding. "But that was a lot at once, and it drains me pretty quickly when I use magic. It must have knocked me out."

Laderic laughed, and the two turned to face him. "Elves can't use magic," he chided, smirking. "You don't have to lie to us. What actually happened?" He crossed his arms, still seated on the floor.

She stared back at him, blinking. "Elves?" She looked between them. "What do you mean? Are you talking about me?"

"You're an elf," he said, staring at her. "You... you don't know you're an elf?"

She shook her head, exhaling loudly, irritated with herself. "I should explain. My name is Alleria, and aside from my name, I don't know much about myself at all. I cannot remember anything from before I turned ten. I'm seventeen now, and even so, I know very little about myself. My memory is not the best.

"My parents told me I was in an accident and injured my head, and that's why I can't remember my past. Although, as I grew, I realized they must have been lying, but I didn't question them. I was curious but believed they had my best interest in mind, and they encouraged that belief by telling me each time I asked them about my past that it was best I did not know. They gave me a hooded cloak, and I was to wear it each day, hiding my ears and even my eyes from those I would meet, especially when going into town. They told me I was just... different. And strangers wouldn't understand and might try to hurt me.

"I only asked about it a few times, my peculiarities and why my ears were different, and of course, why I had to cover them. My mother always said the same thing—that the answers to my questions lay hidden in the north, though exactly where she did not know."

Laderic nodded. His eyes were unfocused as he was deep in

thought. "The north is said to hold the last elvish stronghold—the ancient, legendary city of Nara'jainita. Somehow, your mother must have at least known to direct you toward the city. But... how? And why?"

Alleria looked down at her hands, feeling tears spring to her eyes. She kept her face hidden behind her hair. "I wish I knew... I left before I thought to ask those questions. How she knew what she did... where I came from... and who my real parents were." She stifled a sob, feeling her throat tightening. "I always wondered how I came to be their daughter. It's too late now. I... decided I wanted to discover the answers myself. Just over a year ago, I made my choice. In the middle of the night, I packed my things, and I ran." She looked away, biting her lip and squeezing her eyes shut.

Laderic looked her over, reading her body language. He had believed her story up until that point. Something just wasn't adding up. He narrowed his eyes, skeptical, but kept his mouth shut as the elf continued.

"I had always shown a talent for magic. My powers usually manifested on accident, but my parents told me that I must keep it a secret or it would attract too much attention. So I have kept it buried inside me as much as possible. However, there are times I can't help it... I lose control. About six months ago, I stopped in a small town called Galail, and a man tried to mug me. He forced me out of the crowd and chased me through the alleys. I used my magic to hold him off, and my hood came off my head, only for a second. Just a few people saw, and I didn't think anything of it. The next day, one of the wolf people broke into the room I was renting and tried to kill me.

"I have spent my time since then running and traveling, trying to reach the north. Now and again, the wolf people find me, and I am forced to flee for my life, regardless of where that may take me. I've been as far north as Starpoint, yet have been forced to backtrack so many times, it feels like I'll never reach my destination. I don't know why they are hunting me, and I've tried to avoid contact with anyone, so it's harder for them to track me. This was the longest they had chased me without pause." She looked between Midiga and Laderic, grateful, eyes shining brilliant gold. "If you hadn't found me and split them up, I fear they would have killed me. I was too exhausted to use my magic to stop them all."

Laderic and Midiga only stared, taking in her story. Laderic's eye was twitching slightly. "Let me get this straight," he began, "you didn't know you were an elf until I just told you."

"Yes... What exactly makes me an elf?" she asked, eyes bright with anticipation.

"We'll get to that later," Laderic said, waving his hand in dismissal. "You can use magic... and your eyes do some weird color-change thingy?"

She nodded. "I must be careful to control my emotions on the rare occasions that I come in contact with others."

"And you can kill canidae just by flicking your wrist?"

"Well, it's a bit more complicated than that, but yes. They've been following me for months now. I'm usually able to throw them off my track, but this last time was too close."

Laderic blinked, silent for a moment before turning to Midiga. "She needs to not be here with us," he said, hinting in a singsong voice.

Midiga frowned. "We are *not* going to kick her out. She is exhausted!" She looked at Alleria. "How would you like to stay here today and tonight, to get your strength up?"

She nodded, smiling. "It's nice to be around people who aren't going to judge me for my differences."

"Oh, I'm judging," Laderic retorted. "Midiga, did you not hear anything she said? Do you realize that we could have another pack of canidae on your doorstep *any minute* as long as she stays here?"

"Then we will handle them as we did earlier." Her voice felt colder than ice. "Laderic, if you don't want to deal with the danger, you don't have to stay."

"She didn't even pay us! What, you're going to kick me out for her?" he asked, chest puffed out indignantly. Midiga looked at Laderic, unblinking, raising a single eyebrow without speaking. Laderic sighed, his resolve wavering. Finally, he closed his eyes, conceding. "Fine. She can stay."

"You mean, fine *you* can stay?" Midiga jibed with a smile in her voice. Laderic glared at her before walking to the fireplace to kick up the coals.

"If you don't mind, I have a friend of mine that has been hiding outside. She would like to come in now if that's okay with you." The elf spoke with the meekness of a mouse. Laderic threw his hands up in the air without saying anything. She glanced at him, frowned, and looked back at Midiga.

"Of course, she can," purred the felid. "Do you need to go out and get her?"

"No, it's okay. She can hear my thoughts." With that, she closed her eyes for a brief second and then opened them. "Okay! She is on her way!"

Laderic was staring at Alleria, eye twitching. "Hear... your... thoughts?" he asked, spacing each word out, disbelief filling the voids between them. "Midiga..."

"Come on, Laderic, it's like you've never seen magic before," she scolded, brushing him off and rolling her eyes. "The more, the merrier, I say."

As if on cue, there was a scratching noise at the door. Alleria stood slowly, careful to make sure she didn't pass out a second time. When she got to her feet, she walked over to the door and opened it. A tiny red fox padded inside, and she shut the door behind it. "This is Reia," she said plainly.

Laderic pointed accusingly at the fox, staring at Midiga. "She's an alamorph, too?" His voice was rising in pitch with each new revelation. Alleria looked at him, tilting her head, confused.

"An alamorph? I don't understand..." She frowned.

"How do you not... Gods," he groaned, massaging his temples. "Did that fox find you one day?" he demanded, gesturing at the fox with disgust.

"Yes?"

"And could you hear it talking in your head?"

"Yes, but..."

"And then, was there a flash of light, and *suddenly,* it felt like your souls were connected?" Sarcasm dripped off each word.

Alleria stared in shock at Laderic, wide-eyed. "How did you know?"

But Laderic didn't answer. He just stared at Midiga. "An alamorphic elf? She's a *freak*!" he exploded. "No wonder she is being hunted!"

Alamorphs are people who are born with an innate connection to animals. So much so, that during their lives, at some point, they will meet an animal that they have an unexplainable link to. At that moment when they meet, their minds connect, and they become soul bonded. After that, alamorphs are able to hear the animal's thoughts, and those who are more experienced can even see through their eyes. And, on top of that—

"Hello," said Reia, looking around the room. "Nice place you have here."

The animal also learns to speak the language that their soul partner speaks.

"Agh!" shrieked Laderic. "I forgot about that part!"

"Stop being such a jerk," Midiga growled, growing tired of his demeanor. She crossed her arms, her tail whipping back and forth with annoyance. "If you can't be nice to my guests, you're going to need to leave." She looked down at Reia, smiling with her pointed teeth showing. "Nice to meet you, Reia. Welcome to my den."

Reia bowed her head in respect, and at that moment, her tail suddenly split into pieces. Laderic watched, horrified, as the seemingly normal fox revealed itself to be a *kitsune*, sporting seven tails instead of one and the ability to wield magic with ease. He blinked his eyes, praying that he was seeing things. On her forehead and shoulders, tiny runic symbols appeared, glowing with faint white light.

Alleria bent and picked up the fox, stroking her fur. "We've only known each other for a few months now. She found me when I was on the run again, being tracked from Mariscale. After that... it felt like we had known each other forever." Reia turned her head to face Laderic, a tiny white swirl marking on her face drawing his eye.

Laderic only stared, looking back and forth between Midiga, Alleria, and the kitsune. He was dumbfounded, so he turned back around and moved toward the chair. "Nope. Nope," he said to himself. He sat down, throwing his hands up once again. "You can handle this one, Midiga. I've had enough insanity for today."

And so, as it came naturally to her, Midiga made her guests feel welcome. She opened a trap door in the wooden floor, walking down a few steps to a hidden basement beneath her home. She descended for only a few moments before returning to the surface with strips of dried meat. Below the house was where she kept her food, all of which she had hunted and killed herself. It was lightly salted, dried like jerky, and—

"Delicious!" mumbled Alleria through a mouthful of meat. Reia nodded her little head in agreement, tearing into the food as if she hadn't eaten in days. Both of them dug right in, stuffing themselves without a word.

Midiga looked on, pleased that they were enjoying her food. Absentmindedly, she licked the back of her hand-paw, as she was deep in thought. Her eyes became misty and unfocused. The sun was rising, warming the house with a pleasant glow. Even Laderic had started to relax. Slowly, he let his eyes shut, resting them after having been awake for so long. Exhaustion hit him like a sledgehammer.

"So tell me, Reia," Midiga began after a while, watching the kitsune eat with a smile in her eyes, "why do you have so many tails? I've never seen a fox with more than one, though I've heard stories."

Reia's tails twitched with amusement. "Well," she said, after swallowing another bite, "I'm a kitsune, a special kind of fox. Magical… in some ways, at least."

"Go on," said Midiga, leaning forward and clasping her hands together. Laderic's interest piqued, as well. He forced his eyes open, trying to stay alert. He knew of kitsune only through spoken word. He had never had the chance to see one, let alone speak with one.

Reia sat back on her haunches, tails forming a halo around her body. "We are born with one tail, as all foxes are," she began, "but, as we grow—reaching milestones in our lives—our tails split into more than one, up to nine, where the *real* magic happens." Her tails flicked in excitement behind her. "Once we reach nine, all of our powers are unlocked." She smiled—though since she was a fox, it looked more like a snarl. "Right now, I can only manipulate fire… to an extent. That's really the only thing special about me aside from my seven tails."

"And the fact that you can talk," commented Laderic. But Reia shook her head.

"I can only speak your language because I have bonded with Alleria," she said. "Speech is an ability gained by *all* alamorph soul partners. That has nothing to do with my being a kitsune. Just my limited control over fire." Her tails began to wiggle once more. "When I get my ninth tail, however, I'll be much stronger. I'll be able to control fire with such ease, and even transform into a human! Well, with tails, but I'm not picky. And my fur

EMBER — ECHOES OF ASHES — BOOK ONE

will turn silver or gold—I can't wait!"

"That sounds quite amazing, Reia," purred Midiga, excited by the fox's story. Her own tail was even vibrating in response to Reia's energy. "When will you get your ninth tail?"

Reia shrugged, as best a fox could. She had picked up on body language after living around Alleria. And, while it looked awkward on her, it did get the point across. "You gain them as you get older... but not necessarily with age. Sometimes, you get them after a deeply personal experience, or sometimes even after witnessing death." Her eyes glazed over for a moment, and she was silent. After a second, she snapped out of her trance and continued. "It just depends. It's... based on maturity more than years."

Alleria, who had been listening silently, spoke up. "We hope that she will receive her ninth tail sometime on our journey north... if we make it that far, that is."

Reia nodded, ears flattening back on her skull. "I don't like the wolf people. They're scary."

"I hear you, sister," Midiga agreed.

Alleria sighed, staring out the window, her golden eyes appearing lost. "They are finding better ways to tire us out. I have considered hiring a guide, or a guard, but I don't have the money to do that. Reia getting control of her fire magic, and me learning better control of my own magic, those things might be our only chance of making it."

Midiga stared off at the fireplace where the coals glowed lightly. The two guests continued eating, though slower than before. Sun shone through the windows in beams, and it was pleasantly quiet for a while. The wind gusted outside, causing the house to creak in a nostalgic, comforting way. Midiga, deep in thought, was unaware of most of these things. For Alleria, it almost felt like she was back home for a moment. No one had shown her such hospitality since she left.

After a while, Midiga suddenly broke the silence. "I'll take you to the north."

Laderic, who had been leaning back in the wooden chair with his eyes closed, jerked in shock. The chair tumbled backward to the floor, dragging him down with it. He smacked his head against the floor, hard. "Ow!" He moaned, sitting up on his elbow, turning to face the two. "Midiga, what are you talking about? Gods, that really hurt." He rubbed his head with his hand.

Midiga, without skipping a beat, continued. "Laderic will come too."

"What?" Laderic scrambled to his feet. "What makes you think I'm going to come along with you, I have, er, other things that I have to get done!" He took a few steps back, holding up his hands in objection.

"Like what?" the felid growled, glaring in his direction.

He froze under her gaze, stammering. "I... well, I mean..." His thoughts felt scattered as Midiga's amber eyes stared into his very soul.

"That's what I thought," she stated matter-of-factly. "Now, why don't you consider your next move to be repaying that debt you owe me?"

"What makes you think that going on some crazy escort mission is going to earn either of us any money?" He crossed his arms, skeptical. "Even if we got something, it probably wouldn't be enough for me to pay you back. She already said she is too broke to even hire anyone."

"Well, consider your joining us to be your payment," Midiga snapped, closing the matter.

"Also..." peeped Alleria quietly. Midiga and Laderic turned from their squabble to look at her. "My mother mentioned before when I would ask her questions, you know, that if I ever were to go to the north, I would be met with 'riches both spiritual and physical.'" The last phrase she spoke as if quoting someone directly. She pondered for a moment. "I guess it makes sense, if you say the elvish capital is hidden in the north, and I'm an elf.

40

If I were to find it, I'm sure that the people there would welcome me. Maybe even recognize me." She glanced back and forth between Laderic and Midiga. "Do you think they would know me? Do you… do you think my real parents would be there?"

Midiga opened her mouth, but Laderic spoke first. "All I heard was riches of the physical type... I'm in." He looked at Midiga, grinning. "When do we set out?"

She stared at him, unblinking. "You're *unbelievable* sometimes," was all she could say. She turned back to Alleria. "Seeing as how elves live for thousands of years, I'm sure they would still be there. After all, Daechir is said to still be ruling, even after all this time. Whether or not they would recognize you is a different story. And how can you be sure that anyone would have that amount of money, let alone give it to you?"

Alleria shrugged, not even fazed at hearing she was likely immortal. "I don't know. It's just what my mother told me, but even if my real parents don't have very much, I'm sure they would reward you for bringing me back to them safely." She smiled. "I would if it were my daughter."

"Well, regardless of reward, the journey itself would be enough for me." Midiga sighed. "Just to see Nara'jainita would be a reward on its own."

"Speak for yourself," muttered Laderic. "We better be getting paid. And, Midiga, you better not be thinking you're getting any of my share. You already made it clear me coming with you was payment enough for—"

"Yes, yes, Laderic. I get it. You'll get your share," Midiga interrupted, rolling her eyes. She yawned unexpectedly, glancing out the window where sunlight spilled inside. "I don't know about you guys, but I'm exhausted. Being nocturnal has its flaws."

Laderic nodded in agreement. "I was up all night too. Let's get some shut-eye."

Alleria agreed, as well, as the exhaustion was hitting her

hard, too. Her eyes changed to a deep blue. "I'm full… and sleepy…"

"Well," Midiga began, arching her back, her tail stiffening as she stretched, "it's settled. Let's get some rest. We'll set off first thing in the morning. At dawn. I need to switch my sleep schedule around if we are going to be traveling during the day."

Laderic propped his hands on his hips. "I've got a few ideas of where we could start. I have a friend in Strita who might know where we can find the lost capital. It's not exactly close, but it's the best I've got right now."

"Sounds good. What do you think, Alleria?" Midiga asked.

"Whatever you think is best. I'm—" As she spoke, she yawned hugely. "I'm just so tired."

Laderic grinned. "Agreed. Sleep, for now, talk in the morning."

CHAPTER 5

THE GRASS WAS drenched in dew when the group left Midiga's house early the next morning. After making certain to extinguish the coals in the fireplace, she locked the door and buried the key under a rock beside it. "I don't want to accidentally lose my key while we're gone," she explained, placing the rock on top.

Strita was northeast of Ulandyl, and one could follow The Walk for most of the journey, before taking a side road due east to the mountain city. It would take over a week for them to walk from Ulandyl to Strita. The early part of their journey along The Walk was the least of their worries, as the more southern parts of the road were frequently traveled. This beaten path cut all the way through the Brushdeep Forest to the northeast, and it would take them through another decent sized town fairly soon, just a couple of day's travel from Ulandyl. It was when they would be forced to leave The Walk and turn toward the mountains that they would have to worry.

It would take nearly four days to travel the rough trail eastward off The Walk toward Strita on foot. The road itself was known for being particularly dangerous with bandits, bloodhungry, and vicious monsters lurking in the woods, waiting for unsuspecting travelers to step into their traps. Rarely would sensible creatures walk the road alone, and seldom would foolish souls who chose to try their luck by themselves make it to their destinations.

However, for the time being, the four of them were not concerning themselves with what was to come tomorrow. For today, they had an easy trip down a well-traveled trade route, the weather pristine, and they were full of energy.

They left Ulandyl through the northeast gate, the Brushdeep Forest splayed out before them. Merchants and their carts were both leaving from and coming into the city. The Walk was wide with room to spare on both sides of the path for two caravans to pass each other easily. They nodded cheerily at the salespeople, who waved from their horses and smiled back at them.

Alleria started to sweat as they walked, becoming annoyed and hyperaware of how bad she smelled. She hadn't bathed in days, and it definitely showed. She had dirt caked under her nails and on her hands and face. Her hair was such a mess, she couldn't bear to think about it. It had been rained on, soaked, and then air-dried at least three times since the last time she had washed it. Her pants were a bit bloody, and also covered in dirt. All around, she just felt gross. After about an hour of walking, she couldn't take it anymore.

"Can we... find a creek? Or something?" she asked quietly, avoiding eye contact. She didn't want to burden her new companions with the request, but she was just so uncomfortable, she had to at least ask.

Midiga froze, instantly catching the hint and staring at her with eyes wide. "I didn't even think to ask that!" she cried, feeling terrible. "I'm just so used to licking myself clean, I forgot humans need baths! I'm a horrible host," she said with a moan. "I don't even *own* a bathtub! Of *course,* we can get you cleaned up."

"Yeah, looks like you need it," Laderic joked, looking the elf up and down. Midiga shot him a dirty look, and he smiled, unashamed. Alleria felt like her face was on fire.

Soon, they came upon a thin creek that flowed to the south. Midiga made Laderic sit on his own on a log beside The Walk, and she escorted Alleria into the woods. They pushed through the brush and trees for a few minutes until they reached the clear, running water. Luckily, a small waterfall had formed upstream—perfect for Alleria to wash her hair in.

She started to take her clothes off before stopping and making awkward eye contact with Midiga. "Um…" she began, and Midiga once again got the hint.

"Oh! Sorry," she said, spinning around and looking away. "Modesty is just not my thing, but I'll keep watch!" She planted her feet facing away from the elf, training her ears and eyes toward The Walk.

Alleria smiled at her, looking around one last time before removing her hood from her ears. The wind felt good on their pointed tips. She took off her green cloak, hanging it from a branch, and then took off her bag, leaning it against a tree. She wrenched off her muddy boots, pairing them up beside the trunk of the same tree. Then, she quickly peeled the rest of her nasty clothes off, laying them on the grass. She dipped her foot into the water, cringing at how cold it was.

Reia dipped her nose near the water, taking a long drink upstream from where Alleria was trying to gather the courage to get in. "It's good drinking water," said the kitsune, "but I feel bad that you have to swim in it!"

Alleria took the fastest bath of her life, scrubbing her body with her hands as best she could. She dipped her long, brown hair under the waterfall for as long as she could stand it, using her nails to loosen the dirt that had built up on her scalp. After one last rinse, she practically leapt out of the water, though not feeling much warmer in the late spring breeze.

Shivering, she dug through her bag, pulling out her extra pair of pants and a tan cloth shirt that she had taken from home. She only had a few outfits with her and tried to keep them as clean as possible. She used a strip of cloth to wrap her breasts, holding them in place so they wouldn't hurt if she had to run. Then, she quickly dressed, pulling on her shirt, and stuffing her legs into her pants. Last, she slid on a fresh, clean pair of socks and slipped her boots back on her feet.

Her cloak was the final touch. It was the only one she had, and it wasn't the freshest, but she couldn't go without wearing it. She clicked the silver clasp in place around her neck, feeling it with her fingertips for a nostalgic moment. It had been her mother's, and she had given it to Alleria to wear each time she was in public so her ears would be covered and she would be safe. The clasp was real silver, shaped like two arrowheads with a small chain connecting them. She pulled the hood up over her head.

She took a few minutes to scrub the worst of the dirt out of her other clothes. They didn't get as clean as she would have liked, but she already felt like she had wasted enough of everyone's time. She wrung her clothes out before hanging them on the straps of her bag to air dry as they walked.

"Okay, I'm done!" she called to Midiga. She pulled her fingers through her hair, combing it as best she could, before stuffing it into her hood to dry. Her wavy bangs hung in front of her eyes, and she pushed them back behind her ear.

The felid turned and smiled at her. "You look so much better!" purred Midiga. Then, she backtracked. "I mean, you looked good before... I was just saying, now that you're clean—"

"Thanks," Alleria said, interrupting her. She reached down and picked up Reia, clutching the fox to her chest. Midiga nodded, grinning, and they turned toward The Walk.

46

It seemed like they had only just started walking when they finally stopped to make camp the first night. Reia lit the campfire with a show of magical prowess while Laderic and Midiga watched on, impressed by her skill, limited as it was. Reia was quite humble, bowing her head and insisting she still had much to improve upon.

The night was clear, and the moon illuminated much of the woods around them. Alleria was relaxed, unlike how she usually felt. She normally took turns keeping watch with Reia, spending half of the night staring off into the trees and listening for the howl of bloodhungry canidae, and the other half tossing and turning in restless, nightmare saturated sleep. But tonight was not that way, and she soon fell asleep without any problems, feeling protected by the presence of her new friends.

The next day passed just as smoothly. Alleria, becoming more comfortable with her two escorts, overcame her shyness and started asking them questions. It turned out she had quite a few of them. Her curiosity was insatiable. She switched targets between Laderic and Midiga all day, firing question after question their way about everything from elves, magic, the lay of the land, and even their history together.

When she asked Midiga about her and Laderic's relationship, the felid was amused. She smiled wistfully, eyes glazing over for a moment. "If you mean to suggest that we have a *romantic* history together, you couldn't be more wrong."

Alleria giggled, stealing a glance at Laderic, who, to her surprise, didn't seem offended in the slightest. In fact, he was grinning. The elf was curious, figuring he would have leapt at the opportunity to defend himself. "Yeah, I can see why he wouldn't be what you're looking for, Midiga," poked Alleria, fishing for a reaction.

Laderic only smiled broader. "I think you're misunderstanding her reasoning, Alleria." He and Midiga made mischievous eye contact. "Whether or not I'm good enough isn't the issue. Let's just say, I'm not her *type*." His emphasis hung deliberately on the last word.

"Oh!" remarked Alleria. "You only like other felids! I guess that makes sense." But they were both starting to laugh at her, and her face turned red as she was embarrassed and confused. "What?" she asked, glancing back and forth between them. She crossed her arms. "I don't get what's so funny."

Midiga was nearly crying she was laughing so hard. "I don't mind dating outside of my race. That's never been an issue, as long as it's not a canid," she clarified after she had calmed down a bit, still giggling to herself. "You're getting warmer... It's just still not quite right."

Laderic was wiping tears from his eyes, still smiling hugely. "This is hilarious... No, Alleria, she doesn't care that I'm a *human*, just that I'm, well... a man."

After a brief moment of silence, the pieces fell into place in Alleria's mind. "*Oooohhhh,*" she realized. "You don't like *men,* not just Laderic!" The other two were both laughing again, finding the exchange hysterical. The elf was giggling along with them now. "I guess I can't blame you. I've never dated anyone before, but having the choice, I'm not sure why *anyone* would pick men."

"Hey," said Laderic, still laughing. "We aren't that bad. Don't go looping us all in the same circle now."

Midiga shoved Laderic playfully as they walked. "I don't know if you're the ideal spokesperson for the benefits of dating men. In fact... you might be the opposite," she teased. Her tail whipped back and forth with amusement.

"Oh, hush." He groaned, rolling his eyes. "We've got our perks. You'll see." He winked at Alleria, and she blushed, quickly averting her eyes and struggling to keep from smiling.

They stopped to rest for a late lunch, tearing into the dried jerky and nuts that Midiga had brought along. A thin creek wound its way through the trees, and they drank deeply before setting off once again. Alleria soon picked back up with her questioning, feeling as though each time she got an answer, she came up with twice as many questions to ask.

"I've seen so many things since I went out on my own, but I've been so scared of people finding out the truth about me, I never stopped to ask anyone questions," she explained, after interrogating Laderic for over an hour about the different races of the Far Land. He grunted a response, his mouth dry and jaw aching from answering all of her questions as they walked. He *almost* thought she was going to give it a rest for a bit, but he

49

was wrong. Just a few seconds later, she started back up again, this time asking about swordplay and fighting. A pleasant turn of events for Laderic, since he was quite happy to talk about something he felt he knew much about. They talked until nightfall, making camp in a clearing just off the beaten path.

They rose early the next morning, eager to reach Acrosa, and in particular, to reach a cozy tavern with a warm bed. The Walk divided Acrosa almost exactly in half and was the reason for the prosperous nature of the town. The people of Acrosa were more diverse than those of Ulandyl whose natives were almost exclusively felidae. Acrosa was a catchall for those who traveled The Walk and was home to humans, canidae, dwarves, felidae, and all other sorts of sensible creatures that inhabited the Far Land.

While most of the people in the Far Land had their own self-proclaimed capital cities where their species almost exclusively made their home, many other small towns were quite varied in nature, and its inhabitants got along accordingly. Ulandyl, for example, being home to mostly felidae, housed those with extreme negative dispositions toward canidae. It was, in fact, possible for the two to coexist in the same environment without conflict, and even to become friends.

Alleria made sure to don her hood before they set off, covering her pointed ears and color-changing eyes. Her eyes were curious to Laderic. He had only ever met one other elf and couldn't remember if her eyes had changed color or not. He had never heard of elves having that ability. But, then again, he had never heard of elves being able to use elemental magic like a spectral, or of them being able to form alamorphic bonds with animals like humans. Truthfully, he didn't know much about elves at all. So he let it go, figuring it was probably just a side effect of her being so weird.

"So who is this contact that you have?" asked Midiga. Her footsteps were nearly silent on the path. The morning was sunny and warm, a pleasant day for walking. Sunlight filtered through the gently blowing leaves, speckling the ground with dancing fulgor.

Laderic shrugged, looking side to side as they walked, vigilant, and ready for whatever might try to surprise them. "A friend of mine—we used to work together. His name is Mavark. We've been through some tough times together, and he's requested my specific skillset on a few of his own jobs," he alluded, referring to his own set of illegal talents. "Over the years, we've become good friends. He's referred me to several other clients as well, helping me make some money." Laderic backtracked. "It's actually not him that we need to speak to, though. It's his wife, Ysmira. I met her through him. She's a renegade elf—she might know where the city is."

Midiga nodded, one of her ears flicking with a gust of wind. "Sounds like a good plan. It's a start, anyway. Even if it is fruitless, this small detour could still help us get some information. Who knows? She might know why our friend here is so... different."

Alleria smiled, keeping to herself. While over the last couple of days, she had appeared young, almost childlike in her fear and naïvety, but she now seemed more her age. She was confident in her steps—calm, poised, and collected. "How much longer until we reach Acrosa?" she wondered aloud. "We've been walking for a few hours now."

"We should be there before nightfall," said Laderic, answering her absentmindedly. His mind was still on Mavark.

"You know, I think that's the first time you've addressed me without being sarcastic or rude," Alleria chided, raising an eyebrow toward Laderic. He hardly paid any attention.

"I should tell you guys about Mavark just so you're not surprised," he said cautiously. "He's an alamorph."

Alleria clasped her hands together excitedly. "Maybe he could help me out with some advice?" she asked. Reia, who trotted beside them, nodded her tiny head in agreement.

"I'm sure he could..." Laderic glanced at Midiga. "He's a drake alamorph."

Midiga blinked, snapping her head toward Laderic. "You're joking," she balked, eyes wide. Her tail twitched behind her, fluffed up larger than usual.

Alleria frowned, staring at the two of them in confusion. "What does that mean?" she asked. "What's going on?"

Midiga looked at her, ears lowered near her skull. "A drake alamorph is an alamorph that is bonded with a dragon," she said slowly. "This gives them a frightening amount of power. Because dragons are such strong-willed creatures when the bond occurs, the alamorph takes on a lot of dragon-like characteristics, making them a formidable foe, and quite dangerous." Midiga looked at Laderic, crossing her arms over her chest absentmindedly. She swallowed hard. "Are you sure this guy can be trusted?"

Laderic nodded, unwavering. "Absolutely. He can be a bit hard-headed, but he's a good friend. Fierce. I can safely say he would bleed for those he trusts—and I would do the same for him."

Midiga narrowed her eyes, unsure of Laderic's praise for the drake alamorph. From what she had heard, they were *not* to be trusted. Drake alamorphs often take on more than just the dragon's physical features. She had heard of the human partner being driven mad from the dragon's insatiable craving for gold and jewels. Or how they become sneaky and cruel, acquiring the silver tongue of their partner, knowing nothing but greed and treachery. Then again, these could simply be rumors and old wives' tales. As Laderic appeared to know Mavark fairly well, she had no choice but to trust his judgment.

Alleria was torn, watching both Laderic and Midiga, unsure of whom to believe. She knew little about alamorphs—only what Laderic had told her, really. Laderic was friends with Mavark, sure, but Midiga's reaction was unsettling. She made cautious eye contact with Reia, feeling the kitsune's mind in her own, unsurprised that they were sharing similar feelings about the subject.

The group continued to walk in silence, enjoying the day, each deep in their own thoughts. Warm days like this brought Laderic back to when he was younger, having grown up south of Ulandyl in a small fief just outside of Mariscale, where it was summer nearly all the year. He grew up well protected, the youngest of three boys. His dad was on good terms with the lord who shared his land with them, so they never went without.

His mother had died when he was still quite young of a plague that ravaged the lands in the south. His oldest brother also passed with the same illness. So he entered his adolescence with his father and his next oldest brother, who had stepped up as the eldest son early on in life. After the death of his mother, his father started running with a rough crowd, often abandoning the house for 'work,' leaving the boys to manage their small farm by themselves.

When Laderic was just approaching manhood, his father left for a long time, much longer than ever before. When he returned, he'd been beaten up, his body scraped and bloody. He said hardly a word, but something was horribly wrong. He moved with urgency, his eyes sunken into his skull, flinching at every sudden movement and shadow. He ordered his sons to pack their things immediately, for they were leaving the farm and not to return.

Not even an hour after his arrival, however, a thick, black fog, almost like smoke, draped itself over their farmland. A dozen nightwalker spectrals, trained in the art of dark magic, appeared from the fog and surrounded their home. One of them, in a cloak paler than moonlight, stood watch as his clan formed a circle around the old building. Laderic had run to their storehouse to stash what little food they had left in a bag just before the fog had arrived. He watched from a distance, as the nightwalker spectrals burned his home to the ground with evil, black fire, his father and brother inside.

The days after were a blur to Laderic. Nightwalkers were merely a myth in the Far Land, as any spectral chosen by dark magic at birth was cast out of their society immediately, left to fate and nature. Whispered of and spoken about around campfires late at night, or mentioned in scary stories told to children to frighten them into behaving, these stories were widely accepted as just that—stories with no truth behind them. This is what Laderic had always believed... until that night. However, each time he spoke about this, he was laughed at and quickly hushed. Talking about nightwalkers was a bad omen. It didn't take long for Laderic to learn to keep his mouth shut about what had happened that night. But he knew.

He knew.

Many nights, he would dream of the nightwalker in the white cloak—the day that they would meet once more, and he would wrench a sword through his still-beating heart.

"Laderic!" shouted Alleria, waving her hand in front of his face. He flinched, blinking, shaking his head back and forth to clear his thoughts. He narrowed his eyes, glaring at her. He didn't speak.

"I was just wondering how you met your alamorph friend?" she asked, frowning. "But you ignored me. Twice."

"It's a long story," he said flatly, gloomy thoughts killing his mood. He normally tried his best to avoid thinking of home around other people.

Alleria huffed, looking away into the distance as she walked. "I was just asking," she muttered.

"I'll tell you eventually," he grunted, closing the subject. They walked in silence a while longer.

Midiga kept her ears on alert for anything suspicious in the surrounding sparse woods, but, as it was daylight, and this road was well traveled, it was unlikely they were going to have any surprise visitors. She didn't mind the quiet walk, basking in the sunlight as any cat would. She grinned to herself, as her thoughts drifted to a humorous subject.

"So," she began, "Laderic, when do I get my payback for Padstow?" Her tail flicked with amusement as she bared her sharp teeth in a mischievous grin.

"Please, Midiga, not now," groaned Laderic, preferring to keep quiet and mull his emotions. He was not in the mood to talk.

"What are you talking about?" asked Alleria, eyes widening in anticipation of the story that was to come. Midiga chuckled.

"It's not a big deal, really," she said, though glancing at Laderic to make sure he wouldn't mind her telling the story. He didn't say a word, wrapped up in his own little world again. She shrugged and continued. "Laderic and I have known each other almost four years now. We traveled together a lot, and we share tips on jobs whenever we happen to run into each other.

"Well, one summer—last year I believe—we had a lead on a thief hiding out in Padstow, a city southwest of here on the Servatio River. A lord of the kingdom of Rokswing owned land to the north of the city, and some petty thief had broken into his house and stolen a bust of his late wife. Well, long story short, we caught the guy, took the bust back from him—well, maybe a bit more than that too—and then we hung him by his hood from a three-story window." She sighed, closing her eyes in wistful nostalgia. "Ah, those were the days..." Alleria smiled, amused by the image in her head.

"Anyway, that's not the end. Laderic and I decided to head to the local tavern and celebrate... and some burly dwarf challenged him to a drinking contest. I *tried* to tell him to say no, but Laderic has this problem where he *can't* say no to a challenge, even when he knows he's going to lose." She raised her muzzle in a coy grin. "As you can imagine, he got himself drank under the table. And it wasn't anything to do with the dwarf." She eyed Laderic, jerking a thumb in his direction. "Mr. Tough Guy over here is a lightweight. He had himself two pints and *could not* stand up."

"It was three," interjected Laderic bluntly.

"Whatever. Anyway, the dwarf demanded a prize. Too incapacitated to say no, he essentially robbed Laderic of all of his things. Including the bust that we had *just* got back from the thief earlier that day." The felid sighed. "It was a shame I had to kill him to get it all back."

Alleria, who had been listening intently, did a double take. She blinked. "You... you killed him?" she squeaked. Midiga nodded as if it were no big deal.

"Dwarves won't part with treasure for *anything*. Especially treasure they believe they've won. So, I killed him while he slept. He probably didn't even feel it." The cat's tone was nonchalant as if she were merely recounting a mundane day's events.

Alleria stared, eyes wide. "Couldn't you have just... taken it from him while he slept and left him alive?"

Midiga shook her head. "You can't leave any loose ends in business like that. Technically, he had won the stuff, but *I* had worked for it." She tilted her head toward Laderic. "And sensitive over here just can't say no, even when he knows he's outmatched. He was passed out *way* before that dwarf hit the hay and left me to do all the dirty work."

"I said I was sorry." He moaned as he looked back at Midiga. "Can't you just let it go?"

"We'll see...," she said, winking at Alleria. The elf suppressed a laugh. "I'm sure I'll find a way to get you back, eventually."

Alleria swallowed, uncertain if she wanted to know exactly what Midiga had in mind. The elf picked up Reia, stroking her intently. She felt a new fear and respect for the felid in the back of her mind. She squinted, contemplating for a second. "Wait, isn't he making up for it by coming with us?"

Midiga cackled maniacally. "Oh no, he owes me money for a different reason." She stretched her arms up over her head. "You'll find Laderic gets in over his head quite often, and it's usually me saving him."

"I've saved you too, don't forget," he remarked, still lost in his own head.

"Yeah, but I've kept track. Still not nearly as often as I have," countered the felid.

Laderic didn't say anything back, and Midiga finally took the hint. The sun was just beginning its descent, as it was just after midday. They decided to stop to eat lunch in a small clearing visible from the road. Midiga had brought along her entire stash of dried goods, keeping most of them in Laderic's enchanted bag. She had mostly meat, but some berries too, only because she liked the taste. No vegetables, though no one was complaining about that.

Once they had finished eating, they set back on the road, determined to make it to their destination before nightfall. And they were not disappointed. Only a few hours later, they reached the outermost watchtower of Acrosa. The tower was old and carved from stone, and the forest had grown around it so naturally, the stone itself seemed alive from the moss and vines that laced its exterior. Caravans passed in and out of the city, carrying food, jewelry, and other goods to and from the market. At the city gates, two guards on large horses stood watch. Midiga kept a watchful eye on the guard nearest them. His muzzle stuck out from his helmet, and his tongue lolled out of his mouth as he panted in the heat of the encroaching summer. Her fur stood on end as they passed the canid, but he paid them no mind, doing his job dutifully.

Acrosa was one of the oldest towns in the Far Land with buildings made from ancient hand-carved stone and wood that had been refinished and replaced over the last century or so. The Walk split the city almost perfectly in half, and the market was located on both sides of the road. The vendors nearly smothered visitors with their proposals of limited-time-only deals, discounted prices, and free gifts with certain purchases.

Every kind of sensible being in the Far Land could be seen walking the streets, mingling happily with each other in the diverse city. Acrosa was not only a center for trade but for culture, as well. It was unlike the more traditional Ulandyl, which was one of the first cities settled by the felidae. Acrosa had been settled by a mix of races, and this was clearly visible both in the diversity of its residents and the equal representation of the different gods.

Alleria, fascinated by the diversity around her, began to ask Laderic more questions, this time about the cities of the Far Land. Laderic, being well traveled and knowing much about the history of each race, happily obliged, launching into a lecture on the capitals.

He began with telling her each race in the Far Land had a self-proclaimed capital city—a city in which their race dominated the population, and the foundations of the rich history of their people took root. For felidae, it was Ulandyl, the regional capital of trade. As felids were sly of the tongue and good with business, it was only natural that their kind should flourish in such a strategic location. The felidae in Ulandyl were nearly all nocturnal and very independent. They usually hunted their own food, and whatever extra they had, they often peddled from inn to inn, hoping for some business from hungry travelers. The felidae in Ulandyl were notorious for their hatred of canidae, and rarely would a canid be caught dead anywhere near the city. Acrosa was the closest they would get—if they knew what was good for them.

The canidae themselves had their capital far to the west, in the city of Haust. Haust was located in a beautiful field in the open plains by the Blue Lake. Tall walls made of stone surrounded the city, and while it was open to outsiders, it most definitely remained closed to felidae. Haust was the last friendly city westward before reaching uninhabited lands. The forest beyond was aptly named the Underdark and was widely considered evil and impassable. Filled with undead and hardly explored, it was a treacherous trap for any curious adventurer. The walls around Haust were built originally to keep the dead out until they could clear the forest in the immediate perimeter. In fact, they likely wouldn't have settled near the Underdark at all if not for the Blue Lake being such an important religious symbol to the canidae.

The elves had cities everywhere, though now abandoned. Thousands of years ago, they had towns in every corner of the explored world—before most of the other mortal races had even settled in the Far Land. The elves existed along with the dwarves and fae long before the arrival of the others. The farthest city to the south was an ancient elvish city called Kaina'jainito, located on the southwestern coast. To the east, beyond Strita in the mountains, the elves had another city at the summit of Mt. Ewa, the tallest mountain in the range, called Ewa'jainito. Also abandoned, the city is now said to be home to dragons, griffins, and other fantastical creatures.

During an ancient war with the dwarves, the elves abandoned their cities and fled to the north, no longer revered protectors of the Far Land, but secretive cowards, locked in their own world in the ice. An enchantment was placed on Nara'jainita that it would be lost from the memories of all those who weren't elves. Now the city is rumored, hundreds of years later, to be only myth. Elves were a rarity to see, and those who left often lived secluded and alone. Some considered them a dying race, but others spent their entire lives trying to find the elvish capital in hopes of some kind of otherworldly enlightenment.

The dwarves only laid claim to one city, Terun, but they could be found in nearly every corner of the known world. Their only claimed city was even further to the north than where the elvish capital was rumored to be, in the Skytouch mountain range, where the mountains were so high that no one had ever seen the other side of them. The dwarves made their home within the mountains, having hollowed out many of them, and built their livelihood directly into the rock. The hand-carved caverns were warm year round, which was important in the arctic, especially in the winter.

As for the other races, they generally made their homes all around the Far Land. Humans could be found in virtually every city, but most lived in the south, in the plains lining the western part of the Servatio River and in the eastern city of Mariscale. The two cities of Rokswing and Mariscale were once warring kingdoms but had been at peace for centuries, united under the banner of a single kingdom since their peace treaty was signed.

The fae people were said to consider the Brushdeep Forest—the eastern woods spanning from the Servatio River to the south and the Navanja River to the west—to be their home. spectrals also made their home in the Brushdeep Forest, in the life-giving Tree of Amarantae, but they were much more seclusive than the fae. While spectrals themselves were a common sight in the Far Land, outsiders were rarely welcomed in their own society.

Fae, while mainly found in wooded areas, could also be found in nearly every city, including Acrosa, as was made clear by the number of fairy vendors in the town. Alleria was fascinated by the sheer amount of booths and salespeople, more than half of which were fae. Since the fairies only worked for a quarter of the year in assisting the changing of the seasons, they spent the rest of the year selling and trading wares all around the Far Land.

"And they always try to convince you to—Alleria?" Laderic

said, pausing his monologue mid-sentence. She was nowhere to be found. He whirled around to find her drifting to the right, fascinated by the multicolored booth of one of the fae vendors. The booth appeared to be a small tree growing right out of the stone ground. The canopy of leaves created a nice shady area for potential buyers to scout their wares. From the branches of the tree hung small cages with exotic birds and tiny snakes and other creatures for sale.

"Hello," said Alleria, wide eyes taking in all of the trinkets and magical objects. She looked down at the vendor who was fluttering just above the ground, crinkled eyes smiling at her. The fae woman was only three feet tall, and her skin was tinged green. She had vibrant green hair and long dragonfly wings on her back that buzzed so fast they were almost impossible to see. She wore simple brown cloth pants and a flowing, earth-colored blouse. She wore no shoes, of course, as the fae people rarely walk, and prefer to wear as little clothing as possible so as not to weigh themselves down.

She was a summertime fae, making a living selling her wares in her off-season before the summer started, for the fae control the changing of seasons. They are only in their magical prime during their born season. She was an older woman, well seasoned in the merchant trade, and had the familiar kindness of a grandmother.

"Hello, dearie," said the fairy, fluttering up a few feet to look her in the eye. "You have beautiful eyes," she said, peering at the elf with a searching gaze. Whether or not her flattery was only to help make a sale was unimportant to Alleria, who blushed deeply, looking down quickly in case her irises were to change color.

"Thank you," she said. Reia rolled her eyes, still in Alleria's arms. The elf pointed up at the cages hanging from the tree. "What are those?" she asked.

The fae woman fluttered to the ceiling, gesturing at each

61

cage. "These are exotic birds from the northern forests," she said, pointing first to a large red parrot-like bird with six wings, and then to a bright yellow, slender one with a large, fluffy crest. "They would make nice accessories and would match your hair. And these are drascals from the coasts near Mariscale, they make good pets." She gestured towards another cage, where a tiny blue dragon was sleeping. It was the size of a seagull, with a bright yellow beak and webbed feet. As Alleria watched, it lifted its head and yawned, flashing row after row of tiny needle teeth.

The summertime fae halted suddenly in her sales pitch, noticing Reia, who Allera had clutched in her arms. "Do these old eyes deceive me or is your friend there a kitsune?" She zipped back down from the ceiling to take a closer look at the fox. The wrinkles around her eyes became more prominent as she squinted at Reia.

"How did you know?" Alleria asked, glancing back and forth between the fairy and her soul partner. The fae woman shrugged, lifting the back of her hand and allowing Reia to sniff.

"I've been around a while. I know all about magical creatures. I could tell because her—she's a she, right?" she asked. Alleria nodded, watching as Reia gently sniffed the fairy's hand. "I knew because her eyes are golden and not brown like a normal fox."

Reia grinned, though it appeared like a snarl. "You have a good eye," she spoke, bowing her head to the fae woman, who gasped.

"An alamorph," she swooned, clasping her hands together and doing a quick spin. "Oh, you are very lucky to have a kitsune as your soul partner. I'm quite jealous!"

Alleria blushed once more, stroking Reia's forehead. "I know, I'm so lucky," she agreed. "I can't imagine my life without Reia. We just found each other one day, and since then, it's just felt like my whole life was—"

"*There* you are!" interrupted Laderic, appearing suddenly

behind Alleria and startling her. He put his arm around her shoulders, pulling her away from the booth. "No, we don't want a drascal or a bag of love berries," he said, cutting sarcasm lacing his words, "but thanks anyway!"

"But I—" Alleria began, looking longingly backward toward the nice fae woman, who was scowling in Laderic's direction with her arms crossed. Her wings seemed to buzz angrily, somehow even faster than before.

Laderic looked down at her. "Do you have any money?" he asked rhetorically.

"No, but I—"

"Fae are naturally charming, making them excellent salespeople," Laderic lectured. They wove their way through the crowd, past creatures and people of every type. "I know you enjoyed talking to her, but that's how they make everyone feel if they want to, but trust me, she just wanted a sale."

Alleria frowned, dejected, clutching Reia tightly as she walked, Laderic's arm still around her shoulder. "I guess," she said, not necessarily believing him. Although, she began to think about the woman's words, remembering how she had complimented her hair, which was tucked completely back under her hood. She sighed then, realizing Laderic was probably right.

"You have to be careful in these places," Laderic said, continuing to offer advice. He scanned the crowd for Midiga, who he had accidentally left behind on his mission to find Alleria. "I do my best, anyway. These people target young people like you to try to get an easy sale."

Alleria furrowed her brow, looking up at Laderic. "But you're the same age as me... right?" she asked. There was no way Laderic could have been much older than she was. She looked him over while they walked, noting his young face and neatly trimmed facial hair. He couldn't have been more than twenty years old... *Right?*

He grinned as he spotted Midiga in the crowd. He pulled Alleria along faster, wanting to catch up before he lost sight of the felid again. "I guess I'm close enough to your age, but even so, you're a woman," he said flatly, dragging Alleria behind him, impatient.

"What's that supposed to mean?" Alleria asked, indignant, yanking her arm out of his grip and stopping in her tracks. "I'm a woman, so therefore, I'm easier to trick into buying something?"

Laderic stopped, turning to face Alleria and putting his hands on her shoulders, staring into her red eyes. "*Most* people don't think that, *I* don't think that," he began, quickly defending himself, "but a lot of people, especially salespeople, always try to sell to the women first. They think women are more flippant with their money, or something along those lines. It's just the way it is. Doesn't make it right." He turned to start walking once more, throwing his arm back over her shoulder to pull her along with him, so she didn't drift away toward any other booths. "And, I mean, I can't blame them. You ladies are more likely to buy shiny things and accessories. It's just how it goes."

He flagged down Midiga with a wave while Alleria acknowledged his point. *Women do buy more jewelry and clothes*, she thought to herself. She shrugged, deciding to drop the subject as they reached their felid friend.

"Look," Midiga said, gesturing ahead of them with her paw. There was a side road, taking them away from The Walk and toward a large tavern, which looked to be filling up quickly. A couple of dwarves pushed past each other, squeezing through the tight doorway into the lively bar. As the doors opened and shut, a wave of sound ebbed and flowed—the sound of clinking bottles and hearty laughter. A rusty sign hung outside the doorway swung as each person who entered slapped it with their hands in turn. The sign read, 'The Water Bowl.'

Midiga bared her teeth in a mischievous grin. "While you two lovebirds were off shopping, I might have found us a place

65

to stay for the night." She put her paws on her hips, eying the two of them.

"Lovebirds?" Laderic and Alleria cried in unison. Laderic looked down, realizing his arm was still around Alleria's shoulders. He raised it up quickly, nearly punching her in the back of the head. "Come on, Midiga, you know me better than that," he stammered, and he quickly pulled ahead of them as they squeezed their way to the tavern through the crowd. Alleria's face flushed at Midiga's comment. She was confused why a smile was stuck on her lips.

CHAPTER 6

THE INN WAS nothing special, though it was crowded as could be. Inside, there was an L-shaped bar, tables and chairs, and a small stage area for shows and street performances. But that was it—no paintings, seat cushions, or even windows. The tables themselves were filled, though, with nearly every race in the Far Land represented in that tiny room.

Midiga approached the bar with Laderic and Alleria awkwardly tailing behind. It was loud, the lively nature of the customers adding some flair to the otherwise plain and boxy room. The felid set her elbows on the bar, propping her head in one of her paws. "How much for a room for the night," she purred, twirling her whiskers with one of her claws, her voice catching the barkeeper's attention. He turned, and Midiga nearly leapt out of her fur.

The barkeep was a white canid with a gray-tipped muzzle. His tongue lagged lazily out of his mouth, and he stumbled across the floor toward Midiga, clearly having had some drinks himself. In his paws, he cradled a glass, which he polished with a rag. "Thrice the cost of a lager," he said, wagging his tail and nearly brushing some of the glassware off the lower shelves, "or, if you sit down and have some drinks, it might be free, dependin' on your tab."

Midiga stood up, rigid, her tail stiff and fluffed from the sight of the canid. "We'll just have some drinks then," she said through clenched teeth, and her ears flattened against her skull from the unpleasant surprise. The barkeep wagged his tail again, gesturing over to an empty table on his left. The group headed that direction, Midiga still rigid from her encounter with the canid.

"Relax, Midiga," Laderic said, eyes narrowed in concern. "Are you okay?"

She exhaled hard as she realized she had been holding her breath. Her ears twitched as they slowly unstuck themselves from her skull. "I'm fine," she growled. "Just caught me off guard, and after our little encounter with those canidae the other day, you can't blame me for not being too happy to see one *running* this place." She closed her eyes, folding her paws and breathing slowly and deliberately.

"You really don't like them, huh," Alleria said, watching the barkeep from across the room. He was collecting three full mugs in his paws, preparing to carry them over to their table. "But he seems so nice!"

"He's drunk," grunted Midiga. "Any canid you meet would bite you in the back *in a second* if it meant he could get ahead somehow," she said darkly, mind elsewhere. "That one is probably just waiting until we go upstairs to—"

"Midiga!" Laderic interrupted, waving his hand in front of her face. "Calm down! By the time we go upstairs, he's probably going to be passed out on the floor."

"Here's a round to get you guys started!" barked the canid suddenly, appearing right behind Midiga as he reached their table. He began passing out the three nearly overflowing tankards. He sloshed some beer on Midiga, who hissed in response, but he didn't even notice. "Now, y'all be careful with that. It'll make you want more. Don't wanna end up like me now!" He laughed, howling at the end of his speech. It was loud and drawn out, and answered by several other canidae in the tavern. Midiga's body was flattened against the table, ears pulled back, tail completely fluffed. The barkeep didn't even notice, laughing and stumbling back behind the bar.

"What has gotten into you," Laderic said, watching Midiga carefully with concern. "It's like you've never seen a canid before."

"Usually, when I see them, I'm killing them," she hissed, still trying to become part of the table. "Not socializing with them."

Alleria was staring curiously at her drink. "What exactly is this?" she said, ignoring Midiga's demeanor. Laderic grinned, pushing it closer to her.

"That's a *tasty* drink right there." There was a hint of impish joy in his tone. He laced his fingers, smirking at Alleria as she watched the drink with suspicion.

Reia, who had been quiet for quite a while, raised her little head and peeked over the table from Alleria's lap. She put her paws on the table and stood, slowly leaning her head over the edge of the drink. Immediately, she pulled back, scrunching up her nose. "It smells awful."

"Yeah, but," Laderic replied, taking a drink of his own, "it tastes *so* good."

Alleria looked doubtfully at her cup, watching as Laderic sipped his beer and Midiga downed her own. The elf stared as the cat-woman drank, and drank, and drank, turning her tankard upside down without stopping. She slammed her drink down on the table, glaring over at Laderic.

"Get me three more," she said, serious. "I don't want to go *near* that dog." Laderic sighed and nodded, standing from his seat and meandering over to the bar.

Alleria looked down at her own drink once again, picking it up gingerly by the handle. Reia jumped back down into her lap as she brought the drink toward her nose. The elf sniffed, immediately regretting her decision. The lager was pungent in smell, and she didn't want to imagine what it might taste like. Nevertheless, wanting to make a good impression on her new friends, she took a sip. It bubbled in her mouth, stinging almost. She swallowed quickly, but the awful taste lingered. She forced a smile.

"Wow, this is good," she said, watering eyes turning pale yellow with the lie. Midiga watched her, whiskers glistening with droplets of beer.

"Just don't drink too much," she warned monotonously. "You don't want to get like Laderic does after two of them." Slowly, but surely, she had been sitting up in her seat, no longer trying to blend in with the table.

Laderic came back, holding the three beers. He dropped them in front of Midiga, who immediately picked up a new one and started chugging again. Alleria took another drink, eyes leaking in protest of the flavor. "This is good," she repeated, unable to concentrate enough to think of anything else to say. Laderic watched, knowingly.

"You don't *have* to drink it," he said, remembering the first time he had tasted beer. Growing up with two older brothers, he was just nine. The experience, he remembered, hadn't been a pleasant one. His two older brothers hadn't been nearly as nice to him as he was being to Alleria about it. "If you don't like it, don't worry about it."

Alleria shook her head, taking another indignant drink. "I do like it," she said, after forcing the bubbling lava down her throat. She was going to like beer whether she liked it or not.

Laderic shrugged. "Suit yourself," he said, taking another sip of his own. He was gonna stick with just one tonight. He

EMBER — ECHOES OF ASHES — BOOK ONE

couldn't admit it to himself, but he really just didn't want to look foolish in front of Alleria.

Reia leapt off Alleria's lap, jumping back up to sit in the empty fourth seat at their table. She watched the three silently drink the gross tasting liquid, not quite understanding why they would put themselves through drinking such nastiness. *Humans,* she thought, shaking her tiny head in wonder. *I don't think I'll ever understand them.*

Suddenly, a man in a blue cloak swooped through the door, approaching the canid at the bar. Reia couldn't quite hear what the man said through the deafening noise of the rowdy drinkers in the tavern, but she saw the canid laugh and gesture the man over to the empty stage in the corner.

"Hey, guys," she chirped to the three silent drinkers.

Midiga put down her third beer, picking up her fourth. "What?"

"I think that guy is gonna perform," said the kitsune, perking up her ears and watching him weave his way through the tables and chairs. As he passed other people, they grew quiet, whispering to each other in excitement. Soon, the room was silent, all eyes on the stage.

Once he settled on stage, the man pulled off his cloak to reveal his bare chest, covered in intricate tattoos on his blue-tinged skin. The tattoos appeared to ebb and flow, floating on his skin as if it were a lake. A large golden pendant hung from his neck, the gemstone inside shining with dazzling blue light. The audience clapped, cheering and hooting for the water-breather spectral. His head was shaved, face hairless, save for a single, long ponytail of black hair jutting out from the back of his head.

Alleria clapped too. "Oh, he's gonna do magic! This is going to be good!" she cheered. Laderic watched silently, observant. Midiga continued to drink.

The water-breather lifted his cloak from the ground, revealing a glass vase that seemed to materialize out of nowhere.

The audience clapped again. He closed his eyes, hand hovering over the vase. The water from inside rose into the air in a delicate spiral pattern, sparkling in the tavern light. When it reached his palm, it gathered into a sphere. Once all of the water was in his hand, he tossed the ball into the air, letting it fall until it nearly touched the ground, and then he held out his hand, stopping it just inches from the floor, letting it hover. A murmur of 'oohs' and 'ahhs' filled the room.

He concentrated again, the large sphere now splitting up into hundreds of smaller spheres, each one only as large as a single coin. He levitated them, surrounding his body with the water. He made two circles around himself, both of them meeting right in front of his body, forming an *X*. The circles began to spin, the droplets intersecting perfectly, so they didn't touch. The crowd applauded once more.

Alleria was starstruck, eyes vibrant green in her awe. She sipped on her beer as she watched, hardly noticing the harshness of the flavor anymore. Laderic watched her, amused. Spectral street performers had lost their luster with him as he traveled. He had seen performances of almost every kind of magic. The current performer was only sub-par in his eyes.

The water-breather let the droplets merge once again until they formed four larger spheres. Two of them he held in his hands, and two of them he sent to the floor, forming thin planks beneath his feet. Then, he closed his eyes, and his body began to rise as he stood on the water under his feet, using the spheres in his hands to balance. The audience went wild. He held his hands in front of him, the water pulling him forward as he 'flew' around the room. The drunks in the bar whistled and laughed as he soared by their tables. Alleria clapped, giddy, as he whizzed by their own.

Midiga stood, moving to the bar, now at a point where she didn't care about facing the bartender alone. She sat at a barstool and ordered two more for herself.

Laderic sighed, propping his feet on Midiga's empty chair. He watched Alleria, entertained by her reaction. *She must have never seen magic done this way before,* he thought. Alleria had received no training, so her own magic was based more on emotion rather than will.

The spectral brought himself back to the stage, raising his body higher and higher in the air. He maneuvered the water so that he was eventually lying flat on the ceiling upside down. Suddenly, the water below him gave way, and he fell to the floor. The audience gasped, some people even standing from their seats to watch, but just as he was going to hit the floor, the droplets formed a cushion beneath him, catching him in the air.

The room burst into whistles and cheers, but Laderic shook his head, unamused. *As if no one has ever used* that *trick,* he thought sarcastically. He was, however, amused by Alleria's reaction.

"That was *amazing!*" she said, the water-breather taking his bows, passing the vase around and collecting coins from the crowd. "I've never seen magic used in such a... pretty way! And so artistic! And wonderful!"

"You know, you could probably do that too," Laderic told her. She sat back down, taking another drink of her beer, which was almost gone. It wasn't burning her mouth anymore, and it was starting to taste... good.

"You mean with my magic?" she asked, unsure. Laderic nodded. "I've never been able to use it on command... Only when I'm upset or scared."

"That's just something you'll have to work on," he said, studying her curiously.

"Could you teach me?" Alleria asked with eyes wide and golden once more.

Laderic paused for a moment, unsure. "I can't use magic myself, but I'm sure the techniques for controlling that kind of thing are similar to learning swordplay or footwork." He grinned to himself. "Concentration, meditation, execution."

"Concentration, meditation, execution," Alleria repeated to herself. "Can you show me that stuff?"

"I'm sure I can," he said, more than happy to educate someone else on something that he himself was good at—especially if it could help all of them in the end.

"Also... Laderic?"

"Yes?" he said absentmindedly, now lost in thought, pondering various exercises he could come up with to help her practice.

"Can I have another beer? That one was good." The elf's eyes were bright gold still, not paling in the slightest.

"You... don't have to have another one if you don't want to," he said hesitantly.

"But I do," she said, excited. "I really do."

Laderic sighed, standing up to walk back over to the bar. He flagged down the white canid. "Can I get another beer, and a room for the night?"

LATER THAT NIGHT, when the tavern itself was nearly bare, Laderic finally managed to get Alleria up the stairs and into their room.

"That was *ssssooooo* much fun!" she slurred, concentrating on moving her feet. Laderic was essentially holding her up, scared to let her go to try to walk on her own.

"Mmhmm," he agreed, without even listening to what she said. "Let's get to bed now."

"Where's Midiga?" she asked, sounding like her mouth was moving in slow motion.

"She's already in the room, sleeping on a blanket on the floor. We're gonna sleep in the bed, okay?"

Her eyes widened, their color swimming back and forth

from green to red to yellow and back again like they couldn't make up their mind. "But we can't sssleep in the same *bed*!" she cried. She stood up straight suddenly, glaring at Laderic. "I bare-ly even *know* you."

Laderic closed his eyes, canning his frustration. "I'll put some pillows down so there will be a wall between us. Is that okay?"

Alleria's eyes changed instantly from an angry scarlet to a deep blue. "Okay," she whined, sounding terribly sad all of a sudden. They hobbled over to the bed, and he helped her sit down.

"Why can't I walk?" she slurred, looking up at Laderic in confusion.

"Because you drank four of those beers after I told you that you should slow down," he explained bluntly, pulling back the blankets and helping her get under them. Reia, who had been following diligently behind, jumped up onto the bed beside her soul partner.

"Just... make sure she doesn't throw up," Laderic begged. "Or roll off the bed and hit her head on something. Or get up and start—"

"I got it," Reia interrupted, sounding just as frustrated as Laderic. She curled up next to Alleria between the elf and the edge of the bed, covering her own face with her seven tails.

Laderic sighed as he went to close the door behind them. He locked it, putting the key on the wooden dresser. They had got the free room sometime after Midiga's eighth drink, though the free rooms really illustrated the phrase *you get what you pay for*. The room had one full-sized bed, a tiny dresser, and a single lantern. One thing nice was the large window at one end, which took up nearly the entire wall, floor to ceiling. Midiga had gone to bed early, seemingly unfazed by the alcohol in her system. She had taken a blanket from the bed and made a pallet on the floor for herself, leaving the rest of the bed for Laderic and

Alleria.

Laderic was forced to babysit Alleria for the next few hours after she discovered that she liked beer. He cut her off at four, though he should have at two. He didn't even end up finishing his own. Now, he could finally get some rest, and he stripped down to his undergarments and climbed into bed on his side of the pillows. Alleria was already snoring.

Just a few hours later, something woke him once again. At first, he thought thunder had done it, for the storm outside was raging. As he lay in bed trying to go back to sleep, he realized there was another noise. Someone was quietly crying, and he sat up to see who—though he had a guess. Alleria, still somewhat tipsy, was laying in bed, stiff as a board, terror on her face.

"Did I wake you up?" she whispered shakily. "I'm sorry. I'll get back to sleep soon."

"What's wrong?" Laderic asked. Lightning flashed outside, and Alleria jumped.

"I just don't like—" she started. Suddenly, thunder that sounded like cannon fire boomed from directly overhead. Alleria quickly covered her mouth with her hands, muffling a tiny screech. "Storms," she whimpered, barely audible.

"You're scared?" Laderic said, stating the obvious. She nodded her head. For a minute, the two both sat up in bed, listening to the pounding rain. The silence between them stretched on for a while, filled only by the sound of the pouring rain.

"You know," Laderic began after a while, speaking to her as he would a child, reminding himself that she was still intoxicated. "Things are only as scary as you make them"—he pointed to his head—"up here." Alleria watched, drinking in his words. "When you're scared of something, you just start thinking about it over and over until you can't get it out of your head, right?"

"Yes." Alleria exhaled, eyes flicking back and forth between

Laderic's face and the window. There was another flash of lightning.

"Well, if you can look at the thing—" Thunder interrupted his words, deafeningly loud. Alleria covered her face with her hands.

She stayed like that, unmoving. "I'm listening," she squeaked after a second, keeping her face covered. Laderic rolled his eyes but held his tongue.

"I was saying that if you can look at the thing that scares you the most and say 'I'm not afraid,' then you've won." He watched her, her face covered still. She spread her fingers apart slightly, peeking through. "Can you say it with me?"

"I'm not afraid," she said in sync with Laderic. "I'm not afraid." Lightning flashed again, and her body tensed up once more. She stared at Laderic through her hands. "I'm not afraid," came her muffled voice. "I am not—" Thunder resounded overhead. "AFRAID!" she cried, squinting and then closing her eyes. Her hands began to glow slightly with a faint, golden light. Laderic's eyes widened, nervous.

"Remember when I talked with you about learning to control your magic?" he said quickly, not taking his eyes off her hands. He reached over, resting his hand gently on her shoulder. He could feel her muscles relax a tiny bit. "Remember the words I said? Concentration, meditation, execution. The first one is—"

"Concentration," she breathed. "I'm not afraid," she said again, repeating the mantra. The light in her hands began to fade. "I am not afraid." She slowly moved her hands from her face into her lap, the golden glow having completely vanished. She took a deep breath in and let it out. Lightning flashed outside, and though she saw it through her eyelids, she kept her eyes shut. "I am not afraid." Thunder boomed. She didn't flinch.

Laderic smiled at her when she opened her eyes. "How did you know I should do that?" she asked, looking at him with a feeling of wonder.

"I've used it before many times," he said. She leaned in, listening to his every word, drinking them in. "It's a mental thing. Most of the time, fear is the only thing holding you back from the things you want to do. You just have to convince yourself not to be afraid—just keep telling yourself over and over. Then, the thing you're most scared of isn't even scary anymore. It's beautiful." For a while, the two stared out the window. Alleria watched the wonder of nature through a new lens, still nervous, but feeling more appreciative than afraid. In the back of her mind, she felt Laderic's presence right beside her. A little voice in her subconscious whispered that his shirt was off, and they were in bed together, and—

"What are you most afraid of, Laderic?" she blurted, interrupting her own thought process. She moved her long brown hair out of her face, feeling tiny beads of sweat that had gathered on her brow. She focused on breathing.

Laderic frowned, looking away. "That's a pretty deep question for someone you don't really know," he said, tone shifting suddenly into a dark place. Alleria blinked, his change in mood startling her. "But I guess it doesn't matter," he continued. "My biggest fear is dying."

"Dying?" asked Alleria quietly, unsure of how to feel. Laderic nodded.

"Death frightens me," he admitted, sounding as though he was talking to himself. "I don't know what I would do if I couldn't think, couldn't breathe." His hands absentmindedly drifted to his neck. "If I'm not thinking... what am I? If I can't feel..." he shuddered. "I don't even like thinking about it. Nothingness... I can't even comprehend it, but it scares me."

"You don't believe there is something after death?" asked Alleria. Laderic looked down at his hands, internal battle raging in his mind

"I don't know if I believe in the gods," he said slowly. "It would be nice if there was somewhere to go after you die... but the thought that there might not be, that's what scares me the most." He grew silent then, avoiding eye contact with the elf woman.

Alleria frowned, feeling guilty for prying into Laderic's personal feelings. She hadn't meant to, not realizing her innocent question would bring up such deep emotions. She yawned then, exhausted. Laderic forced a smile.

"Let's get some sleep," he said. She nodded, lying back down and pulling Reia close like a stuffed bear. Laderic lay back down as well, rolling his eyes at the silly pillow wall between them.

He closed his eyes, folding his hands over his chest. "I am not afraid..." Alleria mumbled. Her voice was relaxing. "I am not afraid." Laderic let her words lull him to sleep, confident that he would wake up the next morning, fully alive.

"I am not afraid."

CHAPTER 7

"WAKE UP!" YIPPED Reia, jumping over the pillow wall and landing right on Laderic's crotch.

It was as if a hot iron had landed between his legs. "Oof!" he gasped, sitting up straight and doubling over, covering his sensitive parts. "Oh… gods..."

Alleria laughed, sitting up and noticing Laderic's position, immediately catching on. "Reia..." she said, looking at the kitsune, playfully scolding her, "what did you do?"

"I just wanted him to wake up." She pouted, sitting at the foot of the bed, seven tails curled around her paws. Midiga was up already, leaning against the wall with her arms crossed.

"Oh, he's awake now." She snickered, grinning evilly. "Normally, he takes *forever* to get out of bed."

Though Laderic could hear their conversation, he was unable to make coherent sentences or even move. He continued smooshing his face into the mattress as he held himself, hoping maybe to cut off his air supply long enough to numb the pain.

It took him a few minutes, but he finally rolled back over,

eyes squinted shut. "I'm okay," he wheezed, having finally quelled his urge to puke.

Midiga moved away from the wall, arching her back as she stretched. Her claws unsheathed for a moment as she lifted her arms above her head. "We should get a move on," she said with a yawn, muzzle pulling back taut and revealing her pointed ivories. "We need to make as much ground as possible since we will be camping out again tonight."

Alleria frowned, dreading the thought of sleeping on the hard ground once again. "I had *just* gotten used to the bed." She sighed. Laderic nodded in agreement, trying to find the willpower to stand up.

"Yeah," he grunted. "We should get going." After another minute or so, he swung his legs off the bed, standing up slowly and stretching for a long moment.

Alleria stood as well but quickly became dizzy, sitting back down on the bed, hard. "Oh…" she mumbled, closing her eyes. Her head had started pounding, and she raised her fingertips to her temples.

Laderic, who knew exactly what was wrong, played dumb. "What is it?" he asked, making sly eye contact with Midiga across the room. "What's wrong?"

"My head…" groaned Alleria, holding her forehead in her palms. At the same time, her stomach had begun to hurt, and she felt nauseous. "Oh, man, I think I'm getting sick."

Midiga snorted, unable to hold back her laughter any longer, and Laderic joined in, both of them lacking the willpower to stop giggling.

"Ugh, what?" demanded Alleria, annoyed, snapping at them without looking up from her palms.

"Hey, I told you to stop after two of those beers," Laderic said, holding back another giggle.

Alleria looked up, making horrified eye contact with Laderic. "You mean… the *beer* did this?" she asked. Another

81

wave of pain slammed into her head, and she covered her eyes once again. "It's so… bright in here."

Midiga and Laderic couldn't stop laughing, and even Reia joined in the contagious humor, though she didn't know exactly why she was laughing. After another minute or so, Midiga reached into her bag, pulling out a plump, green berry, and plopping it into Alleria's lap.

The elf looked up, confused. "What? Do I eat this or something?" she asked.

The felid nodded, wiping tears from her eyes with the back of her paw. "Yep," she confirmed, suppressing another fit of laughter. "I always keep them on me. They're called pompouries, but most people just call them 'day-after' berries. They're popular with people who frequent the taverns, and you'll see why in a second."

Alleria eyed the berry suspiciously but did as Midiga instructed. She popped it into her mouth, biting down slowly. It was firm on the outside with a soft, wet inside, almost like a grape. It burst as she split it open, a waterfall of juices flooding her cheeks. She swallowed painfully, not expecting the berry to contain so much liquid.

Midiga was right, though—the berry was truly a lifesaver. Within minutes, she felt much better—her headache was completely gone, her stomach felt normal, and she was full of energy.

"Come on, let's go!" she chirped, buzzing around the room as Laderic and Midiga gathered their things.

Midiga smiled. "You're welcome," she chided, and Alleria nodded quickly.

"Oh, yeah, thanks a *ton*," she said, emphasis hanging on the last word.

Laderic wasn't as pleasant. No amount of day-after berries could ever make him a morning person. "You know, Midiga," he started, securing his clothes in one of the pouches of his bag. "I

EMBER — ECHOES OF ASHES — BOOK ONE

think you should have just let her suffer." Alleria just smirked. She was starting to get used to his dry humor. She shoved him playfully, amused by his sour mood. And Laderic couldn't help but laugh again, pushing her back with one arm.

Midiga watched them, feeling as though she knew something that neither of them did quite yet. She exchanged a knowing look with Reia, but they both kept quiet.

They left a nice tip for the canid barkeep, to Midiga's distaste, before heading out into the morning. They exited the bar into the crisp, cool air. The rain the night before had chilled the breeze, and the air smelled like wet soil and budding leaves. Alleria flipped her hood up over her ears again, wary once more of her surroundings. She had found an old, broken comb on the floor of their room and—she cringed thinking about it—had combed through her tangled, knotted hair. It had grown long, reaching almost to her waist, but she kept it tucked away in her hood, hidden along with her ears.

It was an early start, the sun just beginning to rise. Laderic yawned as he walked, shivering slightly in the morning chill. They passed the merchant booths where some of their owners had already packed up and moved on. Vendors changed out daily in most cities since many merchants were only able to afford a spot in the marketplace for a week or so. Typically, only the fae merchants were able to afford the nearly permanent spots in the marketplaces of large cities. Laderic noted the booth of the fae woman from the day before, still intact.

Which is why he was surprised to see, in the distance, a small green fairy woman marching down the street. Curious, the group walked a bit faster, catching up to her with ease.

"Excuse me?" said Alleria, kneeling down a bit. The fae was walking, something they almost never did, and was violently dragging a large pack behind her. She whirled around.

"Oh!" she said, jumping back with surprise as she recognized Alleria from the day before. "It's you!" She noticed

83

Laderic becoming slightly annoyed. Her eyes narrowed as she looked between the four of them. "What do you want." It was not a question.

Laderic looked at the bag she was trying to carry. It was tiny but weighed entirely too much for the fae to lift. "Looks like you could use a little help," he observed, declaring the obvious. An idea was starting to form in his mind.

"I'm fine," she said, huffing. She reached back around, gripping the bag with her two hands, dragging it a few more feet. "I'll be fine."

"Your booth is still set up back there... Where are you even going?" Laderic asked, taking one long step and catching up with the fairy.

"My brother is a wintertime fae," she said, continuing to drag her pack. "Summer starts in a week. I have to get to work before the week after the solstice ends, the transition period. He's coming to take over the booth for a while. I was... getting a head start." She pulled again, the pack now refusing to budge, stuck on a small rock that jutted up from the dirt road.

Laderic nodded, watching her, struggling to keep himself from laughing. "Isn't the fae city... several days' walk from here?" he asked, pointing down the road into the Brushdeep Forest. "You're not going to make it in time at *that* pace."

The fae finally stopped yanking on her bag, putting her hands on her hips. Her wings buzzed, and she zipped upward, reaching eye level with Laderic in a split second, startling him. "What's with the questions, huh?" she demanded. Laderic was surprised, taking a step back, but the fairy just zipped even closer to his face. "I. Am. Fine. I said I'm fine. What do you want from me, anyway?" she snapped, talking with her hands and almost hitting Laderic in his nose.

Laderic calmly reached down, grasping the handle, and lifting her bag with two fingers. "Well, since you asked," he said, turning on the charm. "We're headed in the same direction

84

as Charandall... but we don't really know the woods very well. If you can take us as far as the fork in the road toward Strita... I'll carry your bag all the way there." He smiled, perfect teeth glinting in the new sun.

The fae woman stopped flying so erratically, settling down and hovering. "Well..." she said, debating with herself, "I'm not going to have to pay you... am I?" she asked.

"Of course not," interjected Midiga, before the word 'yes' could come out of Laderic's mouth. "Your guidance will be payment enough."

Laderic shot a look at Midiga before forcing a smile. "Of course..." he said through his teeth. Midiga rolled her eyes.

"All right, I'll do it," she declared as if it had taken a lot of convincing to come to that conclusion. Now it was Laderic's turn to roll his eyes. She continued, not even noticing. She spun around midair, floating down the road. "Let's get moving then! My name is Emery, by the way."

"Nice to meet you!" chirped Alleria, walking a little faster to catch up to their newest companion. Laderic hoisted the tiny bag on his shoulder. It looked almost comical, him carrying it. But he did it, keeping to his word. He didn't know The Walk as well as he would like, and it was a stroke of luck that they had run across Emery when they had. Fae people love making deals, and he knew she wouldn't be able to refuse his offer—carrying her bag. Especially when all she had to do was exactly what she had wanted to do in the first place—reach Charandall, the fae city, on time.

So, the group began their march as the sun rose over the hills. The Walk sliced clean through the trees, though Laderic knew the closer one got to Strita, the more dangerous and winding the road would become. Lone travelers wouldn't dare take the road any farther than Acrosa if they could help it. Fae were the exception, as they often took the road alone, but only directly to Charandall and back. The fork splitting from The

Walk toward Charandall was well lit and monitored by other fairies and their seasonal magic. If you continued down The Walk, past the fork to Charandall about another quarter day's travel, you would reach the fork to Strita. Once leaving The Walk and beginning the trek off the beaten path to Strita, they would really need to keep their guard up. That part of their trip would surely be the most dangerous. Strita was well out of the way, up in the mountains, secluded from most of the Far Land.

Mavark hadn't always lived in Strita. For a long time, he traveled just as Laderic did, from city to city, taking odd jobs. That's when he met Laderic. The jobs that Mavark could take were unique, as he was a drake alamorph. Laderic's skills were more… illegal in nature, and Mavark would often pay him to do his dirty work.

Somewhere, somehow, on his travels, he came across the woman who would be his wife, a renegade elf named Ysmira. The two continued to travel together for another year or so, before deciding to settle down in Strita. The city was secluded enough and far enough away from the paths of most common travelers. A perfect place for Ysmira to live out her life as an elf without being harassed or discriminated against.

Elves were very much outcasts in the Far Land with most average folk believing elves to be mythical creatures. Those who were more cultured knew elves were very much real and alive today, but even they viewed those who left Nara'jainita as criminals and outliers. To them, a renegade elf must have done something terrible to want to leave the mystical, wondrous capital. They were viewed through a lens of mistrust, which was why most renegade elves lived in seclusion, and sadly, this only solidified their reputation as secretive, sneaky creatures.

It was an easy walk that day, and they made good progress. Alleria and Emery talked nonstop as they traveled, Alleria full of questions for the fae. She had heard of them but had never met a member of the fairy race before, and she was very curious.

"So… you can use magic?" she asked, only guessing. She turned her head to look over at the green-colored fairy, making sure her hood remained tightly attached to her head, so her ears weren't visible.

"Yes, but my powers come and go, depending on how close we are to summer," answered Emery. Laderic and Midiga, who trailed behind, both listened out of curiosity. Laderic himself had never heard a fae discuss their magic. He'd only read about it and heard rumors. "In just a few days," continued Emery, "when the solstice comes, I'll be at my strongest once again." She smiled, looking into the trees with delight. "And then it's my job to make sure the forest prospers, for the good of everyone."

"So… what would happen if you didn't use your magic?" asked Alleria, skeptical of the fact that the prosperity of the forest relied solely on the fae.

"Well… it would be catastrophic!" said Emery, throwing her hands in the air for dramatic effect. "Let me tell you… there's an old history lesson that goes like this:

"Nearly three hundred years ago, there were two warring human kingdoms in the Far Land—the kingdoms of Rokswing and Mariscale. Mariscale was losing battle after battle, and the war was looking to be lost. So, Mariscale, being so close to the Brushdeep Forest, began to kidnap the fae people to attempt to control the seasons and the weather. The humans, exceedingly greedy, kidnapped more and more fae, locking us in jail cells, trying to force us to do their bidding. They did this to try to swing the tide of the war in their favor. However… too many of us couldn't use our magic because we had been caught and jailed.

"The forest began to die… And the humans were unwilling to release the fae needed to restore life to the trees. The next year, there was a terrible drought and famine followed. Rokswing had aligned with the canidae and called a conference with the felidae people, who had aligned with Mariscale,

begging them to switch sides and end the war for the good of all
people. They agreed, and the war ended swiftly after that. A
treaty was signed between the fae and the humans, declaring that
the fae would never be used as a weapon in war as they had been
ever again. Thus, after our release, the forest was restored to its
former glory, and slowly over the years, our relationship with
humans has improved back to where it was before the war.
Better, even.

"And the other sensible creatures learned then, as well, to
never use the fae as leverage in war, because the death of the
forest was not worth a victory." Emery's eyes looked glazed as
she concluded her story, deep in thought.

They walked in silence for a moment. Laderic had only read
that story before and had never heard it told from a fae
perspective, and somehow, hearing it from the fairy woman
herself was much more inspiring. He had never considered the
ecological importance of the fairy people like that. He and
Midiga shared silent glances, sharing the same thoughts.

"So... can you use any magic right now?" asked Alleria,
insatiable curiosity still not put to rest.

Emery shrugged, dragonfly wings constantly buzzing as she
floated along. "Of course! Let's see, what can I show you... I
can heal both plants and animals alike. Um..." she said,
thinking. "Oh! I can do this!"

She paused midflight, turning to the woods, and landing on
her bare feet.

Alleria paused as well, Reia watching from her arms. Emery
stood on the ground, holding her hands in front of her with her
palms up, closing her eyes in concentration. Laderic and Midiga
watched as well, intrigued.

The tree in front of Emery began to tremble, and then it bent
over, extending a branch to the ground. "Thanks!" Emery said,
stepping onto the branch. The tree then straightened back up,
carrying Emery instantly to its highest boughs. Alleria bounced

on her heels with excitement.

"That was so cool!" she said, smiling ear to ear. Midiga was smiling as well, but Laderic was unimpressed. Emery jumped down, gliding to the forest floor.

"Pretty good, I guess," she said, breathing harder than normal. Alleria nodded, as they picked up the pace once more. "It's a bit harder on me before summer officially begins, but I've still got it!"

Laderic could hardly keep from rolling his eyes, completely unimpressed by the fae's 'skills.' He was more interested in what she could do in her own season. "So, can you do anything better, like, during the summer?" he asked.

Emery shrugged. "I can use my magic all year round, just not to its full extent. Some things tire me out more than others when it isn't summertime. All fae possess some variation of nature magic," she said. Her eyes shone with pride for her people. "We are born to our parents in groups of quadruplets. From each mother comes a wintertime, springtime, autumnal, and summertime fae. And all of our powers vary by season!"

Laderic nodded, having heard of the four kinds of fairies, but not knowing that they were born as quadruplets like that. "But what can *you* do?" he asked again, pointedly.

"Oh, I can make things grow faster, control the movements of plants—as I just demonstrated. Hmm... I can heal wounds in both animals and plants..." She stopped. "That's mostly all," she concluded.

"So... basically nothing," Laderic said, prodding. Midiga elbowed him, hard, and shot him a look. He looked back at her, smiling unapologetically.

Emery spun around, getting in his face again. The anger pouring from her eyes seemed to burn into his, but Laderic stood firm, unblinking. "Just wait," she growled, jabbing her tiny finger into his chest. "Summer starts in a couple nights. We'll see if it's 'basically nothing' then."

Laderic held up his hands. "Hey, I wasn't trying to insult you!" he said.

"Then what *were* you trying to do?" asked Midiga, raising a furry eyebrow. He blinked back and forth between them before shrugging once again.

"I'm just stating a fact," he said, still not understanding. Emery's tiny body quivered with anger, and she quickly spun around, flying faster than usual. Alleria and the others had to step up their pace to keep up with her.

Midiga glared at Laderic. "What?" he whispered, confused.

"You come off so... rude sometimes," she hissed, annoyed. She shook her head in disbelief. "Can you at least *try* not to be such an ass to our guide? We're lucky she's still helping us at all!"

"Fine," he muttered, convinced that everyone was just overreacting. They continued to walk, mostly in silence, for the rest of the afternoon.

THEY MADE CAMP a few hours later after the sun had set for the evening. Laderic had a tent, but he didn't pitch it that night, as there was no sign of rain. Instead, he took out his pack, laying it on the ground in front of him. Emery glared at him as he prepped his sleeping area. She scowled, turning and flying up to the top of a tree and staying there, preferring to sleep in the comfort of the trees anyway.

Midiga sighed, glancing at Laderic. She caught his eye, and he looked back, confused. Midiga jerked her head toward the tree, narrowing her eyes. He stared back, blankly, having completely missed Emery make her exit. Midiga shook her head, getting back to her bed—a single black blanket that she spread on the ground.

"Found firewood!" crowed Alleria, skipping out of the woods with an armful. She set it down in front of them, kneeling and setting right into building a small fire. Laderic looked on, genuinely impressed. The elf must have learned a few things about camping after having traveled alone for so long. In just minutes, she had built a makeshift fire. Reia trotted up to the wood and breathed a small flame into its core. Then, she stared at the minuscule flame, concentrating. After a moment, the flames built themselves up until it was nice and toasty in their campsite.

Pleased with her work, Alleria sat back on her heels, smiling to herself. After a brief indulgent moment of admiration for the fire, she looked around. "Where's Emery?" she asked, not seeing the green fairy's glow anywhere.

Laderic looked just as confused, noticing for the first time that she wasn't with them. "Yeah, where did she go?"

Midiga turned her head toward him slowly. Her gaze was filled with fire, a flame Laderic shrank from. She jerked her head toward the top of the tree once more, and something finally clicked in Laderic's mind.

"*Oh*," he said, looking above them. He could barely make out the faint, green glow that was Emery high above them in the boughs of a tree. "Oops."

"Yeah, *oops*," hissed Midiga, chastising him as a mother might her child that had been mean to their sibling. "You better apologize tomorrow," she said, serious.

"Fine!" he said, admitting defeat and throwing his hands up. "I was a jerk. I'll tell her tomorrow." Midiga nodded, satisfied, and turned back to her things. She pulled out a small book with a plain, black leather cover, and started reading, sitting cross-legged on her blanket. Soon, a low purr began to rumble in her chest

Alleria sat next to Laderic, gazing into the firelight, the flames seeming to dance in her golden eyes. In her mind, she recapped the last few days. She already felt more positive and secure about her situation, glad to have finally found some kind people who were truly on her side. She glanced up, checking to find Emery, but she was unable to pick out the fairy's glow as Laderic had. So, feeling confident no one was watching her, she reached up and removed her hood, feeling the cool air on her pointed ears.

Laderic, realizing he had been staring, forced himself to look away, unwilling to admit to himself his infatuation with her.

He had heard of the unmatchable beauty of the elves, but he had always believed himself stronger than his own emotions. He had met Mavark's wife—Ysmira—once before, yet did not find her nearly as captivating as Alleria. Then again, that could have been because, at the time, they were covered in the blood of a band of felid thieves that mistakenly thought they could sneak up on them. Ysmira's own hood had fallen off during the fight, forcing Mavark to decide that day if he could trust Laderic with their secret. It was because of this that Laderic knew he could trust Mavark with anything.

"Are you okay?" asked Alleria, concerned. Laderic looked over. She was sitting just a couple feet away from him. She had her knees pulled to her chest, staring at him, eyebrows pulled together with concern. Reia had curled beside her, sleeping. Alleria's eyes were captivating, gold and wide.

"I'm fine," he said, forcing himself to tear away from her gaze once more. The fire was low, casting a deep orange glow over the campsite. It flickered as a breeze passed by. The night was warm, and they were lucky to have a dry night for camping.

Alleria looked back at the fire, not quite believing him, but letting it go nonetheless. He didn't look like he wanted to talk. She absentmindedly stroked Reia, watching the flames lick the firewood as they died down bit by bit. A wolf howled in the distance, and instantly, she tensed up. Reia sat up, startled, ears laid back. Alleria's hand was on her dagger in a split second, eyes wide with fear. She sat perfectly still, listening for anything coming through the brush.

Laderic watched her curiously. "It's just a regular wolf," he said, experience allowing him to tell the difference between the call of a canid and the call of an animal. "You can relax."

Alleria slowly removed her hand from her weapon. Her palm was glowing with faint white light. Midiga, who normally prided herself on being level-headed, had her ears pinned back against her skull in fear, gripping the book in her hands much too tightly. The encounter with the canidae just days before had really gotten to her, and she didn't like it.

"I'm going for a walk," she said gruffly, standing and stalking into the pitch-black woods. Laderic wasn't too worried. He knew she could see just as easily as if it were daylight. He instead shifted his attention to Alleria, specifically her hands, which were still glowing.

"Tell me more about your magic," he said, curious. If he was going to teach her how to use it, especially as someone who couldn't use magic himself, he needed to have as much information as possible from her. In the back of his mind, a whisper said he was stupid for thinking he would be able to help her at all, but before he could become discouraged, he stuffed that voice back down where it came from. He watched Alleria as he leaned forward, listening intently.

Alleria stared down at her hands. "It only happens when I'm really scared… or really angry," she looked at her hands as the light slowly began to fade away, "and, usually, it just blows up and hurts people."

"That's not always a bad thing," Laderic remarked. She looked up at him, and he continued. "Fire-dancer spectrals can only use damaging magic, and they're regarded as the most fearsome of all spectral magi."

"I guess," she muttered, looking down once more. Reia was awake now, and she stood to pace around the fire.

"If I met one of those fire-dancer spectrals, do you think they could help me with my magic?" Reia asked. She looked at the flames, concentrating. Once again, the fire began to burn brighter and taller.

Laderic shrugged. "Yeah, probably. It just depends on if your magic works differently because you're a kitsune and not a spectral. spectrals aren't human… but they aren't animals either. They're somewhere in between a mortal creature and the very element they control." At this, he stretched his arms up over his

94

head, flexing obviously. He smirked. "But they're nothing special. I could take 'em easy."

"Oh, really?" Alleria asked, amused by his cocky attitude. She smiled up at him, consciously keeping herself from looking at his arm muscles.

Laderic nodded, more to himself than to her. "Easy," he repeated. His mind flashed briefly to the spectral stone buried in his enchanted pack. He cleared his throat—and his mind—and looked back down at Alleria's hands. "Okay, so if you want to learn to start controlling your magic, we'll start tonight. I'm no spectral, but I know a bit about self-control—" Alleria gave him a skeptical look, a laugh escaping her lips. "Okay, self-control when it comes to *combat,* I mean." he clarified, exasperated. The elf pursed her lips, doubtful, but keeping quiet. "Anyway, the first step is not being afraid of using it. You need to try to consciously summon the light to your hands, *without* relying on fear or anger."

Alleria nodded, staring down at her hands and squinting. She laid them on her knees in front of her, palms facing up. Seconds, then minutes passed. The fire popped. An owl hooted deep in the trees. She continued to stare, without anything happening. Then, she exhaled heavily—she had been holding her breath. "Nothing is happening." She sighed, balling her hands into fists.

"Okay, well, if magic is anything like swordplay, you definitely can't hold your breath," Laderic chided. He scooted over until he was sitting right beside her. He took her hands in his own. "Imagine the feeling you get when you use your spells. Not the fear or the anger, but the *feeling* within your body, from your head to your toes. Try to remember the feeling, and just close your eyes, and *feel* it." At this point, Laderic felt like he was talking nonsense, but he was trying his best to translate the discipline in swordplay to magic. With his weapon, he was told to feel the sword as an extension of his body, and with each swing, to memorize the feeling in his arm until it was perfect every time. He figured that part had to be at least somewhat similar to magic.

Alleria closed her eyes as she focused on her hands. She started with her head, recalling the warm, tingly feeling she got just before her magic happened. It moved from her scalp down to her ears, from her ears to her shoulders, and then down her arms into her fingertips. They became tingly, like they were asleep, and felt wet on the outside. Wet and warm. She took a deep breath, remembering what Laderic had said, allowing that feeling move through the rest of her body.

"Slowly, open your eyes," Laderic said quietly, trying not to startle her. Alleria let her eyes flutter open, immediately noticing the white glow from her palms. Sitting in each of them were small orbs of white light. Her eyes grew wider as she realized they were just sitting there, not hurting anyone, nor exploding. Reia paced over too, sniffing at her hands. As she became distracted with her own accomplishment, the balls of light faded away—but her smile did not.

"I did it!" she practically shouted. Reia's tails wiggled with glee, and she spun in circles. Laderic smiled as well, her excitement contagious. "Oh, Reia, it was beautiful! Did you see it? The orbs stayed this time, and they didn't explode!"

"Is that how your magic usually manifests? In orbs?" Laderic asked. He was genuinely happy for her small achievement.

She nodded. "Sometimes. Other times, it's a beam of light as well, but the explosions always start out as orbs that grow bigger until they burst. They never harm Reia or me though."

Laderic nodded, thinking. "That sounds like light-bringer magic. They can direct it in a way that only hurts enemies and washes over allies without harm. They can also heal others, but I doubt you've ever tried that before."

Alleria thought for a second. "I have, actually... but the only person I've ever healed was myself. And only when I've been hurt badly. It's just like a reaction. Like, I see myself bleeding, and then I touch it, and it goes away." She frowned. "I would really like to try healing other people, but I've been too scared. Now I know I can do it! With help, like, your help, I mean," she stammered. She looked up into Laderic's eyes, becoming suddenly hyperaware that they were only inches apart. She felt her face get warm and tingly, but this time, it wasn't from the magic.

Laderic felt hot all of a sudden, looking down into her bright purple eyes. Alleria blushed deeply, staring back at him. Their faces drifted closer together. *I need to make it stop. It's just because she's an elf. She's twisting up my senses—*

"Laderic!" It was Midiga, her voice pierced through the trees. She snapped him back to reality. He tore his gaze from Alleria toward the direction Midiga's cry had come from. The felid burst out of the woods from the west. "Laderic," she panted, her eyes wide with fear. Her tail whipped back and forth with anxiety. She shook with exhaustion, having sprinted the entire way back to camp. "You need to see this."

CHAPTER 8

LADERIC INSTRUCTED ALLERIA to stay put, holding firm even through her pleas to come with them, and followed Midiga back into a deep part of the woods. He had taken a stick from the fire that was burning to carry with him as a makeshift torch, but it was shoddy, to say the least. She led him west for several miles until they reached a small clearing where the trees were more sparse, and the sky was visible. He looked around, the moonlight providing more light than his so-called torch.

"What am I supposed to be seeing?" he whispered, squinting into the darkness

Midiga pointed across the clearing to where the treeline formed again. Laderic peered into the distance, struggling to see what she was gesturing at, and she groaned, frustrated that he couldn't see in the dark as she could. She took a few steps forward with Laderic following right behind her. He only needed to get a little closer before he could make it out.

A thick, black fog—thicker than even smoke—had spread itself along the forest floor in front of them. It seemed to stop when it hit the clearing, unnaturally confined to that side of the woods. And it was moving, heading north, thankfully, not flowing toward their campsite. It lay close to the ground, only rising about a meter or so before dissipating. It was like a sinister river, silently flowing through the night.

To Laderic, it was an omen. "Midiga, do you know—"

"I know," she interrupted, sounding just as worried. She had heard many times Laderic's tale of how his father and brother had died.

"But why? Where are they going? Why are they here?"

"I don't know, Laderic," she said, desperately trying to stop the tremble in her voice. She wasn't sure if she was more afraid for herself or for him. "But I hope we don't run into them. That fog is traveling directly north. If it keeps going the same direction, it will intersect with the path we must take to get to Strita." She watched the fog, struggling to fend off the feeling of impending dread. "We need to pick up our pace if we are going to beat it."

Laderic was unsure whether he wanted to completely avoid them, or whether he wanted to charge across the clearing without another thought, brandishing his sword and killing each one of the nightwalker spectrals that he knew were hiding like cowards in the fog. He had recognized it immediately, as the very same fog had settled over his home just before they appeared and burned his house to the ground with that eerie, black fire.

"Laderic," whispered Midiga, putting her paw on his shoulder. "Not now." It was as if she could read his mind. He opened his hand, as he had been clenching his fist so hard his fingernails had left half-moon impressions in his palm. He grimaced, and it was physically painful for him to turn away from the clearing and walk back to camp. He didn't say a word the entire way back, and Midiga began to question whether showing him what she had seen had been a good idea... or a bad one. They marched through the trees with Laderic leading the way, and Midiga behind, checking over her shoulder every now and then to make sure the fog wasn't slowly creeping up on them, ready to suffocate them at a moment's notice.

"What happened?" asked Alleria as soon as they got back, clutching Reia in her arms like a stuffed bear. Laderic went and sat on his bedroll, taking out one of his daggers and sharpening it on a rock. He didn't say a word.

"Nothing," Midiga said, addressing Alleria but staring at Laderic. She sat down on her blanket. "Hopefully, nothing we have to worry about. Let's get some rest. We have a long day of walking tomorrow."

Alleria nodded, watching Laderic sharpen his dagger with a purpose she knew not. "Okay..." she said, forcing herself to drop the subject. She hugged Reia, the warmth of the kitsune relaxing her, and she lay down in her sleeping bag. She stole one last look at Laderic before closing her eyes.

Laderic was unable to sleep for most of the night. He kept his eyes peeled for any sign of the darkness. Every hoot and howl and rustle in the trees made him flinch, and one time, he swore he saw a looming figure ready to attack, but it was just a deer passing through.

Eventually, his alertness exhausted him, and somehow, someway, he fell asleep.

THEY ROSE EARLY the next day to start their traveling. Emery flew down with the sunrise, rejuvenated for the new day. Laderic, though stoic from the night before, immediately apologized to the fae for being rude to her the day before. She seemed taken aback by his sudden change in demeanor, but she accepted his apology, nonetheless. Midiga and Alleria exchanged smiles, pleased that everyone in their little party was getting along smoothly once again.

It only took a few moments to clean up camp. Laderic took great care to eliminate any trace of their campground. Alleria was curious as to why he was so adamant about making it look as though they had never set foot in that part of the woods, but she figured it was something to do with whatever he had seen the night before. She kept her thoughts to herself, helping him to cover up the smoldering charcoal with fresh green leaves before they turned to the northeast and started down The Walk once more.

They covered a lot of ground that day, though without hardly any conversation. Each one of them seemed lost in their own, dreary thoughts. The weather was dismal—an overcast sky occasionally shed its tears on the travelers below. The rain was more of an annoyance than an impediment, and they pressed on through the depressing weather. They made camp after the sun had already set, finding a patch of dry earth beneath a particularly large tree.

Sleep was evasive that night.

The next morning was cold, and cicadas buzzed without pause in the trees. There was not a cloud in the sky. Alleria looked up as they walked—to her, the trees looked like the sides of a riverbank, and the sky the river, slicing its way through the canopy above them. It was peaceful. In fact, she had felt more at peace the last few days than she had in over a year. She felt safe with Laderic and Midiga there, and she knew she would only feel safer as she learned to control her magic.

New energy gripped them, seemingly bestowed upon them by the weather that day, and thus, their usual conversation resumed.

"So what's your story, hmm?" asked Emery as she flew along the path. She spun around in midair, just a few feet in front of them, flying backward as they walked. She looked pointedly at Alleria. "There's something odd about your little trio."

"Ahem," peeped Reia from Alleria's arms.

"Excuse me—your little quartet."

Alleria paused for a moment. Should she tell the fae about her past? She looked at Laderic for help, but he had zoned out, as he had done quite often over the last couple of days. His eyes stared blankly ahead, looking but not seeing, his mind deep in thought. She then turned to Midiga, who only shrugged.

"We're on this little mission for you. You can tell her as much or as little as you want." Though her words seemed nonchalant, she gave Alleria a look as she spoke—a look that said: *Don't say too much.*

So, Alleria told Emery about her memory loss and her childhood in the south. She didn't mention that she was an elf, but only that her parents had suggested she travel to the north to discover who she really was. She didn't elaborate much on why, and Laderic could tell Emery knew she wasn't getting the whole truth. The fae stayed quiet, listening to Alleria's abridged version of why they were headed to Strita.

Laderic was interested, though, when she reached the part in her story about why she had left home. She told Emery that her parents had sent her off with their blessing to discover her true self and recover her memories. However, Laderic recalled specifically that she had told Midiga and him that she had *run away* from home. It was a strange inconsistency in her story. There was no reason why she would change that part while telling Emery. Unless... she was hiding something, even from Laderic and Midiga. It was what he had suspected before. He watched Alleria's body language, taking note when she looked down and away as she was speaking during that part. There was now no doubt in Laderic's mind that she was keeping something from them, and he intended to find out what it was.

"So Laderic and Midiga are coming with me to protect me from the wolf people. Something about me is making them chase me, and I hope to find out what that is once I get my memories back," she finished. Emery nodded, looking Alleria's two bodyguards over with her hands on her hips.

"Well, they should do well. They look like more than a match for those mangy dogs," she spat.

The fae grabbed Midiga's attention with her clear distaste toward canidae. "Oh? Do you hate them, as well?" She was excited to gossip with someone else about her hatred of canidae. The tip of her tail flipped back and forth with anticipation. "You simply *must* tell us what sort of nasty thing they've done to you to make you hate them!"

Emery scowled. She didn't exactly enjoy telling this story. "My sister, a springtime fae, was murdered in cold blood by a bloodhungry canid several years ago." Midiga, not expecting this sudden, dark turn of events, laid her ears back slightly, feeling as though she had tread on a nerve. Emery continued, monotonously. "Three years ago, it happened. The canid who did it was captured only hours later and sentenced to death by our courts in Charandall. They don't take lightly to bloodhungry, and neither do I. Not anymore. I was first in line to watch the execution."

"I–I'm so sorry," said Midiga, at a loss for words.

"It's fine. Don't worry about it," said Emery, her wrinkled face unreadable. She turned back around and flew several feet ahead of them as they walked, lost in thought.

Laderic was just as stunned as Midiga. Not only because of the horrors Emery kept buried inside her so well, but also because of the apparent harshness of the fae judicial system. A peace-loving and life-respecting people, he had no idea the death penalty was even considered in their culture. Briefly, he wondered what the Ambassadors thought about that before remembering he really didn't care that much. Midiga and Laderic exchanged glances. They ended up dropping the matter completely, as it didn't seem Emery wanted to talk anymore. The group walked in awkward silence for a while.

Soon, they reached a wide creek with an old, wooden bridge

connecting the path above it. Still swollen with rain from the storm a few days before, the sound of the water running was calming. Emery's mood picked up when she saw the landmark.

"We're almost halfway there," she said. Her translucent wings somehow seemed to buzz even faster. "We'll be there in three days, tops."

They decided to rest by the creek, finding a spot where a tree had fallen and opened up the forest around it. Laderic sat on a log and pulled rations from his enchanted pack. He offered some to Midiga, but she shook her head. "I'm going to hunt. I figure while we're able to, we might as well. The rations might come in handy later on when we don't have the option to hunt anymore." She was already prepping her bow. She strung it carefully, hoisting the quiver on her back.

Laderic paused for a second, putting the meat back in the bag. "You're right," he said. "I've got cloth to store extras. We should see about getting a deer or something for the road." After putting the meat back, he rummaged through the pockets and pulled out an empty sack filled with strips of special cloth, made for preserving food. He stood from the log, walking to where Alleria was sitting talking to Emery. "Here," he said, passing her his magically bottomless pack.

"What's this for?" she asked, hesitantly taking the bag from him.

"Midiga and I are going into the woods to try and scrape together some extra food," he explained. He turned, following where the felid had already entered the woods. "Just watch our stuff!" he called behind him. He pushed some branches aside, entering the foliage.

He didn't tell Midiga—though he was pretty sure she already knew—but he wasn't really coming along to help hunt. He had no ranged weapon of his own now, which was kind of important for hunting. He couldn't exactly run through the woods, swinging a sword around, hoping he hit a deer. No, he was coming along as backup. After what they had seen the other night, who knows what they might encounter, regardless of it being broad daylight. He was on his guard, and every noise made him anxious. He followed Midiga's path through the woods.

Midiga finally stopped in a clearing. The grass in the area grew tall enough to reach her waist. She inhaled deeply through her nose, practically tasting the scent of the animals around her. Her whiskers monitored the air currents, and she could pinpoint exactly where her prey was. In fact, it was for this reason that she had come to the clearing—her prey was right in front of her.

The field was large and circular in shape, with a single dead oak tree in its center. Its branches reached upward into the sky and created a canopy of leafless twigs. With her excellent eyesight, Midiga could see where an eagle had made its nest high in the hidden boughs closer to the trunk. Animals scuttled through the grass, and a group of deer grazed peacefully just across the field. Her pupils dilated with anticipation.

Her ear twitched as she heard Laderic tromping through the brush behind her, and she rolled her eyes. He wasn't going to be much help anyway, and she *knew* he was just coming along because he was worried about her. She sighed, annoyed yet flattered. Laderic was getting closer.

"Shh," she hushed as he appeared out of a bush behind her.

"Gods, Midiga," he huffed quietly. "I didn't think you'd got that much of a head start on me." He squinted, peering across the clearing, his eyesight not nearly as good as the cat-woman. "This is all you," he said, leaning against a tree trunk. "I'm good with watching."

Midiga nodded, not having taken her eyes off the herd. She slowly padded around the treeline, paws silent in the grass. She had picked out a small doe, perfect for what they needed. She was on the outskirts of the herd, grazing and unaware.

Midiga inhaled deeply, settling her hands and lowering her center of gravity. She rhythmically raised her bow and reached back with her right paw to grab an arrow. She lined up her shot, nocking her bow and drawing the arrow back, feeling the familiar tension in the flexible wood. The black feathers that she had fletched the arrows with tickled her whiskers as she held the tension steady for a brief moment.

The release was nearly silent, and it was over in an instant. The arrow buried itself deep in the doe's eye socket, and she crumpled to the ground. The rest of the herd had heard the impact of the shot and scattered once they saw the doe collapse. They sprinted to the woods, disappearing in a clatter of hooves.

Midiga finished exhaling and smirked. She was pleased with herself, as always, admiring the cleanness of the shot. Laderic, who had been watching the whole thing, emerged from the woods to her left at a jog.

"Nice shot, Midiga!" he said, genuinely impressed. Her skill as a marksman was always admirable, but she must have been working on her technique since he had traveled with her last. "That was flawless."

Midiga felt almost smug with the praise. "Thanks," she called back to him as she made her way to the corpse. She had put away her bow and drawn a knife to begin cleaning and carving the meat. Her mouth watered as it always did with a fresh kill, and she found it hard to concentrate on anything else.

Felidae and canidae both are vulnerable after hunting, as their primal instincts tend to kick in after taking down prey. This is called their feral state. While feral, it becomes difficult for them to focus on anything but their kill. Midiga, aware of her genetics, usually took precautions to avoid leaving herself vulnerable in these moments, especially when hunting alone, but with Laderic here, she wasn't too worried about it.

Laderic watched her in the distance as she approached the dead deer. He was in no hurry. He, too, knew to stay far between a felid and their prey after they've made a kill. He had gone hunting with Midiga a few times before, but he would never forget the very first time. He had tried to follow her to help clean the carcass and almost lost an eye. Midiga's pupils had shrunk to the size of needlepoints, and she was snarling and yowling at him in feline, a language he still struggles to understand. She apologized after, of course, as she had neglected to warn him about becoming feral beforehand. She had then promised to remind him in the future, though Laderic had never needed reminding again.

Midiga knelt down and busied herself with skinning the deer, her tail whipping back and forth in excitement. Laderic had brought with him a small leather sack that he kept in his bag, and within this sack were many strips of cloth specifically made for wrapping and preserving meat. He would likely cook whatever they retrieved when they got back to camp, dousing it with salt to dry it out and make it last longer.

These thoughts and more filled his head when he spotted a shadow in the woods.

It took him just a second to process it, but that was one second too late. "Midiga!" he shouted as loud as he could. She turned to look at him, still feral, but panicked by his tone of voice. She turned to look back into the woods where Laderic was pointing behind her. Laderic broke into a sprint, drawing his sword as he did so.

Midiga had no time to move as the bear landed its full weight on her. She heard a snap from behind her back and struggled to roll over and get on her feet. The very size of it was overbearing, she could barely move. Her fur stood up, and she hissed, yowling and cursing in feline, trying to flip over to defend her kill. Her feral instincts had kicked in hard, unsheathing her claws and swinging for the bear's face, aiming for its neck. She hit nothing but fur, and then grazed its arm. The bear only seemed to become more enraged and raised its paw to deal a crushing blow.

"No!" roared Laderic, seeming to appear out of nowhere. He

sliced upward, filleting the bear's arm where Midiga had left but a scratch. It stood on its hind legs, rearing backward a few steps in pain. Laderic crouched between Midiga and the bear, sword at the ready. He noticed how skinny the bear was, and—though tall and broad—Laderic could see its ribs clearly defined in the sunlight. The bear landed back on all fours, charging forward to attack once more.

Laderic stayed to the bear's left—on the side of its bad arm—and jumped out of the way just in time. The bear barreled past, unable to make a sharp turn because of its injury. Laderic kept his sword out to the left, slicing down the bear's back as it thundered by. The bear roared in agony, collapsing partially to the ground, unable to support its left side.

Laderic panted, though he wasn't tired yet, the adrenaline keeping him on his toes. He held his sword at the ready as he watched the bear's every move. Briefly, he wondered why the bear was still fighting. Most animals, when hurt this badly, would have already turned tail. However, the bear turned around again, standing on its back legs and lumbering toward Laderic. Unable to use its upper body to attack, it now seemed the bear was going to simply try to crush him to death.

To the bear's surprise, though, Laderic ran straight at it. Caught off guard, it could do nothing more than watch as he plunged his sword into its chest.

Laderic wrenched his sword out of the bear's torso and rotated his body out of the way just as the behemoth fell forward into the dirt, immobile. He wasted no time and ran straight to Midiga, throwing his sword on the ground. "Midiga!" he cried, dropping to his knees. She rolled over and winced, facing him.

"I'm... okay," she said quietly. The pain had brought her to her senses, and she was no longer feral. She sat up again, cringing. "I think one of my ribs is broken."

Laderic stared at the ground behind her. "That's not all that is broken," he said mournfully. He grabbed a piece of what was left of Midiga's bow, passing it to her.

Her eyes welled up with tears, and she looked away. Laderic looked down at the ground. He knew the attachment that a warrior has to their weapon, and Midiga had had that bow for years—as long as he had known her. Her bow and nearly all of her handcrafted arrows had been smashed—under either the bear's paw or Midiga's own body—as the bear had pinned her to the ground.

She winced again, feeling her side. When she moved her hand, blood was on her paw. She made panicked eye contact with Laderic for a brief second. "*Oh—*"

That was all she said before falling back on the ground, unconscious.

"Midiga?" said Laderic, eyes widening. She didn't move. "Midiga!" She showed no response, her ear not even twitching in his direction, as it usually did. "No, stay with me!" Suppressing his panic as much as he could, he reached down and hoisted her up with all his might. So much adrenaline raced through his blood, he could have lifted the bear if he had tried. He turned and sprinted back across the clearing and into the woods, speaking words of encouragement to the unresponsive Midiga, and praying to the gods for some kind of miracle.

CHAPTER 9

ALLERIA WATCHED LADERIC as he disappeared into the woods after Midiga, clutching his enchanted pack in her arms. She frowned as she wondered again what it was a few nights ago that had put him so on edge. All day he had been looking over his shoulder, hands flinching to his sword whenever he heard something snap in the woods. Everyone had noticed, but no one said anything to him. No one wanted to.

Reia had left as well, scouting the forest and searching for berries to bring back and share with Alleria. She somehow always knew which ones were the sweetest and would bring them back wrapped in a giant leaf for both of them to enjoy.

Months ago, Alleria had been very sick while they were fleeing from the bloodhungry canidae. They had only just met, still not quite understanding their alamorphic bond, but knowing in their hearts, they were in this together. They struggled to push through the woods, and eventually, found a cave by a thin creek that flowed with crisp, clear water.

Reia spent all day and night—for several days—running into the woods and finding different kinds of berries that the animals in the forest would eat when they themselves felt sick. Using a shallow bowl, she would collect water from the creek and bring it back to Alleria to drink, making sure that she stayed hydrated. They tried dozens of different berries, but none of them seemed to work. Both Reia and Alleria finally realized she would have to get real medicine from the nearby city of

Wakeston, and the kitsune ended up having to sneak into an apothecary that night to steal some medicine that Alleria knew would break her fever.

Alleria's adoptive mother was an apprentice in their village's apothecary, and Alleria herself was always fascinated with medicine and the different compositions of both herbs and magic used to make potions and powders for healing. Her mother had always sworn by dusksand—a midnight blue glittery powder that was to be mixed with water and drank. It had the power to cure most common illnesses, and if not cure them, at least lessen the symptoms enough to help build back the body's natural strength to fight the illness itself. Her mother always kept a clay pot filled with dusksand in their pantry and used it for practically everything.

And so, at night, Reia was able to squeeze through a crack in the floorboards of the Wakeston apothecary, and it didn't take her long to find the dusksand. Her sense of smell was better than most, and Alleria had told her that one of the prominent ingredients was mint. Humans could only taste the subtle hint of mint when drinking the dissolved powder, but Reia could smell it quite strongly in the pantry. She grabbed a small bag of the powder and sprinted back to Alleria with all her might.

It worked like a charm, and they were able to get back on the move that next day. They did everything they could to hide Alleria's scent since she was sure it was all over the cave, but they knew they wouldn't be able to hide it completely. Instead, they decided to backtrack and throw the wolf people off her trail, knowing that if they continued on their current path, the canidae were sure to catch up with them once discovering the cave. Changing their route caused them to get lost for a while, but she hoped if they themselves were lost, then the canidae might lose her as well.

Alleria shook her head, clearing her thoughts from the past, gently setting Laderic's pack on the ground beside her. Emery

JESSICA E. SCHMIDT

had landed on the forest floor and was walking around inspecting the greenery around her, occasionally lifting a branch or stroking a leaf, muttering to herself and shaking her head.

Her wings, when still, were gorgeous in the sunlight. They looked just like the wings of a dragonfly. Alleria admired them from her seat on the log, as this was the first time since they had started traveling together that the fae woman had stayed still on the ground long enough for her to get a good look. They were long and thin, as summertime fae have the longest wingspan of any type of fae. Her wings layered in three pairs on her back. The top pair, closest to her shoulder blades, had the broadest wingspan. They were delicate and appeared scaly, extending far past her shoulders horizontally. In the layer below, there was another pair of wings, just slightly shorter and fatter than the ones above. Finally, below those sets of wings was a final third layer that attached close to the small of her back. These two looked very different, appearing triangular. They were not translucent, and looked like upside down, vibrant green butterfly wings, with the downward facing corner extending out wide in a curved hook. These smaller wings were what allowed the fae to make sharp turns, even when flying fast.

Alleria watched as Emery walked slowly around on the ground, analyzing the foliage. She came to a thick tree trunk, finding a spot where it appeared a deer had sharpened its antlers and held her hands over the marks. Her palms glowed, and slowly but surely, green wood sprouted in the gash, healing it as though it were skin over a cut. The fae admired her work, nodded with affirmation, and continued her search.

"Can you heal people too?" The question burst out of her, her curiosity unable to be contained.

Emery nodded without looking back at the elf, distracted. "Of course I can, though I spend most of my time healing the creatures of the forest."

Alleria coupled her hands, squeezing them, nervous. "Could

112

you... teach me how to do that?"

Emery paused briefly, now glancing up at the nervous young girl. For a moment, she was reminded of— "Of course I can," she said quickly, interrupting her own train of thought before her emotions could become derailed. "Well, if you can use healing magic at all, that is."

"I can!" Alleria exclaimed excitedly. "Well," she backtracked, "I have only ever healed myself. I'm not sure if I can heal other people..."

Emery nodded, her wings buzzing as she lifted off the grass to float in front of Alleria. "Healing magic in young fae first presents itself that way. You fall, cut your knee, and when you look at the cut, it starts to close up. It's like... magic." She smirked at her own joke, crow's feet crinkling around her eyes. "Healing other living things, though, is more difficult. You have to feel the pain of whomever you are healing, and make that pain your own, and will it away."

She flew behind Alleria to another tree, searching its trunk for blemishes. After a moment, she smiled, motioning for Alleria to join her. The elf girl stood, pacing over to where Emery was hovering and pointing to the tree. The trunk had gashes all over with markings from deer sharpening their antlers. "Just lay your palm on the wound," she instructed, taking Alleria's hand and placing it on the trunk. "Now concentrate. Feel that cut in your very soul... and will it away."

Alleria stared at the bark, trying to picture it as whole again, and trying to force the magic out of her, but nothing was happening. Canning her frustration, she tried to do what Laderic had told her before—to remember the feeling of the magic flowing from her core the last time she had used it. But still, nothing. She huffed, scowling at the tree, but refusing to give up.

"Oh!" chirped Emery, breaking Alleria's concentration. She snatched her hand back from the tree and looked back at the fae, slightly irritated. The fae continued, oblivious. "I just remembered, there's a sap we use to help encourage the flow of magic in young fae. It helps them more easily draw upon their power at will. It might just work for you, too!" She clapped her small green hands and looked around, excited. "I'm *sure* there's some around here," she said, and she took flight, zipping into the forest. "I'll be right back!" she called behind her before disappearing into the trees.

Alleria stared after her, slightly bewildered, before turning back to the bark. She closed her eyes, clearing her head and trying once more to heal the bark on the tree. She took a breath and forced herself to remember how the magic felt the last time she used it. Tingly and wet, like a coating on her skin, and just beneath it. She opened her eyes—and nothing. The tree was just as gashed as before.

She frowned. *What did she say again?* Emery had said she had to feel the cut in her very soul. *But what does that mean?* She stared again at the gash in the tree and remembered the last time she had to heal herself. She had been bitten by one of the canidae. The pain had opened the floodgates of her magic, and it was nothing for her to blast him away with her light. But the cut was still there, and it stung like nothing she had ever felt before. Blood was soaking her pants, along with rainwater. A layer of skin hung like a thread from her calf, and the wound was starting to slow her down. In the pouring rain, she sat on the ground, and with Reia keeping watch, she had *forced* the gash to close itself.

She looked back at the tree where a deer had carved long and abrasive cuts from the bark. She tried to recall her emotions from before, the desperate need to heal herself. She imagined feeling the same antlers cutting into her, and tried to visualize the pain, and will it away. Eyes closed, she steadied herself against the tree, both hands now on the trunk.

The cool wetness of her magic began to spread itself out from her core, onto her skin. She noticed it, but kept her concentration, willing it toward the tree with anticipation. She felt the coolness spread through her wrist, to her fingertips, and out from her body. She could feel herself inside the tree then as if they were connected. Her magic was like an appendage, seeping into the trunk and exploring its recesses. She felt the gashes in the bark as if they were part of her own skin. Then, they began to shrink, until she felt whole again. She opened her eyes and gasped. The tree was perfect once again, and a faint, white glow was fading from the bark. She removed her hands and felt the connection disappear, and instantly, she felt tired. She placed her hand back on the tree to steady herself, familiar with the lightheadedness she was feeling. But even her exhaustion couldn't wipe the smile off her face.

She looked around for Emery, but the fae was nowhere in sight, probably in the forest looking for that tree sap still. She went and sat on the log again, feeling hungry. She decided to get into Laderic's bag to find that meat from before since she didn't think he and Midiga would be back for quite a while from their hunt.

In his bag, she found the strips of meat and took a couple out, careful not to snoop too much through his things. She would be mad if someone went through her stuff and tried her best to be respectful. She chewed on the delicious jerky as if she hadn't eaten in days, enjoying the weather, and the cool, spring breeze.

She sat for a while on her own, waiting for someone to come back. Then, in the back of her mind, she felt Reia coming back into their range of telepathic connection. Since their bond was new, their range was quite short for an alamorph. Midiga could have shot an arrow farther than Alleria could feel Reia's presence. She felt comforted for a moment as her partner neared, but the closer she got, and the stronger the connection, the more Alleria became concerned that something was wrong. She stood and began to walk toward the forest, toward where Reia would appear any second, when suddenly—

—Need your help! Can you hear me? Alleria!

Reia! Alleria began running toward where she felt the kitsune's presence. *I can hear you now. What's going on?* She stumbled for a moment on a root, regaining her balance, and then picked up her pace.

It's Laderic! I heard running... Just hurry! Alleria could feel the panic in Reia's mind, and she felt a lump in her throat. The adrenaline in her veins kept her running for a moment longer until she spotted them in the trees.

"Laderic!" she cried. She saw him turn toward her voice and shuffle toward her through the woods. He was out of breath, and it was plain to see why. He had hoisted Midiga over his shoulders like a sack of potatoes.

He looked tired and worried, scanning the forest frantically. "Where's Emery?" he gasped, looking over her shoulders. "We need her!"

"What happened?" asked Alleria, looking Midiga over, trying to decipher what had happened. The felid was unconscious, and Laderic looked roughed up. He had blood on his face and arms and a grim look on his face.

"I need Emery!" Laderic said, not really hearing Alleria's questions, and sounding slightly panicked for the first time since she had met him. She swallowed, anxiety gripping her gut, watching as he gingerly set the unconscious Midiga on the ground. Laderic looked around again. "Where is she?"

"She..." Alleria tried to talk, but her mouth was dry. Midiga wasn't moving and was hardly able to breathe, barely gasping for air in her passed-out state. Alleria licked her lips and tried to talk again. "She went into the woods to find some plant or something, for me—"

"What?" Laderic seemed to panic more then. "Emery!" he shouted into the woods, seeming to forget about his previous desire to draw as little attention to their group as possible. "Emery, we need you, please! Emery!" He was calling out into the forest in all directions. He was yelling so loud, his voice

116

cracked. "Emery!" His words were desperate, dousing Alleria with dread like ice-cold water.

"I'm going to go find her. You guys stay here and take care of Midiga," Reia said, tiny voice shaking. Her ears flattened against her skull as she stared at the cat-woman. She took a couple steps backward before she turned tail and dashed into the woods back toward the campsite, trying to find the fae's scent.

Alleria stared blankly at Midiga. Her fur was matted around her ribs where something had torn a hole in her thin, leather armor, and dried blood was crusted around a gash. Something was poking from the wound. Alleria bent on her knees to take a closer look. As she got closer to the felid, she could hear gurgling each time Midiga breathed. She peered at the wound, feeling her stomach suddenly tie itself into a knot. The thing poking from the wound... was a bone.

She felt dizzy, sitting suddenly on the dirt to steady herself. She could feel herself panicking. Laderic was still standing and calling into the woods frantically, but his voice sounded muted, and she could clearly hear her heart pounding in her ears. Everything was spinning... spinning...

After a few minutes, Laderic stopped shouting, realizing that it was doing them no good. He ran his hands through his hair, pulling at it for a moment, hoping the pain would clear his head. He had noticed the rib sticking out of Midiga's body while he was running, but he had pressed on. His only hope was Emery, remembering the fae had told him she could use healing magic.

He looked down at Midiga, her face scrunched up in pain, even while unconscious, her gurgles getting louder. They were running out of time. Soon, she wouldn't be able to breathe at all... Laderic felt his eyes tearing, and he blinked hard. Now was not the time. He looked at Alleria, sitting on the ground, staring up at the canopy of the trees. Alleria... Something clicked.

"Alleria, can you heal her?" he asked, turning to face her, a wild look in his eyes. He knew she had never healed anyone but

117

herself, but it didn't matter. It couldn't matter. She didn't move, continuing to stare up at the leaves. "Alleria!" he shouted, louder than he had intended. She jumped, startled, bringing her attention back to him.

"Can you heal her?" Laderic asked again, pleading this time. Alleria looked down at Midiga, frozen. In this state, she could barely focus her eyes, let alone focus her magic. But Midiga... Alleria stared at her face. Her muzzle would scrunch up each time she breathed, and it sounded like she was inhaling through a straw. Midiga, who welcomed her into her home, fed her, gave her a place to sleep... Midiga, who saved her life...

"I...," she said, her voice cracking, "I can try." She clenched her fists as she said the words, digging her nails into her palm, hoping the pain would bring her back to reality. She shifted into a kneeling position, crawling closer to Midiga's body. Carefully, she placed her trembling hands on either side of the gash. She closed her eyes, trying to steady her breathing. She could feel Midiga's chest rising and falling, her breaths somehow more shallow than they were a few minutes ago. The air around Alleria suddenly felt heavier, thicker, and it was harder to breathe.

It was much harder for her to concentrate than it was when she was practicing on the tree. Every time she started to feel any magic in her body, Midiga would wheeze, and she would lose her concentration. And it only got worse. The pressure was suffocating, and soon, she wasn't able to feel any magic in herself at all.

Laderic watched her as he became more and more anxious by the second. Midiga's condition was declining rapidly, and he could see he had made a mistake by asking Alleria to heal her. Nevertheless, she was trying, and if even the slightest amount of magic slipped out, it would be better than sitting around doing nothing.

Alleria was now also starting to slip into a panic. She took a deep, shaky breath, and squeezed her eyes closed. She breathed in and exhaled harshly. She imagined herself with a wound in her side. Imagined the pain she felt. And the blood... and her bone sticking out from her side... She felt nauseous and had to consciously stop herself from vomiting. She felt the magic retreat back into her body.

"I *can't!*" she finally cried, jerking her hands off Midiga then as if they were on a hot burner. She covered her face and pulled at her hair. "Argh!" she cried to herself, tears springing into her eyes.

Laderic's patience finally wore out. "If you don't do something, my friend, *your friend*, is going to die!" he roared. He drew his fist back, and lashed out, punching the side of a nearby tree. Alleria began to cry harder.

Laderic pulled his fist back and looked at it, mutely noting the split skin over his knuckles. His mind was buzzing with static as if he couldn't form any thoughts of his own. He saw red, and the edges of his vision were becoming cloudy as if he were about to pass out. He sat down suddenly on the ground. *What are you doing,* he thought to himself. *This is not helping—*

"I found her!" It was Reia, suddenly bursting through a bush into the small clearing, followed closely by Emery.

"Gods," said the fae woman when she saw Midiga. Without question, she knelt down next to where Alleria was still crying and placed her hands on the wound. She closed her eyes, and her skin began to glow. Tendrils of wispy, green magic were flowing from her fingertips into Midiga's body. Midiga's breathing instantly improved, and her skin began to regrow over the cut.

After a few minutes, Emery pulled back her hands and sat back roughly, looking exhausted. "She... will take a while to come to. Her body needs time to heal in its unconscious state before she can come back to us—but she will live."

It all happened so fast. So easily. Alleria, who had peeked out from behind her hands to watch Emery's process, immediately covered her face again. She shuddered with a silent sob and didn't even move when Reia came to curl up at her side.

Laderic breathed a heavy sigh of relief, still sitting on the ground. He felt like the weight of the world had just been lifted off his shoulders. He and Midiga had been through worse fights than this but never had he come so close to watching her die. *Just dumb luck. Bad luck.*

The group sat in silence for quite a while. Laderic eventually stood and walked off into the forest alone. No one followed him, but Alleria watched him go through her fingers. Emery sat cross-legged on the forest floor, meditating with her hands on her knees. The forest around her shone and sparkled. The dirt was sprouting tiny grass spears and little flowers. A breeze ruffled the leaves above them, scattering sunlight and shadows all around the forest floor. Alleria slowly removed her hands from her face, taking a deep breath of fresh, crisp air from around her. The weather really was beautiful, and if she hadn't just endured a near tragedy, she would almost be enjoying herself.

Laderic came back from the woods a while later, his pack slung over his shoulder. Alleria had left it on the ground back at their previous stopping point when she took off to find Reia. Someone could have easily found it and stolen all of Laderic's things. Feeling even worse about herself, she brought her knees to her chest and buried her face in them.

Laderic's mind was somewhere completely different. He was so thankful that Midiga had been saved, repeatedly thinking to himself how lucky they had been. His guard had been down, and it had almost cost them her life. And he could never let that happen again. If he hadn't been traveling with Emery, Reia, and Alleria... There's no telling what would have happened.

"We should stay here tonight," he said finally, looking at Emery. "We can continue on to Charandall tomorrow. Midiga has to sleep, though." His voice nearly choked up, and he swallowed a lump in his throat that he hadn't realized was there.

The fae opened one eye, nodded slightly, and closed it again. Alleria didn't move. Midiga sighed in her sleep. Laderic moved to the ground beside the felid, sitting near her head. He gently scratched behind her ear like he knew she liked and stared off into space.

They were all mostly quiet for the rest of the day into the night. Emery eventually flew up into the branches to continue meditating as the sun went down, absorbing the last rays of sun possible before nightfall. Alleria was sure Laderic had fallen asleep sitting up. She eventually stood and moved beside a tree, the same tree Laderic had punched earlier on. She leaned against its bark as she sat down, closing her eyes and hoping for some rest. She had slept this way many times since she left on her journey, and the familiar feeling of the bark against her back was almost comforting. She drifted off shortly.

It took Laderic a bit longer to silence his mind and sleep, but his exhaustion had finally caught up with him. He hadn't slept hardly a wink the last few nights since he had seen the river of black smoke, but that combined with the stress of the day acted like a tranquilizer. He lifted Midiga's head to rest on his lap, leaned his own head back, and was soon fast asleep as well.

CHAPTER 10

IT WAS MIDIGA who rose first in the morning. Her head hurt, her side hurt, and her legs were stiff as could be. It was just before sunrise, and everyone else was still asleep. She was confused, gently raising her head from Laderic's lap and looking around. *Laderic's lap?* Emery was nowhere to be found. However, she could hear quiet breathing coming from above her head in the branches. Alleria was directly across from her, leaning against a tree, fast asleep. The clearing she was in was different from the one they had stopped at the day before.

Laderic was passed out on the ground beside her, drooling slightly in his sleep. When she saw him, her memory clicked into place. She remembered hunting, she remembered the bear, and she vaguely remembered speaking with Laderic before... nothing. She had no memory after Laderic had killed the bear.

She gingerly reached and felt her side where she remembered the pain had been. She felt dried blood, but no wound, and only a dull, achy pain. She sat up completely, stretching and yawning. The only thing she felt now was hungry.

She scanned the area for Laderic's bag, finding it in no time and digging for some of the jerky he had brought for them. She found it but frowned when she realized they had less than she thought. *If only I had been able to get that deer... It's long gone now.*

"You're up," peeped a small voice. Midiga looked toward where it had come from to see small golden fox eyes glowing in the twilight.

"Reia," she breathed, quietly. "What happened? Where are we?"

"We aren't far from where we originally stopped. Laderic didn't make it that far with you on his shoulder." Reia walked over to sit near Midiga, her seven tails curled around her body. "I was so worried, Midiga. I thought I was going to get another tail yesterday."

Midiga grimaced, remembering that kitsune get their tails after moments of personal growth or strife, including witnessing death. "I was that bad, huh?" she mumbled. She looked at Laderic again, shaking her head. She couldn't believe he had carried her all this way. "Is everyone okay?"

Reia's ear twitched, and she bared her teeth in a grimace. "Sort of. I had never seen Laderic panic that way, though I've only known him a short time. And Alleria... she feels guilty." Reia quickly relayed to Midiga how Alleria had been unable to heal her, and Emery had come in the nick of time. "So Alleria feels like you almost died because of her. And Laderic feels like you almost died because of him. So really, they're both feeling bad. But they'll be glad to see you up and moving. Surely, they'll feel better," she said hopefully.

And they did, a little at least. Laderic awoke several hours later and panicked slightly when he realized Midiga was no longer next to him. He was relieved, though, to see her up and chatting with Emery near where he was sitting. Alleria woke shortly after and was also thankful that Midiga was okay, but her gut still clenched when she thought about how close the felid had been to death, and how she herself had been unable to even slow the bleeding down, let alone heal her ribcage.

Thank the gods for Emery, she thought as she watched the fairy pantomime the events from the day before. Midiga was smiling, nodding every so often as Emery gave an exaggerated reenactment from her point of view.

"And then we *burst* through the trees where you were hanging onto your life by a very thread! Alleria had put forth a valiant effort, and I continued her work by healing the rest of your side," she finished, panting slightly from the wild movements she had made with her arms. "Also, I find it weird that the bear was this far south… Bears in Brushdeep live much farther north. Something must be happening to their food supply…" she frowned. "I'll have to investigate when I get back to Charandall. I haven't been home since last summer, you know."

Midiga nodded, placing her hand on the fae's shoulder in solidarity. "Thank you, my friend," she said seriously. Emery blushed slightly at the word 'friend.' "If not for you, I certainly would not be here today." She looked at Laderic. "And you." She turned her head toward Alleria. "And you, too."

Alleria frowned, nodded, and looked away. Emery had spoken highly of her a few moments ago, but she didn't feel at all like she had helped the situation. If anything, she felt like she had made it worse. She felt her throat tighten with guilt, and she shook her head to clear it. *It's fine. Midiga is okay. It's fine...*

Laderic seemed back to his usual self. "Thank you, Emery," he said genuinely. "I had never been so worried about Midiga in my life. And that's saying something. She's always getting herself into some kind of trouble..." Midiga laughed and shook her head.

"Says you! You are the one always getting yourself nearly killed. I remember this time that Laderic got into a fight in

Starpoint..."

And so, they spent the rest of the morning recounting tales of times each of them had nearly been killed, which were amusing, to say the least, but didn't make Alleria feel any better.

They got back on the road, heading northeast toward Charandall. They had just two more days left until they were to part with Emery, and they kept a good pace. Alleria lagged behind most of the time, quieter than usual. Even Reia was up toward the front, participating in their conversation and laughing at their jokes.

Emery was the one who noticed Alleria wasn't near them first. She looked behind her, seeing how far behind she was lagging. Frowning, she flew a little slower, letting herself fall back to where Alleria was walking.

"Hey honey, what's up?" she asked kindly. Alleria shrugged and kept walking in silence. She looked up at Midiga again, walking up front with Laderic, and looked back down, dejected.

"Ah," Emery said, grinning. "Jealous, are you? Well, don't worry. If they've been friends this long without becoming any more than that, then I'm sure you don't have anything to worry about!"

"What?" asked Alleria, realizing Emery must think she was jealous of Midiga. "No, that's not it at all. No... I'm just..." she looked down again. "I'm useless."

Now Emery was shocked. "What? No! You aren't useless, dear. Don't feel that way." She was flying backward, looking Alleria in the eye. "You did your best. And your best is all you can do! So you did everything you could." Alleria shrugged, not having thought about it that way, but not really comforted, either. Emery noticed, and kept talking. "Midiga is very appreciative of everything you did for her... she told me this morning when she woke up. She told me everything she remembered that had happened, and when I told her the rest of the story, she was so thankful!"

"Really?" Alleria asked, looking back up at the felid woman. She didn't seem upset. She was joking with Laderic just like usual. But Laderic— "Laderic was so angry," she said quietly. "He punched a tree, he was so mad at me…"

"I don't think he was mad at you. I think he was just scared." Emery shrugged, watching the two of them walking in the front. "When people are frightened, they say and do things they might not normally."

Alleria frowned. "I guess," she said, unconvincingly. She wanted to believe what Emery was saying, she really did.

Emery gently grasped Alleria's hand, holding it in her own two tiny green ones. "Don't be so hard on yourself. I've really come to like you these last couple days, and it pains me to see you so upset." Though she could hardly admit it to herself, Emery had found herself enjoying Alleria's company more than she had enjoyed anyone's company in years. Alleria's personality was so much like Wyndi that it was uncanny. And she missed her twin sister deeply. Emery had always seemed like the older, more mature sibling, and had acted almost motherly toward Wyndi. She felt the same maternal feeling toward Alleria. It was comforting to the fae—soothing, even.

Seeing Alleria still upset, she made up her mind. "Give me just a minute," she said, holding up a tiny finger. Then, she whirled around to catch up with Laderic, and Alleria could see them talking. Emery was waving her hands dramatically as she often did. Laderic looked back at Alleria and said something. Emery threw her hands up in the air and pantomimed a punch, and pointed her finger in his face. Laderic shrugged his shoulders and nodded, and said something to Midiga, who nodded and pointed at him accusingly. Alleria knew they must have been talking about her, but the exaggerated hand signals and finger pointing were too funny for her to be self-conscious about it.

When Laderic slowly started drifting back toward her as

they walked, she had to force herself to stop smiling. He fell into place beside her, stretching his arms up over his head nervously. They continued to walk in silence for a while, and Alleria watched Reia now in front of them. Reia was telling another animated story to Midiga and Emery.

"So…" began Laderic. Alleria looked up at him expectantly. He was looking up at the sky. "Nice day for walking, thank the gods."

"Yep," she said. An awkward silence enveloped them. He was right though. It was another beautiful day, and they had really been lucky with the weather so far.

Laderic took a deep breath and exhaled loudly. "I am not mad at you," he said without much context.

Alleria knew what he was trying to say, but pushed him to say more. "What do you mean?

"The… the thing. The punching thing?" he tried to explain through his awkwardness. "I don't want you to think I was mad at you. I just have issues sometimes expressing how I'm feeling, and sometimes it comes out that way, and it gets misinterpreted, and I just don't want you to think I'm mad because I'm not," he stammered. He looked at her eyes, which were bright gold. "I'm thankful if anything. You did what you could, and so did I, and so did Emery, and in the end, Midiga was all right. I think that's the best outcome that there could have been."

Alleria nodded, feeling instantly as though the world was off her shoulders. She went from being anxious and upset to those feelings being overshadowed by sheepish pride. But Laderic wasn't finished.

"I have always had problems with expressing my emotions," he said softly, looking away. "Especially negative ones. I… I think it probably comes from my childhood. I grew up without my mother and in a house of all boys. When your dad hangs out with a rough crowd, and your older brother runs the farm, you're not supposed to let your emotions get the better of you. It makes you less of a man.

"My dad had a pretty bad run in before—got involved with some stuff he should have stayed out of. He came home one day and told my brother and me to get our stuff together as fast as we could because we needed to leave. Well, I went outside to the shed and tried to get together what little food we had saved up, and that's when they came."

Alleria stared at Laderic, drinking in his every word. Midiga had fallen back slightly to listen to the story she had heard many times before. She placed a paw on his shoulder in solidarity as he spoke. The words were spilling out of him now, and he didn't know why. He hadn't told this story in so long since he had told Mavark for the first time, a little over a year ago. And he just couldn't stop himself from telling her.

"They came, a dozen of them—nightwalker spectrals. I don't know what Dad had possibly got into that involved them, but it must have been bad, and they—" He choked up for a second and cleared his throat to continue. "They surrounded my house and burned it to the ground. A black fire. Burned it and left while it was still burning. The leader, he wore a white cloak, and I'll never forget it. It shone in the moonlight. The others followed him back into the woods once he started their retreat. And I came out of the storehouse when they were gone, to try to search for their bodies, but there weren't any... just ashes."

Alleria then realized she was crying, as a gust of wind chilled the tears on her face. She wiped them off, still looking at Laderic. He, too, had tears wetting his face, but it was as if he didn't notice. His eyes were misty, staring into the distance. The tears fell down his cheeks, dripping onto the ground.

He had opened up to her so soon that it almost scared him. It must have been because of what had happened with Midiga the day before. Such serious experiences often bring people closer together more quickly, and this was no exception. Such a thing he would not have dreamt of telling her just days before, but now it felt so easy—and so necessary—for her to know.

"I didn't know nightwalker spectrals could use fire magic," Emery commented, having listened to his story.

Laderic shrugged, blinking away more tears. "That's the same response I always get. But I know what I saw. These spectrals weren't like any other nightwalkers I'd seen. They were... demonic."

It was silent for a while. With Laderic setting the mood, and opening up to her like that, Alleria felt compelled to do the same. It had been weighing on her mind, what she had been keeping from them, and she had been waiting for the right time to come clean. And there was no better moment than now. She hadn't been sure she could trust him or Midiga before with details of her past before. She wasn't certain how they would have viewed her, or if they would have wanted to help her, but after Laderic told her such a thing, she wasn't worried anymore. And the similarities... they were uncanny. "Something like that happened to me too," she said slowly.

He looked at her, wordless and confused. Something like *that?* "What do you mean?"

"I wasn't completely honest with you before," she began. She wrung her hands. "I hadn't planned to leave my parents' house in the south, where I'm from—at least, where I can remember I'm from. Like I said before, they were my adoptive parents, and my memory before my mid-teenage years is essentially nonexistent.

"We lived on a small farm also, outside of a village on the outskirts of the kingdom of Mariscale. The lands around Mariscale aren't the best for farming, but we raised livestock and chickens, and sold cheese and eggs to our neighbors, making a decent enough living. My mother was also an apprentice at a local apothecary, learning how to mix medicine, potions, and such, so we could sell the farm and move into the city.

"It was just after she had completed her training to start

making a living as an alchemist when they came. My father caught word of the canidae in town, searching for me. I didn't know for the longest time how he knew they were looking for me. I only realized it after you told me that I was an elf. They were bloodhungry, and they were asking about renegade elves in the area. Mother told me they had known this day would come. They told me that we must all travel to the north and that I had to get there to discover who I truly was—to recover my memory.

"They said, when they found me, lost in the woods without even knowing my name, I was clutching a letter that insisted I reach the north when I was ready, and warned whoever found me that one day people might come looking for me. People with bad intentions.

"With no time to explain completely, Father said he would fill me in on the rest as we traveled. He never got that chance. They told me to hide and sent me into the woods before them, saying that they would catch up. They took an old blanket from our nursing sow and covered me with it to mask my scent. It smelled terrible, but that was the point—I just couldn't smell like me.

"I ran into the woods, but stayed within sight of the house, hiding behind a thick tree stump. That was when they came out of the woods. A pack of them. There were nearly twenty—I couldn't count them all—and they caught my parents as they were trying to run away. They dragged them into the house and—" She choked for a second there. Her words couldn't come out. She cleared her throat but still couldn't speak. From her bag, she drew a water skin that she had filled up in the creek the day before and took a long drink. Her voice steady again, she continued.

"They dragged them inside and locked the doors. From the barn, they took straw and lined the outside of the house. I could hear my parents screaming, I saw my mother try to jump out of a window, but she was shot with an arrow from one of their archers... I saw another canid outside with a blanket from my bed. They were passing it around, inhaling deeply. I don't know why I remember that detail, it just sticks out in my mind so vividly... because that was what I noticed right before they lit the straw.

"It caught quickly and spread to surround the house. The smoke was so thick that it masked the windows and kept me from seeing them anymore. Now that I think about it, I'm glad it did. Because I would have watched my parents as they were burned alive."

Laderic had known she was hiding something before, but he didn't expect that, and he didn't expect how eerily close their fates had been. He was more than shocked, staring at her with his mouth agape. But she wasn't done.

"I came from the woods then, as the fire still raged, and it was like something was controlling my body. I was so angry... They saw me coming, but they were too late. Excited at first, they pointed and howled. Some began racing toward me, their red eyes wide and crazed looking. The magic flowed from inside me as it never had before, and bursts of white light shone from my fingertips, piercing their chests, ripping them apart..."

Alleria's eyes glazed as she recalled that moment, detached almost. It was frightening. She continued, monotonous. "I killed them. I killed them as they ran toward me. I killed them as they ran away. I would say nearly half of them escaped, and the other half..." She shook her head as if she remembered where she was. "Sorry, I always feel lost when I think about it..."

"It's okay," muttered Laderic, concerned. He, too, had done some terrible things. He knew how she felt as she recounted the story. He and Midiga made eye contact, sharing the same thoughts. Alleria seemed not to notice.

"After, it felt as though life had left my body. I could no longer stand, and I blacked out. When I came to, the sun had just set, and I was surrounded by our animals." She smiled, the tears finally coming to her eyes, her words laced with sobs. "I could tell they knew something terrible had happened. They'd kept my body hidden while I was passed out. I managed to stand and looked toward where my house had been—but it was leveled. Just like you said." She said the last sentence as a whisper. She looked Laderic in the eye, seeing through them, into his very soul. "Just ashes."

She said it so quietly that the wind took the words away. But Laderic knew—he knew before the words even came from her lips. Slowly, during her tale, the group had stopped walking, and Emery and Reia had both turned to listen as well. The sky was now overcast, and the wind had picked up, filling the deathly silence. Alleria was staring at the ground, viciously wiping the tears from her eyes. "I'm sorry," she said through her tears. "I don't know why I told you. I'm so sorry."

"Don't be sorry," Laderic said, her words nearly breaking him. He could feel her pain in his chest. It was his pain. "Don't be sorry." He moved forward, embraced her, and felt her body tremble with silent sobs. He held her while she cried. He held her like he wished someone had held him. The others averted their eyes with mournful reverence. Slowly, after a while, her tremors began to subside. The wind blew again, scattering leaves and dust around them. When he felt it was right, he released her.

She took a step back, breathing deeply. "Sorry, everyone," she said, a faint smile drawn on her face. They each responded in a chorus of their own versions of Laderic's response—not wanting her to apologize for opening up.

Reia padded over to Alleria and stood on her back legs, pawing at the elf's waist. Alleria picked her up, hugging the kitsune tightly, breathing in the calming scent of her fur. "I love you, you know," said the kitsune softly. If Alleria hadn't already run out of tears, surely she would have started crying tears of joy at that moment.

"We all care about you, you need to know that," said Midiga

firmly. She put her arm around Alleria's shoulders as they started walking again. "Please, don't ever feel like you can't talk to me. We are a family now if only temporary."

"Or longer," chimed in Emery, floating beside them. Discovering Alleria's true identity as an elf hadn't shocked her in the slightest.

"Well, not much longer for you," Laderic interjected. He pointed up the path. "We'll be reaching Charandall tomorrow."

"Yeah..." said the fae slowly. For a reason she couldn't quite place, she was actually dreading arriving at Charandall. Which had never happened before. Normally, arriving in Charandall at the start of the summer made her feel happier than anything else in the Far Land. But, at that moment, after all that had happened just in the last few days... she just didn't know how to feel anymore. After all, she already felt so close to everyone in the group. They were like her... friends. The first friends she had made in many years. Even Laderic, which shocked her even more.

And Alleria—she couldn't stop seeing her sister in the elf's every move. She already felt so protective of her, and she hadn't felt that way about anyone since Wyndi was killed.

"Emery, are you okay?" called Midiga. Emery looked up, realizing she had drifted behind the rest of them. She picked up her pace, beating her wings faster.

"Yeah!" she said, catching up to them. "Just... thinking."

"What's wrong?" asked Alleria, in a better mood since they'd started walking again. The sun had dried the tears on her face.

"I just—" They were listening expectantly. "Well, how long will you guys be in Strita?"

"We're just there to get some information," said Laderic. The wind blew a leaf into his face, and he brushed it off, annoyed. "We shouldn't be there for more than a day. We'll probably stay with Mavark for a night just to get some solid rest before we set off in whatever direction he points us." He eyed her, knowingly. "Why?

"I was just thinking, maybe I might, I could, I guess—I'll take you the rest of the way to Strita?" she stammered. She kept going, talking quickly. "I just, I know the woods in the area pretty well, and we've already had some unpleasant surprises, and you might need to be healed again. Who knows what could happen?" She was blushing, embarrassed that she was asking to tag along, but her determination allowed her to hold her ground.

Laderic shrugged, indifferent. "If you want to. I'm fine carrying your bag a little longer." He had stuffed the fae woman's bag in his own expanded one, so it really wasn't bothering him at all.

"I do want to!" she chirped, a little too excitedly. "I mean... I've made better time than I would have thought. I've been in a bad place with myself for the last few years, and honestly, traveling with you guys has taken my mind off things—if even only for a few days. I'd like to extend that feeling as long as I can, and if you're only in Strita for a day or so, and you don't mind escorting me to Charandall afterward..."

Laderic grinned. "Of course not. I'm sure we'll be heading back that direction anyway. Relax." Emery was quivering as she flew, with excitement and relief, since she had been legitimately worried they wouldn't want her to come. The anxiety she hadn't realized she'd had was lifted off her shoulders, and she felt as if she could breathe easier.

"We can always use an extra hand," Midiga agreed, feeling a sense of empathy toward the fae. She knew all too well what it was like to be stuck in a mental hole—an adventure being the only rope strong enough to pull yourself out. "You've saved my life already. I'd be honored for you to take us the rest of the way."

"Yeah, you have so many stories," Alleria agreed. "You make it more fun to do all this walking." Midiga and Reia nodded in agreement.

Emery sighed happily, grinning. "Well, in that case, onward to Strita! The fork is just a few miles from here." With the smile still on her face, her tone became serious. "But, really, thank you guys for this. You have no idea how much I've needed it."

CHAPTER 11

THE TRAVELERS PASSED by the westward, glittering path to Charandall the next day. An unnatural archway of vines and flowers framed the entrance to the fae city, a work of art sculpted each season by the residing fairies. This archway was still the one that the springtime fae had created.

Emery waved sheepishly at the two fae guards posted outside the entrance as they passed, making sure to avoid eye contact with them. They stared at her, conflicted on whether or not they should stop her and ask why a summertime wasn't on her way to the city this late in the season. But they let her go, remaining silent at their post.

For Emery, passing by Charandall without turning left had been a thrill in itself. She was immensely proud of herself for making that decision. It had been so long since she had made a choice for herself instead of for what everyone else wanted from her. It was rejuvenating, and the buzzing electricity of life shocked her old bones. She felt like a new fairy.

They reached the split to Strita the following morning,

taking a turn toward the east. A tense air settled over them as they headed deeper into the woods.

They had only been off The Walk for less than half a day when the weather began to turn wild. The skies were quickly darkening, and what had started as a few clouds and a breeze was now compounding into a vicious storm. Occasionally, the wind would gust, and a few ominous raindrops would sprinkle on their heads—raindrops which had been blown astray from the downpour marching toward them.

They picked up their pace to a swift jog. Emery was flying quite fast, and Midiga was just behind her, baring her teeth with displeasure each time a raindrop plopped onto her fur. The droplets felt like icicles, occasionally pelting her in the shoulder or on her ears—which twitched each time this happened, though they were flattened against her skull.

"It's this way!" shouted Emery behind her so Laderic, Alleria, and Reia could hear. They were lagging behind, but not by much, as they hustled their way down the dirt path. Reia ran beside Alleria, who was gripping her hood tightly to keep it from blowing off her pointed ears, on the off chance they were spotted by someone—or some*thing*.

They had left The Walk only hours after waking up that morning, carefully making their way through this new section of woods, a persistent paranoia suffocating them. This new road to Strita had no name and was significantly narrower, and perilous more so. The spidery branches of the thin trees loomed, and the thickets were wild with thorns and vines. All sorts of nasty creatures lay in wait in these woods. However, that was the least of their worries now. The forest was silent, as even the most terrible of monsters had taken shelter from the looming storm.

"Come on!" called Emery again. "We are almost there!" The fae knew the Brushdeep Forest like the back of her hand, even in these most dangerous of parts. And she knew, coming up in just a couple more minutes, the remains of an ancient fort lay nestled in the trees. Long ago, it had belonged to the elves who laid claim to this eastern section of the woods, but, like everything else, the elves had abandoned the fort years ago to seclude themselves in the far north.

Having been abandoned for a long time, it would provide excellent shelter until morning, but Emery was worried about whom or what else might have that same idea.

As they rounded a corner, they could see the tiptop of the once-elegant watchtower of the fort. A stench like rotting flesh hung in the air, invading their lungs. A thin dirt path overgrown with thorns and roots led toward the building from the road, and they wasted no time pushing their way through. It wasn't long until they reached its front, and they were surprised by how close it actually was to the path. While the watchtower appeared to be quite far away, the fort itself was only twenty yards from the main road. It was so overgrown with foliage, it was impossible to see the faded gray and green stone unless one was right next to it. Moss and ivy covered the crumbling walls, and carvings of griffins and dragons cast shadows each time lightning flashed.

The abandoned fort, called *Ewa'faita*, was the largest fort the elves had built to guard their city on the summit of Mt. Ewa, the tallest mountain in the eastern Cliffside Mountains. Strita lay nestled at the foot of the mountain range, on the banks of a river that flows from the north. In Strita, the river cuts east into the side of the mountain range, and over millions of years, it carved out a path through the base of the mountains to the ocean. The people who settled Strita did so because the mountains provided shelter from enemies from their eastern front, but the river provided a relatively quick path to the ocean, as opposed to taking days to hike over the mountains to the other side.

The Cliffside Mountains were aptly named, as their leeward side was located right on the shore. The drop on that side was sheer as could be and very dangerous to traverse. One misstep could send an innocent traveler over the edge to their death. And it was on this side of Mt. Ewa that the elves built one of their crown jewels: *Ewa'jainito*. The city was chiseled into the mountainside with tunnels carved deep into the rock. Windows were cut into the cliff itself, facing the ocean. The view they provided was phenomenal but treacherous. In the summer, the ocean breeze would circulate throughout the man-made caves, providing fresh air and keeping the caves from getting too hot. In the winter, the windows would have been shut with boards to keep in the warmth.

Even now, though it had been abandoned for thousands of years, the wind continues to blow. Boards no longer shut the tunnels off from the elements, and the ocean breeze pushes through the narrow halls each time it gusts. The cave system in the mountain acts as a giant pipe organ and the mountain plays its song all year round. Some days, it is a peaceful humming whistle. Other days, it is an eerie, mournful howl.

"People around here call Ewa the Singing Mountain," finished Emery, sating the curiosity of the others. They had all settled inside the fort. It was damp and dark, with just the fading light from outside illuminating the space through the windows. It had a creepy feeling, cobwebs covering the walls and crevices, and the opaque darkness of the hallways could have been hiding any manner of evil things. And again, the stench of rotting flesh, though faint, was ever present.

"I don't like it in here—" started Reia. Suddenly, thunder boomed outside, the very ground vibrating beneath them as it rolled. "Eep!" she cried, crouching and covering her face with her seven tails. "But I guess it's better than out there!"

With that clap of thunder, the realm of the gods seemed to open. The downpour began quite suddenly. It was loud and constant, pounding the ground outside and slamming into the sides of the fort.

"Ah!" cried Alleria, moving her things away from the old stone windows. In ancient times, wooden panes would have provided protection from the elements, but that wood had worn away many years ago, leaving gaping holes in the sides of the stone wall. The group scooted their belongings deeper into the darkness of the fort, as rain streamed through the window.

"Reia," Laderic said, fumbling around in his bag. From within, he drew two unlit torches and oiled rags, wrapping the rags around the tips of each torch. "A little help here." He grasped one in each hand, holding them out to her.

The kitsune puffed up her chest and blew a tiny flame, each torch blooming to life and illuminating the damp room. The doorframe they had entered through was agape, the wooden door itself having long since decomposed. The hole was covered on the outside by wild thickets, ivy, and branches, which Laderic had partially cut away so they could scramble inside. In the back of the room, stone steps led up to a second-story landing that continued to extend back into darkness. Two long hallways stretched back on the main floor, one to the left and one to the right. The torches only lit their paths so far before inky blackness took over. The rain continued to pour.

They each began to make themselves comfortable for the evening. The thick rain clouds cast the forest in a dark shadow, and nighttime seemed to be approaching quicker than usual. Laderic wedged one of the torches in the cracked stone ground in the center of their group, using a loose stone jammed into the floor and pinching the wooden handle of the torch so it would stay upright. The other he placed in an ancient sconce in the back of the room, away from the gusty wind and invasive rain.

Midiga pulled from her belongings her single woolen blanket which she spread on the floor in front of her. Her pack felt much lighter without her bow, and her quiver was dreadful looking, having only a single arrow to boast. She sighed, ears lowering slightly with disappointment. She not only felt saddened but also, useless. Without her bow, she still had her claws, though they were her only line of defense. She had become so accustomed to taking out foes before they even reached her, she was nervous about being limited to melee combat.

Alleria pulled her sleeping roll and an extra blanket from her bag and did her best to find a spot on the floor that was neither too damp nor too uneven. Eventually, she had to settle on a spot that was a little of both. She laid her things out, frowning slightly. Outside, thunder boomed, and she jumped, feeling panicked for a second before she remembered what Laderic had told her in Acrosa. "I am not afraid," she muttered to herself as Reia helped her straighten the corners of their bedding. The kitsune's tails were standing at attention, quivering with anxiety. Through their alamorphic bond, she shared a bit of Alleria's fear of storms.

Emery, who usually slept in the trees, grumbled to herself as she dug through her tiny bag that Laderic had been carrying for her. From within, she drew an intricate golden and emerald colored quilt. Its fabric glistened in the firelight. It caught Laderic's eye immediately. He knew very well when something was valuable, and that quilt was no exception. He silently cursed Midiga for not upping their price on carrying Emery's things to Charandall—he would have got her there in half the time for that quilt alone. Every so often, he glanced over into her little suitcase, wondering what other valuables she had hidden away.

"That's beautiful," Alleria said, eyes shining shimmery gold. She had been staring at the quilt since the fae had taken it out, unashamed. "Can I feel it?"

Emery looked down at it. "This thing?" she said, trying but failing to sound nonchalant. "Oh, sure, if you want. Be careful though!" Alleria had sprinted over to feel the fabric, and Emery had become quite nervous. "Please... be gentle."

"Wow," Alleria said, wide-eyed. The quilt was made of some of the softest fibers she had ever touched. She glided her hands over it, feeling the hand-woven patterns. The border of it had been sewn with green thread into hundreds of small forest creatures—rabbits, snakes, bears, wolves, squirrels, foxes—every creature in the Brushdeep Forest was represented.

However, in the center of the tapestry was where the beauty truly lied. A large portrait of a doe was embroidered into the golden background. The deer stood at an angle, her whole body visible, and from her back sprouted giant eagle's wings, flared up over her head like a halo.

"What is *that*?" asked the elf, pointing toward the deer on the quilt.

"That's Kune," said Emery, smiling to herself as she looked at the embroidery. "Kune is the goddess of spring for the fae people. She is one of our four gods."

"But aren't you a summertime fae?" asked Midiga, curious as well.

Everyone was staring intently at Emery now, and she felt a bit embarrassed. "Well, yes, this was my sister's. I carry it everywhere."

"Oh," said Midiga, feeling bad again. "I'm sorry—"

"No, it's fine!" said Emery quickly. "I don't mind talking about it. She actually made this quilt herself. She used to make all kinds of them during her off-season for us to sell in Acrosa and Starpoint. I just kept it when she... passed away. She loved the spring goddess, and she was more devout than my brothers and me combined, really."

"That's amazing," said Alleria, sincere. She looked between Laderic and Emery then, puzzled. "I thought the goddess of spring was Lisia?" she questioned, referencing one of the human gods.

Emery's eyes crinkled in a smile. "Each race of mortal beings in the Far Land has their own gods and goddesses, and some of their domains overlap. They all came from the same place, though—the domain of the Celestials. The fae only have four gods, one of each of the seasons. Humans have more gods than all of the other races combined. Felidae have only a few gods, I believe..." She glanced at Midiga for confirmation. The cat-woman nodded, grinning and showing her pointed canines.

"Indeed, though I'm partial to Fazaith, god of the hunt, myself." She felt another pang of sorrow, thinking about her bow again.

Emery nodded, looking back at the quilt fondly. "She made one for my two brothers and me, as well, with our respective gods adorning their face. Mine, which I left back in Charandall, has Uruso on its front, the god of summer, and also of heat, growth, and courage. He has several forms, as do all of our gods, but on our quilts, she embroidered them in their animal forms. For Uruso, that would be a bear. For my brother Issio, my autumn sibling, she sewed Hie, the god of fall, and also change, rain, and rebirth. He looks like a griffin, with the front end of a barred owl. For Ponchi, my winter brother, she sewed Lupia, goddess of winter, and also ice, death, and silence. She is a white wolf. Personally, I think Ponchi's quilt is the prettiest." Emery scowled with playful jealousy.

"Ice, death, and silence..." murmured Alleria. "Is Lupia... evil? Those don't seem like very positive domains."

"Nonsense!" said Emery, quite passionately. She was talking with her hands once again. "None of the gods are purely evil, just as no gods are purely good. They all fall on a spectrum, somewhere between the pure domains of the Celestials. Do you—how educated are you on the heavens?"

Alleria frowned, embarrassed. "I have no memory from before I was a teenager, remember? And my parents only worshipped a few of the human gods, but they never really explained any of it to me. I just know we were to leave offerings for Lisia, of spring and harvest, and Saina, of storms and growth. Both of them were really important to the farm, I guess, but I never really noticed a difference between days when we made offerings versus days when we—well, when I—would forget."

She looked sheepish, wringing her hands as she spoke.

"Oh, well, don't worry! It's really quite simple." Emery got comfortable on her quilt, crossing her legs and clearing her throat. The fae people were known for being very devout, and for good reason. Their magic stemmed directly from their gods, and they were able to see firsthand the work of their deities. "So, each of the races in the Far Land has their own gods, as I said before," she began, in full teaching mode. "This includes all sentient races, even creatures like dragons and griffins."

"And kitsune?" asked Reia, looking puzzled. Emery shook her head.

"I don't believe so, but I'm not a kitsune so I couldn't tell you. Seeing as how kitsune are only partially sentient, I wouldn't think that they have their own gods. All animals, though, technically answer to the fae gods of nature. So, since you have gained your full sentience through your alamorphic bond with Alleria, it would likely be appropriate for you to worship a fae god of your choosing. And, might I suggest Uruso because of your affinity with fire, and his command of flames as well? And also, well, he's the best." Emery puffed out her chest a bit, delivering her sales pitch.

Reia thought for a moment. "I'll... have to do some thinking," she said finally.

Emery looked disappointed but shook her head, moving on. "Anyway, before there were any mortal creatures, and before there were any gods, there were the four Celestials: Caine of Chaos, Ostro of Order, Gildia of Good, and Evon of Evil. Each pure of their domain, seeing all things in black and white. There is no gray area for the Celestials, and so they created the gods, hoping to expand their influence over the others.

"However, the gods were not as the Celestials wanted them to be and fell between their domains—none of them completely good or evil, none completely ordered or chaotic. Like I said, they fell on a spectrum.

"From the many gods came the mortal creatures of the world, also created in their own image, hoping to expand their own influences. They created the animals first, before groups of gods began to unite, conspiring with each other to try to create the perfect beings to worship them and thus gain power. From these groups of gods, came the first sentient creatures of the Far Land: the dragons and mythical beasts. Though sentient, they were still quite similar to their animal counterparts. Then came the felidae, the canidae, and the fae. These were the closest true sentient beings to nature, with the fae worshipping the same gods as the animals, and the others taking on the appearance of animals.

"Then came the humans, another step away from nature. More gods united to form the humans than any other race, so the gods expected them to be the best. This was not the case. Humans were courageous and insightful but had the shortest lifespans and the most fragile bodies of any of the sentient creatures.

"Soon after came the dwarves, stout and strong. They were gruff and not the most, er, *aesthetic* of the gods' creations. However, they lived longer than humans did, and though they were smaller, they were definitely tougher.

"After that... the elves.

"The elves were perfect beings, created by only two gods. These two gods did not collaborate together for the same reasons as the others, who sought power, worshippers, or influence. No, these two gods were in love. Dietha and Bathur. The first elves were born from the womb of Dietha, created out of love between them. Because of this, the elves were as close to godlike as they could be. They lived forever and had the beauty of the goddess herself. They were smart, athletic, and the kindest peacekeepers there ever were. It's a shame they have all disappeared. The elves, dwarves, and fae were the first people to settle the Far Land all those years ago, and only thousands of years later did the felidae, canidae, and humans finally arrive from across the sea."

"And the spectrals?" asked Alleria, completely absorbed in Emery's storytelling. But Emery only shrugged, and Alleria frowned.

"No one knows very much about the spectrals," Emery pondered. "They just... appeared. Amarantae, the tree of life in the Brushdeep Forest, gives birth to spectrals, and they live secretive lives. They don't really talk about their history much, and, if I remember correctly, they don't worship *any* gods."

"Wow..." Alleria said, staring off into space, lost in thought. She had been worshipping human gods for as long as she could remember, but... hearing the names of her own gods... it was like a bell had chimed in her soul. She felt tears coming to her eyes. *I have my own gods,* she thought. *No wonder it had always felt so strange worshipping Lisia and Saina!*

"Or," interjected Laderic, standing and adjusting the weapons on his belt, "you don't have to buy into this worship nonsense."

Emery scowled at him. "You shouldn't speak that way of the gods..."

He shrugged, pulling the torch off the wall. "The gods have never done anything for me. Why should I do anything for them?"

"They've done *everything* for you," Emery snapped. "And you would do well to respect that."

He shook his head. "Half of them probably don't even exist. Humans have dozens of gods, literally. It's sad, really. At least the fae have it together. One god for each season and you get your powers from them. That makes sense! But really, where I'm from, religion is a cult." He frowned. "I'm not going to be part of something that I don't believe in just for the hell of it, especially if there isn't anything in it for me." He turned and started walking off, deeper into the fort.

"Where are you going?" asked Alleria and Midiga at the same time. Emery was shaking her head, stewing in her frustration.

"I'm going for a walk. All this god-talk is boring me. Who knows what kinds of valuable things there are hidden in here? An ancient abandoned elven fort? It's like a gold mine!" He was beyond their sight now, disappearing down one of the dark hallways, calling back to them as he went. The word 'mine' echoed around them as his voice dissipated, and the light from his torch faded into the blackness soon after.

Alleria sighed, filled with worry. "I hope he'll be okay," she muttered. Emery laid on the ground, pulling the quilt around her body and facing the wall. She stayed silent.

Midiga strained a smile. "He will be," she said, unconvinced. "He always is."

CHAPTER 12

LADERIC MADE HIS way through the damp tunnels of the fort, shivering as he went. The path he had taken circled around into another main room, dusty and filled with vines and moss. Cobwebs draped over the walls like sheets, shifting slightly in the wind as Laderic walked by. The darkness was oppressive as he kept walking, with no windows on the walls in these inner parts of the fort.

He came to a set of stairs, one leading up to his right, and the other leading down to the left. The upper staircase most likely led to the watchtower they had seen from the road. He grinned, starting up the stairs. *If there's anything worth taking, it's gonna be up there.* However, he had only just started up the steps when he heard a noise.

He stopped, looking around, but he didn't see anything. He remained motionless, listening, when sure enough—he heard it again. It sounded like a rhythmic rapping—as if someone was tapping two stones together to a slow, repetitive beat. And it was coming from below him, down the other set of stairs.

Instantly on alert, Laderic turned and began slowly descending into the basement of the fort, moving carefully to muffle his footsteps. He held his torch behind him to keep its light from preceding his entrance and alerting whatever was down there to his presence before he wanted. He went down, down, the steps spiraling around several times before he started to notice something new—it was getting brighter. A soft, yellow glow was illuminating the staircase before him.

He quickly doused his torch, sliding it into his bag and arming himself with his daggers instead. He continued to creep his way down, moving slower with every step. He could still hear the rapping noise, louder now, and still just as rhythmic. He eventually reached the bottom of the steps, the yellow light flickering brightly in front of him, and he carefully peeked around the corner.

A small dungeon lay before him, a torch burning in a sconce, and a table with two chairs pushed against the wall. He stood frozen as he realized where the noise was coming from. It wasn't a rock. It was bone. A skeleton paced in front of another doorway, an ancient sword propped on its shoulder. Each step of its bony heel rapped against the floor as it moved, repetitive and constant.

It hadn't noticed Laderic yet, who still watched in shock. "A necromancer," he breathed. Where there was undead, there was someone bringing them to life. He cursed silently, berating himself for not anticipating this after having smelled the telltale rot of risen bodies.

He knew this lone skeleton was the least of his worries. He scanned his foe, carefully looking for the eerie glow that he knew marked the dark magic's fixation. He had dealt with undead before, and slicing limbs and breaking bones wasn't quite enough. But simply destroying the glowing seal on their body would release their souls back to the Otherworld where they could continue their search for the heavens. This skeleton had a soft, green glow inside its ribcage, the seal likely on the inside of its sternum.

Once it turned around again, Laderic quietly tumbled into the room, quickly hiding behind one of the chairs in the skeleton's line of sight. He was successful, as the boney soldier continued his mournful watch without pause. On its next turn, Laderic made his move.

He sprinted up behind its body, and it turned around much too slowly to prevent its demise. "Hey there." Laderic grinned as he jabbed one clean strike into the creature's bony chest. Green magic burst from the wound for a few moments, and then the skeleton collapsed before him into a pile of bones.

"Easy," muttered Laderic, sheathing his weapons once again. He inspected the corpse, but there wasn't anything unusual about it, aside from the fact that it had been very much alive a few seconds ago. *I should probably go warn everyone,* he thought. He had started to turn back toward the staircase when he heard another noise, this time from behind the door the skeleton had been guarding.

Curiosity was definitely one of Laderic's weaknesses, and this was no exception. He drew a dagger, grasping the ancient door handle in his hand—briefly wondering why every other wooden door in the fort had rotted away, but this one was somehow still intact—before he swung the door open.

"Aha!" he proclaimed, leaping into the dimly lit hallway. But... there was no one there. "Huh, that's weird," he said, taking a few steps forward. The hallway was empty, the end of it blocked by what looked like a cave-in from the upper floors. To his right, though, was a large hole that had been cut into the wall and seemed to lead into a winding, underground cave system. While the cave itself looked ancient, the hole dug through the walls to reach it was fairly new compared to the surrounding fort. It descended down into the dark, branching off in several directions, with no end in sight.

150

"That's weird..." he muttered before he felt a sharp pain in the back of his head. "Ah!" he cried out loudly in pain. He tried to turn around and confront his attacker, but his sight was already starting to fade. "That... hurt..." he mumbled as he slumped to his knees, his vision going black.

"LADERIC!"

Midiga woke with a start. She had only been halfway asleep—a catnap if you will—when she had heard him cry out. She sat up, her ears perked up on high alert, drinking in every sound—but there was only silence again. She had heard it though, no mistake—he had cried out in pain.

"What's wrong, Midiga?" asked Reia, yawning sleepily.

"Laderic is in trouble!" she said, standing up and reaching for her quiver. She saw the single arrow, remembering that she had no bow, and cursed. "We have to help him. I heard him cry out—something is wrong."

Alleria sat up, yawning hugely. "What's going on?" she asked, rubbing her eyes. She had only been asleep for a half hour or so and felt quite disoriented.

"Get your stuff, we are going to help Laderic," Midiga said. "Emery?" The fae hadn't moved from her spot on the floor, lying down, facing away from everyone else.

"No thanks," she said, clearly not having slept a wink. She continued facing the wall. "He can do it on his own, remember? Doesn't need the gods? Doesn't need me."

"Ugh," Midiga groaned, making her way toward the dark hallway. "This is *not* the time to be petty."

Alleria was putting on her shoes with haste. "Come on, Emery," she said, pulling the last one on and standing up, running to join Midiga. "We need you!"

Emery said nothing, and Midiga shook her head. She pulled

Alleria's sleeve, heading into the darkness. Alleria stared wistfully at Emery, who still hadn't moved an inch. She sighed, turning and jogging after Midiga, with Reia at her feet.

"It's dark in here," Alleria said, looking around. She could barely see the walls around them and couldn't see Midiga's smoke colored fur at all.

"Sorry, I forgot you can't see in the dark. Can you not use your magic to light the space?" Midiga asked without turning around.

Alleria frowned. She hadn't ever used her magic like that, but it couldn't hurt to try. She focused, remembering how it felt when the magic ran through her, from her scalp to her collarbone, down through her shoulders and into her fingertips—

A golden light began to shine from her palms, and she raised them to her face, staring. Fist-sized golden orbs had manifested in her hands, and they weren't hurting anybody.

"Hey, Midiga, look I—*oof*!" She ran straight into Midiga's back, blinded by staring at her light for too long.

The felid had stopped suddenly. "Down there," she whispered. Alleria looked around her. To their right was a staircase leading up, toward another floor. To their left was another staircase, leading down into pitch-blackness.

"What's down there?" she asked nervously, keeping her hands lowered so the glow from her magic wouldn't blind her again.

"There's light down there, I can see it. It's dim. Laderic must be down there," she said, sure of herself. Reia nodded in agreement. She could also see the light—if very faint—with her night vision. Kitsune could see in the dark, but not to the same level as a felid.

They hurried down the stairs.

Alleria's eyes adjusted as they walked down the spiral staircase. The glow from her hands illuminated the area around them just enough for her to see a few steps ahead. Soon, she started to see the glow in front of them and panicked a little bit, worried that they might see her magic's light.

"Midiga," she whispered. "What if they see—"

"Can you make the lights smaller?" asked the felid, stopping. "If not, you'll have to stay back while I go in first and make sure it's safe."

Alleria nodded, staring at her hands. She took a deep breath, steadying herself, and concentrating on shrinking the balls of light, but not making them go away entirely. She stared at them, and slowly, but surely, they began to shrink, until they were the size of acorns. She could close her fists completely around them, and hide the light entirely.

Midiga smiled, impressed by her progress already. "Good job," she purred, patting Alleria on the head. The elf blushed.

They carefully made their way to the bottom of the stairs, taking one step at a time as they got nearer, peeking around the corner. Alleria had to bite her tongue to keep from crying out in shock. In front of them, a bony skeleton with bits of rotted flesh sticking to its body marched back and forth, guarding a wooden door. The smell was atrocious. It hadn't appeared to notice them yet. On the ground beside it was a pile of bones.

Midiga reached behind her back, grasping at only air briefly before remembering once again she no longer had a bow. Groaning, she flicked her wrists, unsheathing her claws. She took a deep breath, steadying her nerves. She eyed the skeleton, searching for a glow. Then she remembered Alleria.

"Have you ever fought undead before?" she turned and whispered to the young elf. Alleria shook her head, still staring wide-eyed at the skeleton that was *walking* right in front of them. "Okay, well, you have to look for a glow on their body. That's where the necromancer will have placed a seal to bring them back to life and bind a soul to their body. You have to destroy the seal to take them down. Do you understand?" Still silent, mouth agape, Alleria nodded again. "Good."

Midiga turned and lunged then, jumping from behind the wall. "Mrrrrow!" she yowled, striking out at its chest with her right paw before it had a chance to react. She shattered it's sternum with one strike, cracking the seal. It crumpled to the floor, right beside the other pile of bones.

"Looks like Laderic made it past here," she said, bending down and examining the two skeletons. The sternum of the other skeleton had also been shattered in a similar fashion.

Alleria crept around the corner, looking around the room carefully. A torch burned in a sconce on the wall, looking like it was soon to run out of fuel. Alleria focused, letting her magic flow freely once more, expanding her orbs in her palms for more light. She walked over to Midiga, examining the door. "I wonder what it was guarding?" she asked, peering closely at the wood. It didn't seem nearly as old and run down like everything else in the fort. It was quite out of place.

"Knowing Laderic, he didn't wait to find out. Watch out," Alleria moved out of the way, as Midiga crouched beside the door handle. Then, she yanked the door open, teeth bared, ready to strike. But... there was nothing. She looked around, taking a few steps inside. Then, she turned back toward Alleria. "Okay, coast is clear, come on in—"

"Midiga!" Alleria cried. "Watch out!" A skeleton had fallen from the ceiling, right behind the felid, holding a large rock poised over her head. Without thinking, Alleria raised her arm, firing two golden orbs at the skeleton, blasting it back away from Midiga. Midiga had leapt out of the way, claws raised, but the skeleton was out for the count. On the ground, bones scattered everywhere, its fingers twitched, and jaw wiggled.

Midiga searched the floor until she found its ribcage. Just as she had suspected, the seal was in the same spot. She smashed it, and the bones stopped moving. "Nice work," she said to Alleria, nodding. Alleria was still breathing hard, crouched in a battle stance, adrenaline pumping. "You can relax," Midiga said with a

154

smile. Slowly, Alleria lowered her hands.

"I–I controlled it!" she shouted as she jumped up and down. She quickly clamped her mouth shut. And then, more quietly, "I *controlled* it, Midiga!"

Midiga was genuinely happy for her. "I know. It was good. You did well. But Laderic—" she pointed toward the wall, "is down there."

Alleria took a few steps forward and examined where Midiga was gesturing. An opening had been carved into the stone wall of the fort, and it opened into what looked like an ancient, natural cave system. It descended sharply, the dirt floor having crude steps crafted into it. "I bet that trick got Laderic, and whatever, or whoever, dragged him down there."

Alleria nodded and gulped nervously. Carefully, the three of them passed through the hole and into the caves. Reia took point as they began descending into the darkness, wondering what had become of their friend.

CHAPTER 13

LADERIC FOUND HIMSELF walking through a misty forest, squinting to peer through the fog, but only able to see a few feet in front of him. Shapes moved in the mist, but he couldn't make them out. Occasionally, something would laugh or howl or whisper. He felt uneasy and vaguely wondered how he had gotten there, but the thought was fleeting, and he pressed on, driven by something intangible that made him feel uneasy.

"Laderic..." whispered a voice to his right. He turned, startled, but nothing was there except for more mist and the outlines of trees. "Laderic..." another voice said, right behind him this time. He spun around, only to find more fog. "Laderic... Laderic... Laderic..." The voices seemed to come from everywhere now.

"What!" he roared as he spun in circles. His vision went blurry, and he rubbed his eyes with his knuckles, seeing stars for a moment. When he opened them again, the mist was gone, the forest was clear, and a path had appeared in front of him, leading out of the woods.

He frowned, puzzled, but started down the path. It was drawing him to its end. He reached the edge of the woods, rounding a corner and freezing in his path. It was an open field, and in front of him, his childhood home—the farmhouse.

"Laderic!" It was Alleria's voice, unmistakable, coming from the house. As she spoke, dark shapes began to manifest, surrounding the building. Nightwalkers, they were drawing close. "Laderic!"

"Alleria, no!" he cried, starting to sprint, but it seemed, no matter how fast he ran, the house never got any closer. "Stop! Please!" He pushed harder. His vision blurred.

"Laderic!" she cried out again. He could see her now, standing in the window. The spectrals had begun to cast their spell, the black fire rising around the house, flames catching easily and climbing the wood. To his left, he caught a glimpse of a cloak as pale as moonlight.

"Laderic." Her voice was eerily calm now, nearly soothing. As he watched, her face seemed to magnify until it was right in front of him. Her eyes were blue and sad. "It's okay."

"No!" he begged. "You're going to die!" He was still running, now toward the pale-cloaked spectral. "You won't get her too!"

"Laderic, wake up," she said, calmly. "Wake up."

"No!" he roared, nearly there.

"Wake up."

"*Wake up!*"

Laderic was freezing, his face numb and wet, and he woke with a shock. Water dripped off his hair and onto the dirty, metal ground where he was laying. He blinked, sitting up and looking around to gather his bearings. He was in a cage—that was certain—with bars surrounding him at every angle. He looked behind him and was greeted with another splash of ice-cold water.

"Finally!" barked a loud voice, annoyed. "I was starting to think you were never going to wake up." Laderic rubbed the water out of his eyes, opening them to find himself staring at a middle-aged man, cackling at him. His nose was curved, his skin pale as parchment, and he was as skinny as could be.

"Oh, I'm sorry," he snapped. "Do I have something on my face? What's wrong with you? You look like you've seen a *ghost!*" On that last word, he lunged toward the cage, slamming into the metal bars with a bone. Laderic flinched, more from surprise than fear, and the necromancer chucked, cold. "You're pathetic, but you will be fun company for a while until I get tired of you."

"Who... who are you? Where am I?" Laderic looked around, but he couldn't make out many details beyond his prison. He was in a still in a cave, that he was sure of. A small fire that had burned down to coals was beside him on the ground, and against the wall across the room, a pool of glowing purple water was bubbling up from below. Several dozen skeletons stood guard around the edges of the room, all of them glaring in his direction.

The necromancer grinned, his teeth surprisingly well manicured compared to the rest of his body. "Me, you ask? I... am Elwyse!" he boomed, raising his arms toward the ceiling dramatically. He paused, for effect, before continuing. "I *own* this fort and all beneath it! And, well, you're the first company I've had in a long time," he admitted, slowly lowering his arms. He looked at Laderic, disappointed. "This introduction thing went differently in my head. You're supposed to, I don't know, cower in fear or something."

Laderic rolled his eyes, instinctively reaching for his sword, but finding all of his belongings had been stripped from him. "Where's my stuff?" he demanded.

"I'm not *stupid*," said Elwyse. He gestured behind him where another door was carved into the cavern walls. "I'm not taking any chances. Don't want you escaping, now do we? Not like it would matter if you did." He smirked, cocky. "No one knows this cave system better than I. Even if I let you go, you would never find your way back to the surface before dying, either from starvation or madness, whichever came first."

Laderic frowned. "So, what?" he asked. "You're just going to keep me here and torture me? Make me your undead slave?"

"What? Of course not," balked Elwyse. "The undead aren't proper company." He began to pace the room, lecturing as one might to a classroom. "When raised, they take on a false soul, fragments of those still wondering the earth, one that simply mimics life. It is impossible to bind a sentient soul to a corpse. I'm just raising bodies, not bringing the dead back to life." He said all of this with such an air of superiority as if Laderic couldn't possibly understand.

As he spoke, from the shadows a new corpse emerged. Laderic peered in its direction, realizing after a second that it wasn't a human skeleton, but one of a large dog. Elwyse noticed Laderic's gaze and gestured toward the canine. "I see you've noticed my greatest success."

"What *is* that thing?" Laderic asked, unsure of whether he was more fascinated or scared. The undead zombie dog was much more intimidating than the mindless skeletons. It seemed to actually have a mind of its own, moving with purpose rather than instruction. He stood waist high, with a thick, boxy skull, and a chain of clattering keys dangling from his neck.

"That's Odie, my first and only successfully bound soul," Elwyse mused wistfully. He continued pacing. "When I was but a boy, Odie was my faithful companion. I had been teaching myself the arts of raising the dead for a while when Odie tragically passed away. However, by taking swift action and performing a ritual within moments of his death, I was able to bind his soul permanently to his dead body."

"I thought you just said you can't bind souls to corpses,"

Laderic asked, backing away from the vicious looking dog that was now only inches away from his cage bars.

"*Sentient* souls," clarified Elwyse, exacerbated. "Dogs aren't quite sentient, though they are intelligent. And, although what I did was difficult, it was done in the ideal circumstances and was a true success." He walked over next to Odie, stroking his skull fondly. "And my faithful companion has been with me ever since, guarding all that I own, right by my side."

Odie turned his zombie head toward Elwyse, wagged his fleshy, rotting tail, and lolled a disgusting, reeking tongue out of his mouth. Elwyse grimaced briefly. "No panting, remember?" he said, quickly taking his hand off Odie's head. "You'll stink up this whole room." Odie lowered his head, ashamed, tucking his tail between his bony legs.

Laderic slowly relaxed, realizing Odie was not a vicious hellhound, but simply an undead pet. While he had been speaking with Elwyse, his mind was working overtime, trying to figure out how he was going to escape. *Midiga will come look for me, right?* But he sighed. If what Elwyse had said were true, no one would be able to find their way in if they also couldn't find their way out. *Guess I'll have to talk my way out of this one.*

"So, what now?" Laderic yawned, appearing bored.

Elwyse opened his mouth to speak but said nothing. After a moment, he frowned, snapping his mouth shut. "I... don't know, honestly. I haven't had company for so long." He turned away from Laderic, muttering to himself as he went to sit in the lone chair beside the purple water.

The geyser intrigued Laderic. "What's that," he asked, pointing toward the glowing purple pool. Elwyse looked at him, and then back at the water.

"Ha!" he laughed, excessively loud. "As if I would tell you any of my secrets!" His words echoed back at them from the walls.

"Well, aren't I here to keep you company? And you're just

161

going to kill me eventually, right?" Laderic was reeling him in. "And there's *no* way I could possibly escape to the surface?" His words were smooth and convincing.

Elwyse went to talk again, blinked, and then shook his head. "I suppose you're right." He seemed worried as if he were breaking some unspoken rule. But, after a moment, he grinned. "Okay, I'll tell you," he said, seeming much too eager to talk about it, like a child doing something he knew was wrong. "This water is magic," he said softly, walking over to the pool and crouching beside it. "It amplifies my powers beyond their usual, awesome power." Laderic rolled his eyes, suppressing a groan. Elwyse didn't notice. "It comes from underground, and is deeply connected to Amarantae, the spectral tree of life."

"What?" Now that caught his attention. Amarantae was one of the most mysterious magical places in the Far Land. No one knew where its power came from, or how it had the ability to birth spectrals. "This... is connected to the spectral life force?"

Elwyse nodded, solemnly. "Yes, and I alone have its power," he said. "It allows me to raise many more dead than I normally could and gives me the power to guard this place against all others!" He dipped one of his hands into the water, holding the other one out toward Odie. He closed his eyes, muttering a quick incantation. Purple energy flowed up through his arm, entering his body and exiting through his outstretched hand in the form of eerie, green light. Odie began to grow even larger. His large teeth protruded even farther out of his mouth. After a moment, Elwyse stopped, removing his hand from the energy source.

"You see," he panted, newly exhausted. "This power source makes me unstoppable! But..." he frowned, crossing his arms, "it means I can't leave here without taking the chance that someone else could find it."

"Why don't you just leave and take some of it with you?" Laderic asked. Elwyse, without saying a word, picked a bucket up from beside the wall. He filled it with the glowing water, walked to the center of the room, and dumped it onto the floor. It came out clear, and cold.

"It turns into regular water if it is removed from its source," said Elwyse, monotonous and strangely sad. "I can't leave."

"What do you mean you can't leave?" asked Laderic, confused. "You could leave here at any time. This power is more important to you than... daylight? Friends? Even just social interaction?"

"Why, of course," said Elwyse quickly. "This power means more to me than anything. I could never leave it!"

His forced tone piqued questions in Laderic's mind. Something wasn't adding up. "What use is all of this power if you just sit down here alone and rot for the rest of your life? No offense," he said, directing that last part toward Odie. The zombie dog lolled his slimy tongue out of his mouth again, panting happily.

"Well, I..." Elwyse seemed to be struggling internally. Before he could speak again, however, there was a loud bang from one of the tunnels.

Elwyse looked relieved for the distraction. "Ah, I see my minions have captured someone else!"

Laderic's heart sank as he heard a familiar felid yowl. He watched as Elwyse walked toward the tunnel, motioning for something to follow him. From the doorway emerged a group of skeletons, dragging two struggling bodies behind them.

"Let! Me! Go!" Alleria cried, struggling and kicking each time she spoke. The skeletons mindlessly continued to drag her across the floor, unwavering in their steps. Another skeleton emerged from the doorway shortly after, restraining Reia in its rigid arms.

Reia was flailing about to no avail. "Put me down!" she yipped, gnawing on its bony arms. It paid her no mind, following the others into Elwyse's dungeon.

The skeletons pulled their captives to the center of the room. "Laderic!" Midiga cried, seeing him in the cage. Alleria turned to look as well, smiling for a brief moment when she saw him.

Elwyse looked back and forth between them. "Ah, that makes a little more sense. You guys know each other!"

"We came to find you," Midiga said to Laderic, ignoring Elwyse completely. "But... we got lost in the tunnels. I thought we could follow the scrape marks, but some places didn't have any dirt at all, and we got lost. We stopped to get our bearings and were ambushed. These guys are pushovers." As she spoke, she jerked her arm out of a skeleton's rigid grip and tried to shove the other off her, but another bony hand grabbed her wrist as soon as she could escape their grasp. "There's just too many."

"Ha, ha, ha!" laughed Elwyse far too dramatically. "You have fallen right into my trap! My minions are much too powerful for you to escape!" There was a drawn out awkward silence. Midiga and Alleria stared at him, perplexed.

"Who are you?" asked Alleria with skepticism in her tone.

"I am Elwyse! I own this fort and all beneath it!" He raised his arms into the air as he had done with Laderic, awkward and rehearsed. After another moment of silence, he scowled, lowering his arms. "Oh, come on. You guys too?"

"Let us go," growled Midiga, impatient, straining to pull her arms from the grasps of the skeletons, but there were four of them holding on to her, and even she couldn't break their grip.

Elwyse cackled. "You think that's how this works?" he asked. "No, you are doomed to remain trapped down here with me. Forever!"

"So, you're trapped down here?" asked Laderic, musing.

Elwyse backtracked. "No, no, no. I mean, *you* are trapped down here, with me, who is free to come and go as he pleases."

"So... you could leave right now then," Laderic said, pushing all the right buttons.

Steam was beginning to pour from Elwyse's ears. "Enough!

No more questions. My minions!" he called toward the skeletons. They looked at him blankly. "Restrain them! I wasn't expecting to ever have more than one guest in my lair. So, you lovely ladies get to be tied up... um... over there!" He waved his arms, and the skeletons followed him, dragging the unwilling travelers with them.

Elwyse helped his minions tie them to the wall where a couple of old hooks were hanging near the ground. Alleria attempted to put up a fight, kicking one of the skeletons in the rib cage and knocking several of its bones to the ground. The skeleton was not even fazed, continuing to tie Alleria's wrists to the hook, and eventually, she gave up, slumping to the floor with a scowl.

Midiga didn't resist at all, muttering to herself as she held her wrists behind her back and sat promptly on the dusty cave floor, scanning the room with her amber eyes. Though the room was dimly lit, for Midida, it was bright as daylight. She could see every nook and cranny in the dungeon where they were held, and was searching intently for a way out of their situation. She frowned, pausing for a moment, shutting her eyes. She could feel the ground... vibrating? In the distance, she could faintly hear a rumbling, almost like thunder.

Elwyse had Reia tossed in the same cage as Laderic. "Don't want you burning your way out of those bindings, kitsune," he jeered as he threw her into the cage.

"Reia!" cried Alleria, straining against her bindings. "Don't you hurt her!"

"I got you," Laderic assured, catching Reia as she was thrown. The fox buried her head in his armpit, whimpering and shaking.

Midiga stared at Elwyse darkly. "You will pay for treating my friends with such disdain."

Elwyse turned up his nose. "You're all pathetic." He barked, judging them each in turn. "Haven't you realized yet that friendship is a *lie*? The only person you can truly depend on is yourself." He spat into the cage that held Laderic and Reia. "I have grown beyond such things, my mentality far more advanced than your own. I have become self-sufficient, living without the need for things like companionship and intimacy. I have, dare I say, overcome my humanity!"

"And that's a good thing to you?" Laderic sneered with disgust. "Throwing away your humanity, living as a heartless monster? You'd rather live your life down here, alone, with just some mindless skeletons, and a stupid rotting dog?"

"You leave Odie out of this!" roared Elwyse into the cavern. His voice bounced off the walls, reflecting back in an eerie echo.

Laderic smirked, amused. "See? No matter how you try, you're so unconvincing. You *love* that dog. You're just like everyone else! You haven't overcome anything, least of all your humanity."

"I–I— You have no idea what I've overcome!" cried Elwyse, his voice breaking in the midst of his sentence. There was a long silence to follow, and Laderic stared into the necromancer's eyes, refusing to break eye contact. Elwyse suddenly turned away from the cage, throwing the hood from his cape over his head.

"Come, Odie." He sighed, weariness overtaking him. Odie, who had been cowering against the wall during the exchange, tucked his tail between his legs and stood to follow Elwyse. Slowly, they marched into the back of the dungeon where they shut themselves away in the back room. The slamming door echoed through the hollow cavern, a mournful, lonely sound.

Midiga's ear twitched, as she swore she heard the rumble of thunder again.

CHAPTER 14

LADERIC WATCHED ELWYSE carefully as he left and waited until he was sure he wasn't coming back before he addressed Midiga. "Where's Emery?" he whispered. He glanced at the skeletons who were stationed around the room, but either they hadn't heard him or couldn't hear at all. They continued to stand against the walls, staring blankly ahead, cold and silent guards.

"She didn't come," Midiga growled quietly. "She was upset with you about that conversation about the gods." She narrowed her eyes, frowning at Laderic. "How does your ego always get us into trouble like this?"

"Don't blame me," he whispered back. "If Emery had come down here with you, she would probably have just been captured too." He smirked, crossing his arms. "If anything, I *saved* her by making her mad. Just wait until I can rub that in her face too and—"

"Would you just stop," interrupted Alleria, glaring at him. "Please, for the love of the gods, *stop*."

Midiga jerked her head in Alleria's direction. "See? Even

she thinks you're being a jackass."

"Whatever. She'll probably still come down here looking for us, eventually. And then we'll *all* be captured," grumbled Laderic, looking away. He stroked Reia, who was resting in his lap, stewing in his thoughts.

After another long silence, Laderic spoke again. "How did they catch you?" he asked Midiga. She shrugged, as best she could with her hands tied behind her back.

"The cave system is intricate and confusing," she said. "Even with my night vision, I couldn't figure out where we were going. Locked stone doors seemed to block our path at every turn, but we continued on as best we could. We walked around for almost an hour until Alleria started to feel a bit panicked..." Alleria nodded, face stoic. "So we stopped to gather our bearings, find where we had come from, and start over, but, as soon as we had stopped... they ambushed us."

"Had you seen any of the skeletons before that point?" asked Laderic, thinking of the one who had knocked him out.

Alleria nodded. "There was one guarding a wooden door, just down the staircase. And then another one who tried to hit Midiga with a rock. Oh! I forgot to tell you!" Alleria was smiling now, somehow still positive in their dismal situation. "I controlled my magic and stopped one of them, without hurting Midiga!"

"That you did," Midiga praised.

Laderic waved his hand. "That's good, real good, but do you know what's better?" he asked. They shook their heads. He smirked. "Elwyse *must* know a way out of the cave! I had already taken out one of those skeletons guarding the door up there. He must know the path through the tunnels if he can cast spells from here and raise another skeleton that quickly."

Midiga shook her head. "There's no way he could have cast a spell that far away, though, especially without being able to see what he was doing. I mean, those bone bags dragged Alleria and me down here for what felt like *forever*. I tried to keep track of all of the turns, but there were just so many. They took us through all these stone doors, and the doors only opened for the magical seal on the skeletons' chests."

Laderic pointed over toward the spring of purple, glowing liquid. "You see that?"

Alleria craned her neck to see. "What is it?" she asked. "It's so... pretty."

"It's some magic-enhancing water. He's been using it to amplify his spells. I'm sure using it, he could easily cast a raising spell from that distance, keeping his army freshly stocked. He says it has something to do with Amarantae... the spectral tree of life."

Midiga stared at the spring, wide-eyed. "But... *no one* knows how the tree gets its power!" She glanced at Laderic, almost fearful. "Do you think... this spring welling up down here... do you think it's the tree's power source?"

"Either that or it's runoff from the tree itself, building up underground," said Laderic. "Regardless, it's extremely powerful and valuable. And dangerous, in the wrong hands." He shook his head. "Honestly, we should be glad that this incompetent pushover is the one who found it in the first place. In the hands of someone *actually* dangerous... this could be catastrophic."

Suddenly, the ground vibrated, and a faint crashing like thunder resonated above their heads. Laderic sat up straight. "What was that?" he asked, nervous.

"I've been hearing it for a while now," Midiga mentioned. "I have no idea what it is, though. I wonder if our captor has taken notice."

They waited a moment, but there was no movement from Elwyse's chambers. "I wonder what it could be," Alleria mused.

Midiga looked around them, scanning the ceiling above. "Whatever it is, it's coming from up there. And it's getting louder..."

They sat again, quietly. "What's the plan?" asked Laderic, inspecting his cage. "This thing is locked, but I could probably pick it if I had a knife."

"I might be able to heat it up enough where you could break it," piped Reia from Laderic's lap. She stood up, yawning deeply and stretching her front legs out in front of her.

"Good idea," agreed Laderic, scooting back away from the cage door. Reia shook herself off, making her way toward the lock.

She peered at the mechanism, thinking. "It might take time. I'm not sure how long we have before he comes back out here."

"I could probably burn through these bindings with my magic if I tried," Alleria said, nervous but excited about getting to test out her skills in another real-life situation.

"I've been working at mine with my claws," Midiga said, concentrating. "I can feel them starting to give, but it's gonna be a while..."

As she spoke, the thunder rumbled again, and this time dust fell from the ceiling as everything around them vibrated. "Is it an earthquake?" wondered Alleria, scared.

The door to Elwyse's room burst open. "*What* is going on!" he demanded. "What are you doing! Casting some sort of spell, hmm?" He was sweating, and the whites of his eyes showed as he frantically scanned the ceiling. "Some sort of earthquake glyph? Well, I won't be having it!" He gestured for Odie to follow him, but the undead hound was cowering in the other room, refusing to budge. Elwyse threw his hands up in frustration. He stalked toward his captives, muttering to himself.

"Calm down, it's not us," Midiga said, irritated. "We know about as much as you do." But Elwyse wasn't having it.

"I know one of you *pests* is causing this!" he said, marching over toward Laderic's cage. "Is it you?" He smirked, shaking his head after a moment. "No, I doubt you could use magic. You lack the refined intelligence necessary for a talent such as spellcraft."

Laderic opened his mouth, paused, shut it, and then held his finger up. "You're not wrong." Midiga stifled a laugh.

"And you, felid," Elwyse barked, whirling around to face her. "I see no weapons with you, but that doesn't mean anything. However, felidae and canidae both struggle with the arcane arts, so I doubt you could cast such a spell. Perhaps you are simply too unskilled to use magic *or* a weapon!"

Midiga lunged forward, pulling against her restraints. Elwyse flinched. "If I had my bow, I would have struck you *all* down before me!" she hissed, snarling and laying her ears back. She bared her teeth, vicious and menacing.

Elwyse stood up straight, kicking dirt toward her with his shoe. "No... you could not have cast the spell." He reiterated, muttering. "And the kitsune would have mastered fire magic. Which means..." He slowly, deliberately, turned his gaze toward Alleria. Laderic stiffened. Alleria was looking down, and Elwyse knelt in front of her.

"Look at me," he ordered softly. She continued to look away, staring straight ahead. Elwyse narrowed his eyes. "I said, *look* at me!" He grabbed her face, jerking it toward his own and forcing her to make eye contact. She stared him down, a single tear falling from her red eyes. The ground began to tremble once more.

"Leave her! None of us are doing this!" Laderic roared. As he spoke, the shaking increased, violently this time, and the thunder sounded like a roar, coming from the tunnel leading into the cavern.

Elwyse's eyes were wild with panic. "No! It must be one of you!" he cried. "It must be one of you. They aren't supposed to be here yet!" He drew from his side a long, jagged dagger, gripping it tightly, his knuckles white.

"They?" asked Laderic, grasping the bars of his cage.

"Elwyse, no! Who is *they*?" The necromancer was staring at his dagger as one might a lover. "Elwyse! Who are you talking about! We can help you!"

The thunder rumbled again. "It must be her," he said, flat and emotionless. "It can't be them." He raised the dagger above his head, preparing to bring it down on Alleria. Alleria was pulling at her binds, struggling to escape but to no avail.

"Please stop!" cried Alleria. "Please, I... I can't use magic!"

"Don't lie to me!" Elwyse sneered, hesitating for a moment, still holding the dagger above his head.

"No really! I'm—" As she spoke, she leaned her head back, tears streaming down her face as her hood fell off her head to reveal her ears. "I'm an elf!"

Elwyse stared, slowly lowering the dagger to his side.

"Alleria!" Midiga cried. "No!" Thunder roared, and the ceiling and walls shook so hard that chunks of rock began to fall.

"So, it's true," Elwyse spoke, mystified by Alleria. "You're the one they want."

"What?" she asked, confused and panicked. "The canidae?"

"No, you fool!" he scoffed. He gently raised the dagger then, placing it on her throat with care. "Maybe..." he whispered, "if I'm the one to kill you... they'll finally let me leave!" He pulled his arm back, swinging it forward to cut her throat.

"*No!*" snarled Midiga, lunging forward, tackling Elwyse, and breaking his grip on Alleria. She had managed to loosen her restraints enough to break through, and just in time. She wrestled with Elwyse on the ground, her claws unsheathed, slicing at his arms and face while attempting to take the dagger from him.

"Get her!" Elwyse shrieked, and dozens of skeletons which had been stationed around the room began to close in, eyes glowing an eerie, cold green.

"Reia!" Laderic cried, but she was already on it, conjuring a steady flame on the lock, hoping to weaken it enough for Laderic to snap the door open.

Alleria was in shock, watching Midiga tumble around on the ground with Elwyse. They seemed to be moving in slow motion.

She saved me...

Midiga pinned Elwyse's hand to the ground, the dagger clattering to the floor. He raised his free fist and swung, and the cat-woman narrowly dodged it, grabbing his wrist and slamming it back down on the ground, as well. She hissed, tail whipping back and forth. Her pupils were like needlepoints.

Even though I couldn't save her...

Elwyse kicked Midiga in the stomach, and the cat-woman yowled, falling to the side, holding her ribs. He scrambled over to the dagger, gripping it tightly and rounding on the felid, a crazed look in his glassy eyes. He walked toward Midiga as she gasped for air. He had kicked her in the same spot where her ribs had been broken only days before.

That won't happen again!

A burning feeling began in Alleria's chest and made its way down to her hands, and they started to shine. She strained, pushing herself to her limit. "Agh!" she cried, pulling her wrists apart. The magic shred through the bindings, freeing her with a flash of blinding light.

"Yes! Alleria!" Laderic cheered, throwing himself against the bars of the cage again as he tried to break free.

"It's no use!" Reia yelled, concentrating on the intensity of her flames. She could not make them any hotter, though—try as she might.

Laderic was not even close to breaking them out. He looked around, seeing the swarm of undead encroaching on Alleria and Midiga. He was completely helpless.

"No!" Laderic begged. Elwyse towered over Midiga, the knife in his trembling hands. He raised it above his head, preparing to bring it down upon his enemy.

"Stay back!" ordered Alleria over the sound of the ground

tearing itself apart, the thunder growing louder and louder. Her eyes glowed a brilliant white as power flooded through her. The magic came naturally, and the undead were unable to withstand her might. Cold and confident, she moved with devastating purpose. Left and right, she cast orbs of light from her palms and into their chests, shattering the runes that kept them animated. But their sheer numbers were overwhelming—faster than she was taking them down they were replacing themselves. They formed a barrier between herself and Midiga.

"I should have killed you *all* when I had the chance!" A crazed Elwyse was taunting Midiga as she lay on the ground in pain. "But now… there will be no more mistakes." He swung the dagger down toward her neck, and Midiga closed her eyes, accepting her fate.

"*No!*" screamed Laderic.

Boom!

The wall behind Elwyse exploded, and the force of it blasted everyone off their feet. A monster roared, a deafening noise piercing through the smoke and dust that shrouded the entire cavern. As the dust settled, Laderic couldn't believe his eyes.

"M-Mavark?" he gasped. He blinked. He must be seeing things, right? There couldn't have been a more welcoming sight.

An elegant dragon the size of a large horse stood poised and ready in what used to be the entrance to the dungeon. On her back, a fearsome warrior with huge, azure wings and a giant greatsword sat in a leather saddle.

"Alleria!" Over the warrior's head, a glowing green dot zipped into the cavern. Emery landed next to the elf, who was splayed out on the ground, completely dazed from the explosion. "Are you all right?"

Around them, the dead began to stand, continuing their mindless onslaught. "I think so…" Alleria groaned. She looked around, grimacing. "But if we don't stop them, none of us will be."

174

"Where's the necromancer?" Midiga asked, panicked. She sat up, still holding her ribs.

"Worry about that later. You have bigger problems!" Laderic shouted from the cage. The dead were encroaching on the three, mindless and unfazed by the blast.

The dragon roared again, swinging its tail like a whip, cleaving four skeletons in half in one mighty swoop. At the end of its tail, two sweeping blades curved into a point, turning the entire limb into a halberd.

Mavark leapt from the saddle, gliding on his own wings, swinging his sword over his head and taking out two more in front of him. He began slashing left and right, all while knocking more undead back with his powerful tail, carving a path to Laderic's cage. He sliced through them like butter, a sea of bones turned into dust with every movement.

"Mavark!" hollered Laderic when his friend reached the metal bars. "Man, you have no idea how good it is to see you."

The drake alamorph motioned for Laderic and Reia to scoot back and, with a single swing, shattered the superheated lock into pieces. The cage door swung open, and they quickly jumped out. Laderic took Mavark's hand warmly, briefly embracing his comrade. Mavark pulled back, removing his helmet and taking a deep breath. His long dreadlocks fell out of his helmet and down his back.

"How is it that I always find you knee-deep in the jobs *I* get hired to handle? You always beat me to it." He grinned, looking around the room at the chaos. "You must be an artist—only someone that creative could get themselves into these kinds of messes." He observed the pandemonium, impressed. "Seriously, I'm jealous. How do you *do* this?"

"We can chat later," Laderic promised. "For now, I need my weapons. Reia." He looked at the kitsune, who was frozen with fear. "Go help Alleria." She looked up at him, nodded stiffly, took a deep breath, and darted off into the swarm of undead toward where Alleria, Midiga, and Emery were holding their ground. Laderic watched her go, feeling a twinge of worry grip his insides, but he stuffed it down inside of him, turning his attention to the drake alamorph.

"Mavark," he said, smiling mischievously at his friend. "Let's stop this necromancer." As he spoke, hysterical laughter pierced the sound of fighting. Laderic and Mavark glanced toward where it was coming from, and Laderic's heart skipped a beat.

In the chaos after the explosion, Elwyse had crawled his way to the pool of magical energy. He was now knee-deep in the purple water. His body was glowing, and with each second that passed, he grew taller and taller. "You *fools* thought you could best me?" he shrieked. "What part of unlimited power do you not understand?" He raised his arm, and around him, glowing, shadowy phantoms manifested from thin air. "*Kill them!*" he screeched, and the phantoms joined the fight.

"Prysmi!" Mavark roared. The dragon marched over to them, having cleared another path through the undead. "Can you smell Laderic's weapons?"

The iridescent dragon nodded, lifting her head and inhaling deeply. "There," she said, nodding toward Elwyse's chamber. "Somewhere in that room." She tilted her head, watching Laderic fondly. She winked at him. "Hey there, long time no see."

"No better time than now. Can you get me over there?" Laderic asked. She nodded, crouching down. He reached up, grabbing onto to the worn leather saddle and pulling his body up into the seat.

"I'll go and help your friends. It sounds like they might need it. You guys stop *that* guy." Mavark used his sword to point toward the necromancer, whose entire body was now glowing a vibrant purple. He was cackling, manipulating the undead with his wild gestures.

"On it," said Laderic. He hooked his boots into the stirrups, gripping the built-in handles tightly so he wouldn't be thrown off. He looked back at Mavark, face stoic and grim. "Promise we'll catch up over tea later?"

Mavark grinned impishly. He pulled his helmet back on and pounded his chest with his fist. "Of course, brother. But, after this, I might need something a bit stronger than tea." With that, he turned, and dashed into the swarm, carving a path toward the others.

CHAPTER 15

"HOLD ON," PRYSMI warned, fanning her metallic-yet-feathery wings. With a mighty thrust, she catapulted herself into the air, leaping over the swarm of undead toward Elwyse's room, and Laderic's effects. The ground shook when she landed, and she roared—a haunting, terrifying sound. More and more phantoms seemed to be appearing out of nowhere. She swung her bladed tail, slicing through their forms and shattering the magic that held them together. But, as quickly as she dissolved them, more were materializing.

"Laderic! Go!" she cried, backing toward Elwyse's door and extending her wing toward the ground like a ramp. Laderic leapt from the saddle, sliding down her wing and plowing his full body weight into the door, which caved in instantly.

Inside, Odie was cowering under the bed in fear, and he flinched when Laderic burst into the bedroom. The room was sad and plain, with a single bed, another table with one chair, and a chest at the foot of the bed. He slid over to the chest, lifting with all of his might, but he found it locked.

Suddenly, he remembered Odie's collar of keys. "Come here, boy!" he called, whistling at Odie under the bed. The zombie dog cocked his head, ears perking up slightly. "Yes, that's it, good boy!"

Odie slowly crawled out from under the bed, the keys around his neck dragging across the floor. Laderic held his hand out, and Odie gave him a cautious lick. Laderic wanted to vomit but fought to keep a smile on his face. "That's a... good boy," he said, eyes watering from the smell.

Odie wagged his tail, coming all the way out from under the bed, nuzzling against Laderic, who was trying his best to breathe through his mouth. He fumbled around Odie's neck, coaxing the dog as close as possible to the chest, and then set to work figuring out which key would unlock it. "Down boy, down. Let's see... not this one—aha!" The third key he tried popped the chest open and sitting right on top were his weapons. He grinned, scratching Odie's skull. "Who's a good boy?" Odie barked, lolling his tongue out of his mouth with glee.

Laderic grabbed his sword and daggers, swiftly attaching them to his belt as he ran back out into the fray. He scanned the chaos, drawing his sword in his right hand and a dagger in his left. It was dim, but across the room, he could see flashes of white light every few seconds, marking where Alleria and the others were standing their ground. Elwyse was to his right, facing the group of them, casting spell after spell in their direction.

Midiga hadn't felt so alive in a long time. Though her bruised ribs were throbbing, the adrenaline in her blood kept the pain pushed to the back of her mind. The rush, it was addicting. And without her bow, using only her claws... Something about going back to her primal instincts was absolutely riviting. Left and right, she pierced through the bones in their chests, shattering the runes that held them together like they were eggshells and she a baker. When the shadowy phantoms came, she hardly noticed, shredding their physical forms with a flurry of claws and teeth.

Alleria had searched inside of herself for that feeling of retribution and called it into her mind. Her sole purpose, right now and always, was to protect her friends, to protect Midiga, who had now saved her life on two separate occasions. To protect them all. Orb after orb of light appeared in her palms, and she cast them from her hands with so much force, the skeletons were blown into pieces. The orbs vibrated with such energy that, on some occasions, they would explode on impact in a brilliant flash of light, damaging a group of undead instead of only one at a time.

"Emery! I think I've got the hang of this!" she shouted, blasting another skeleton to pieces that was encroaching on Midiga. "Emery?" she said again, turning her head toward the fae. What she saw almost knocked her out of focus, and all she could do was stare, mouth gaping, at the scene before her.

Emery was floating just a couple feet off the ground, eyes closed, moving her arms in a flowing, rhythmic pattern—an ancient, musicless dance. Around her, roots had sprung from both the floor and the ceiling and were sweeping entire groups of skeletons off their feet, knocking them into the walls. Roots from above were wrapping around their bony bodies, lifting them from the ground and sucking them back up, shattering them with such force when they hit the ceiling that bones were raining down upon the battlefield.

The roots were writhing, keeping Emery safe independent of her movements. She danced in the air like a snake charmer, animating the roots but not controlling their movements herself. They protected her as she did them—their symbiosis a perfect union of power.

From the fray, Reia leapt to Alleria's side. All seven of her tails splayed in a halo around her body as she summoned orbs of fire around her, firing them into the horde of undead. They were holding them off, steadily for the moment, but it was only a matter of time before they began to tire. The undead, though mindless and weak, did not tire as the living did. Soon, their sheer numbers and persistence would become too much to bear.

The four of them stayed near each other, strength in their united front. Emery's plants were doing the job of ten men on their own, and the others felt safer near the fae's powerful magic.

Suddenly, flying over the wall of skeletons, a new form appeared. It soared over them, capturing the attention of the fighters for a brief moment. Powerful wings beat downward as it landed, a gust of wind buffeting the undead onslaught. A mighty warrior clad in silver armor had landed in their midst—gigantic blue dragon wings sprouting from his back. A long, muscular tail protruded from his backside, whipping side to side and repelling the monsters attacking him.

"Is that—" Alleria wondered, eyes wide in a combination of fear and awe.

"The drake alamorph," Midiga finished, instantly nervous. He was in front of them, holding back the waves of skeletons with swing after vigorous swing of his giant greatsword. He was actually managing to push them back, and Midiga took notice, snapping back to reality and the battle before them.

"Come on, give it everything you've got!" she roared, renewed fire in her eyes. The others around her redoubled their efforts, and they slowly began to chip their way through the undead toward Elwyse.

The necromancer had grown into a near giant, standing almost two stories tall, glowing violet with magic energy. He cackled, eyes wild with insanity. "Yes! Yes!" he boomed, voice deepening as he grew. "Rise! Fight!"

"Elwyse!" shouted Laderic from below. The necromancer turned his head, looking for Laderic on the ground. "You don't have to do this!"

"You know *nothing*," he cried, devoid of reason. "I must

protect this power!"

"Elwyse, we can help you!" Laderic roared, turning to slash at a phantom that had approached him from behind. The ghast was made of a thick, black mist, with glowing green eyes as its only distinguishable feature. A clawed hand formed from the smoke and slashed at Laderic's side. He dodged and swung upward with his dagger, cleaving through its eyes and shattering the magic holding it together.

"Prysmi!" he called to the dragon. She snapped her head toward him, immediately leaping in the air and gliding in his direction. Laderic ducked, barely evading the swipe of another ethereal claw, sidestepping before slashing backward with his sword, severing the magical seal in the phantom's eyes. Prysmi landed hard, swinging her tail as she did so, cleaving another row of ghosts with her tail. The situation was getting dire, and the undead were becoming unmanageable.

"We have to get him out of that purple water!" shouted Laderic over the noise of the battle. "Time is not on our side!" He backed up toward Prysmi, letting her metallic body cover his rear.

"How?" asked the dragon, using her wings as knives, slicing over Laderic's head to take down yet another group of undead, but as soon as she took them down, nearly twice as many seemed to take their place.

"Look, he's growing!" Laderic pointed toward Elwyse, who had become distracted again in sending his minions teeming toward the others grouped in a tight circle and barely holding their ground. As the necromancer cast his spells, he continued to get bigger. His legs almost completely filled the geyser now, as it was only a couple of meters in diameter.

"We have to knock him out of it! Once he gets stuck, we can take him down!" Laderic sprinted to Prysmi's side, pulling himself into the saddle once more. "Can you fly well in here?"

Prysmi nodded, swiping in an area around her to fend off the

182

undead. "I think so, the ceiling is high enough." The ceilings of the cavern were tall and arched, at its highest point being over six stories tall, but Prysmi's wingspan was quite large, and maneuvering would be a challenge.

"We have to try! We have to ram him—it's the only way!" Laderic held on tight as the dragon took flight, beating her wings in the dead air to get some lift. She faltered for a moment, scraping her wing on the cavern wall and wincing in pain, but she pulled away, soaring into more open space.

"Oh, look, it *can* fly," Elwyse sneered, his voice even deeper than before. He reached his arm out, swiping at the dragon. She dipped and angled her wings, evading his giant hand by a thread. She took aim at his body, preparing to ram him, but forced out of position again, she only nearly dodged another swing.

"It's no use!" she cried, folding her wings to fly lower to the ground. "If he grabs me, we'll both die!"

"Stay airborne. We just have to wait for him to grow a little more!"

Elwyse's head was nearly touching the ceiling now, though he didn't seem to notice. The others on the ground couldn't help but see him now, looming over them, a significant presence even as the battle around them kept them fully engaged.

"Look!" shouted Alleria, pointing at the ceiling. A small dragon was dipping and diving, flying extremely fast around the cavern, keeping Elwyse distracted. Someone was on its back. "Is that... Laderic?"

"I would hope so!" boomed the drake alamorph fighting alongside her. "I sent him with her, after all!"

Alleria continued to watch the dragon, gasping when the necromancer almost caught it in his hand. As he was distracted, the undead on the ground stopped replacing themselves as quickly, and the group of fighters began to gain more ground, but the longer the dragon was in the air, the closer Elwyse got to smacking her into the floor.

"Emery! Midiga! Reia! And... um..." Alleria could not remember the name of the drake alamorph at all.

"Mavark," he said, completing her sentence. He leapt to her side, startling the elf until she realized why he had done so. He folded his wings around her back, shielding her from a skeleton's sword. It bounced off his blue scales, and he unfolded his wings with a powerful thrust, launching the skeleton across the room as he did.

"Thanks," Alleria breathed, throat tightening as she realized how close a call that had been. She shook her head, getting back to her point. "Laderic and the dragon are trying to take down the necromancer. We have to help him!"

Emery zipped beside Alleria, landing hard on the ground, watching the aerial battle unfold. "I don't know how much help I would be... I am pretty much spent. Nature magic like that without any sunlight is exhausting."

Midiga shook her head, fending off a few more straggling undead as she, too, watched the dragon zipping around in the air. "We just have to distract him long enough to give Laderic a chance!"

With that, she took off, zigzagging her way through the last groups of undead, heading straight for Elwyse's ankles. The others turned to follow, charging in as a group, with Reia sprinting ahead to catch up to Midiga.

"Hey!" Midiga snarled at Elwyse. He either didn't hear her or paid her no mind, continuing to try to snatch Laderic and Prysmi out of the air. Prysmi was tired, and it was starting to show. Her movements were becoming more sluggish. It wasn't long before Elwyse would be able to catch her.

"Leave him alone!" cried Alleria, firing a bolt of white light at his ever-growing legs. It didn't do a ton of damage, only singing a hole in his giant pants, but it was enough to get his attention.

"What—*you!*" Elwyse boomed, voice deep and sluggish sounding. He turned his gaze to the ground. The others had circled him, slashing, biting, and clawing at his legs. To Elwyse, it was nothing more than a minor annoyance. "I should have ended you when I had the chance. Now... I will crush you all!"

He bent his knee as if he were going to raise his foot and smash them beneath it, but his foot was stuck. The ground bulged under pressure but did not break. "What?" he growled, trying again to lift his foot, but it was wedged beneath the cavern floor. As he tried to rip it out of the ground, he lost his balance.

Laderic seized the opportunity. "*Now!*" he roared, pointing toward Elwyse's chest with his sword. Prysmi bared her teeth, folding her wings in a steep dive, and ramming into the necromancer's chest with her shoulder. Her metallic scales acted as a wrecking ball. The force crippled him, his ribcage cracking loudly. He fell backward, displaced so suddenly that he could not catch himself. His feet tore through the earth as he came down on his back, ripping from their rocky graves. Boulders cascaded from the rubble into the pool of water, filling it nearly to the brim with dirt and stone.

The instant his feet came out of the geyser of magical water, he began to shrink. As he shrunk, the power left his body in a mass exodus, pouring from his pores in a swarm of purple light. It was blinding. Alleria and the others on the ground shielded their eyes and turned their heads to avoid looking at it directly.

When the light died down, they breathed a sigh of relief. Elwyse was unconscious but still breathing, back to his normal size on the ground. The risen undead scattered around the room had collapsed, the magic holding them together dissolving into the air.

The geyser had been completely clogged, the glow vanishing as whatever connection it had to Amarantae was lost beneath the rubble. All that was left appeared as a normal pond. Reia walked over to sniff it, gingerly dipping her paw in and pulling back quickly in case it was still dangerous. But it was naught but cold and wet.

Prysmi and Laderic landed hard on the ground, Laderic nearly falling out of the saddle. His heart was racing—the dive they had taken to tackle Elwyse had been terrifying, to say the least. Prysmi was breathing hard, her muscles shaking beneath Laderic's legs, trembling with exhaustion.

Mavark ran to the dragon as she landed, putting his forehead against hers, and closing his eyes, murmuring soothing and comforting words. Laderic slid down her back, onto the ground, his knees nearly giving out as he hit the floor. Alleria and Midiga ran to his side.

"How do you feel?" asked the felid, concerned. As he leaned on his thighs, he gave her a thumbs-up without speaking. She eyed him, unconvinced.

"That was amazing!" cheered Alleria, clasping her hands together. She glanced around at them. "All of us, we did it! I can't believe it's over so... suddenly." Reia ran to her side, and she picked up the kitsune, stroking her russet fur tenderly. "And you were so great, too," she said with a smile, squeezing her soul partner tightly.

Laderic stood up straight finally, noticing Emery hanging back near Elwyse. "Glad to see you made it." He grinned, making his way toward her slowly so he wouldn't get dizzy.

"Well, if the dragon-man hadn't got here when he did, this might have been a different story," she admitted, scratching her arm. She was inspecting Elwyse's body. He looked sound asleep. "So, what exactly happened?"

Laderic filled Emery, Mavark, and Prysmi in on what had happened to himself, Midiga, Alleria, and Reia in the last several hours. "He was *this* close to killing Midiga when you burst in," he finished, holding his thumb and pointer finger a hair's width apart. Midiga subconsciously held her hand to her neck, swallowing hard.

"So, I guess now, the question is, how did you find us?" Laderic asked Mavark directly. "He said the tunnels were intricate and vast, impossible for anyone to find their way in or out without knowing the way... So how?"

Mavark grinned, white teeth seeming to glow against his dark skin. "Well, I was on my way to Ewa'faita for a job, actually. I was hired by the Ambassadors. There has been unusual undead activity in the area, and the Ambassadors' mages had tracked the energy to the fort." As he spoke, he was inspecting Prysmi's iridescent scales for injuries.

"You're actually *working* for them?" Laderic asked, incredulously. He held his tongue, though. While the Ambassadors were not exactly his favorite people in the world, he knew insulting them wouldn't go over well with Mavark.

The people of the Far Land were loosely governed by an elected council of representatives for each of the different races. The council, called the Ambassadors of Unity, generally kept the peace in the Far Land, controlled the rule of law, and regulated trade and commerce between the smallest of villages to the largest of capitals. The major exception to this rule were the two human factions of Rokswing and Mariscale to the south, which were now united under the banner of a single, gigantic, human-controlled kingdom, after their devastating civil war almost three hundred years ago. They had their own monarchy and their own laws, but even they had a representative in the Ambassadors to promote peace and trade between their government and the citizens of the rest of the Far Land.

In fact, the only race that did not have a representative in the Ambassadors was the elves. This was yet another reason regular people distrusted the elves and even believed they didn't exist. The Ambassadors of Unity was formed thousands of years after the elves disappeared into the ice, so it was only natural that the elvish race was missing from their council.

Laderic hadn't exactly had the best experiences with the

Ambassadors in the past, but he wasn't trying to get into *that* conversation with the altruistic Mavark now.

Mavark, ignoring Laderic's outburst, was now inspecting the dragon's claws. "Before we had even landed, Prysmi could smell you, Laderic."

"That's not a surprise," teased Midiga. Laderic scowled at her.

"I do *not* smell that bad," he snapped. Mavark was smiling, shaking his head.

"No, you don't. But Prysmi is a silverback dragon. They have the most acute sense of smell of all dragons. She can track a scent for miles, which brings me to how we found you. We landed and entered Ewa'faita, and found your fae friend in the main room. She seemed quite worried, and obviously shocked to see us, but when we brought up Laderic, she jumped into action. She told me that she was with you, and you might be in trouble, so we set off to find you. It was easy for Prysmi to follow your scent through the tunnels, but eventually, we ran into these giant, locked, stone doors—but they were no match for a dragon." He grinned mischievously.

Prysmi bared her teeth in her equivalent of a smile. "They gave pretty easily after I smashed them down, but sometimes, it felt like the entire cave system was going to collapse as well."

Alleria's eyes lit up with a realization. "That's what the thunder was!"

Mavark looked confused. "Thunder?" The others nodded.

"The entire cavern vibrated every time you smashed down the doors," Midiga confirmed. "I could hear it through the walls before the others could. It sounded like an earthquake." Prysmi looked pleased with herself.

"I guess a formal introduction is in order," Mavark said, changing his tone. He had finished inspecting Prysmi and walked over to Midiga. He removed his right-handed gauntlet, extending his hand toward the felid. His wings flared slightly, and he bowed his head. "I am Mavark. This is my soul partner, Prysmi. I'm sure Laderic has mentioned me before."

"Only recently," confirmed Midiga, shaking his hand after a moment. She eyed his wings and tail, the true markings of a drake alamorph. He was the real deal.

"In fact, Mavark," Laderic interjected. "We were on our way to see you. Well, to see Ysmira, that is..."

Mavark's eyes twinkled, knowing. "Ah, yes... Is this about the elf that is traveling with you?" he mentioned casually.

Alleria looked shocked. "But... how could you know?" Her hood had remained snugly on her head, save for when she removed it to 'prove' to Elwyse she couldn't use magic. She had quickly replaced it during the battle. She was still wearing it now.

Prysmi angled her head toward Alleria, inhaling deeply. "Mavark's wife, Ysmira, is an elf, and your scent is quite unique," she stated. "It is impossible to mistake for anything else."

"Well, I hope I don't smell bad," muttered Alleria, self-conscious. She crossed her arms over her chest.

The dragon's chest rumbled, arcing and falling in pitch in a deep, throaty laugh. "Of course not. You smell just fine." She turned her gaze to Midiga, blinking slowly. "Though, not nearly as decadent as your felid friend here."

Midiga blushed, feeling uneasy. She was unsure whether or not that was a compliment from the dragon, or whether she smelled like dinner to the beast.

Laderic was still speaking to Mavark. "We can fill you in on the way—for now, we should continue on to Strita." As he spoke, his stomach rumbled almost as loud as a dragon's roar. "And we should eat, too."

"I could go for some food," piped Reia, tails wiggling with anticipation.

"Well, first thing's first," Mavark said, pulling a thin rope from Prysmi's saddle. He walked over to Elwyse, who was still unconscious on the ground, quickly securing his hands behind his back. "Don't want any surprises from our friend, do we?" He hoisted the necromancer over his shoulder. Prysmi walked over beside him and crouched down. Unceremoniously, he slung his body across the saddle like a sack of potatoes, fastening him to the seat with leather bindings normally used to keep him secure while flying.

"All right, let's get out of this dungeon and back into the sun!" Emery zipped toward the exit, vibrating with anticipation. Fae disliked being underground, especially summertime fae, who thrived in sunlight.

"Okay, let's go—huh?" Laderic had started toward the exit but heard a strange noise behind him. "What the..." Coming out of Elwyse's room was a tiny yapping creature.

"Arf!" it yelped, galloping across the floor toward their group. It was... a *tiny* zombie dog, with a giant collar of keys dangling from its neck.

"—Odie?" Laderic asked, bewildered. The dog yipped again, doing a spin and sitting, lolling its tongue out of its mouth.

Odie looked completely different. What was once a menacing hellhound now appeared to be nothing more than a small lap dog, but it was Odie, all right. that same collar of keys, now much too big, hindering the undead pup as he tried to walk.

Laderic knelt down and pulled the keys off of his neck, giving the pup a kind rub. In return, Odie licked his hand with a disgusting, rotting tongue. "Good... boy..." coughed Laderic through the stench.

"Arf!" yipped Odie happily.

Midiga was looking at Laderic with disbelief. "Don't even *think* about it," she accused, pointing a clawed finger at his chest. He smiled, apologetic.

"I mean... we can't just *leave* him here," he cooed, bending down and gingerly stroking the decomposing skin of the zombie puppy. "I mean, he's so… cute?" Odie did another spin.

Midiga shook her head, at a loss. "I'm not watching that thing. If you wanna watch it, fine."

"Can we please just get out of here," Alleria whined, impatiently standing by the exit with Emery now, waiting for the rest of them.

"On our way!" Laderic grinned. "Come on, boy!" He whistled at Odie.

And so, together, with Prysmi in the lead, they fumbled their way back to the surface.

CHAPTER 16

THEY GATHERED THEIR things from the fort's entrance and exited into the fresh air. Well, comparatively fresh. The area still stunk of rotting bodies. The sun had just begun to rise, and exhaustion hit them like a sledgehammer.

"Oh, man," Laderic said with a yawn. This sparked a chain reaction, each of them yawning in turn. "I forgot about sleep." He squinted in the brightness, stopping and stretching as they exited the darkness of Ewa'faita.

Midiga arched her back, baring her teeth as she yawned deeply. "We should get some ground covered, but stop to make camp early tonight." She looked over at Mavark. "How long is the walk to Strita from here?"

He frowned, scratching his head, readjusting his dreads since they had been crammed in a helmet for hours. "Normally, we fly, and it takes less than a day... but since we have a prisoner, and will be escorting you guys, I would guess another two days from here at minimum."

Emery seemed the most energetic of all. "But it's a beautiful day!" she cried, zipping up into the branches. "We shouldn't stop early!" Odie, who was also excited about being outside in who knows how long, yipped and barked, turning in circles over and over again, enough to make anyone dizzy.

"Says you. You got the most sleep out of all of us," growled Reia, plopping her butt down on the forest floor and scowling in Odie's direction. "I don't know how far I could walk if I tried!"

Alleria knelt next to her soul partner, scratching behind the fox's ears. The kitsune closed her eyes, panting slightly with enjoyment. "I'll carry you, don't worry." Soothed the elf, lifting Reia into her arms.

Mavark looked on, smiling fondly. "So, you're an alamorph too?" he asked.

"Yes," started Alleria. Then, it seemed another thought interrupted her original train of thought. "Wait, *you're* an alamorph!" she realized, stating the obvious. Mavark nodded slowly, amused by her thought process. "Can you help me? I mean, can you answer some of my questions? And, like, help us, I don't know, get stronger?"

He thought for a moment, before nodding again. "I suppose I could show you some things while we travel," he conceded. "Though, as a drake alamorph, our situations are a little different."

"Nonsense," Prysmi said, pushing her forehead against Alleria's side. "She is one of us. They and we are the same. Of course, we will help you." Alleria giggled, patting Prysmi on the head. The dragon hummed warmly.

Odie looked at Laderic expectantly. "Arf!" he barked, wagging his fleshy tail. Laderic grimaced, patting his side gingerly. Odie ran beside him, bouncing and spinning around his legs.

"Okay! Let's get a move on, then," Laderic said, taking off with Odie trailing close behind. They turned back toward the road, pushing their way out of the woods and back onto the path.

It felt good to be moving once again, even though they were exhausted. Through it all, they kept each other motivated, laughing and joking, and generally feeling positive about the days to come. Their second wind was fleeting, though, and it wasn't long before they needed to stop and rest once again.

"We should stop up ahead," Mavark said, pointing down the path. "There's a clearing not far from here and a sheltered place to make camp."

As he said, just a few minutes later, they came upon an opening in the woods, abruptly ending in a rocky cliff-face. They began to clear an area against the wall, making things comfortable, as they would be staying there until the next morning. A small overhang jutted from the side of the rock, and they arranged their things beneath it, in case it was to rain.

"We should reach Strita by tomorrow night, if we make good time during the day," Mavark assured, watching as they set up their things. He himself had a tent and bedroll fastened to Prysmi's saddle, which he unhooked and set up within minutes.

Midiga laid her blanket down as usual, and Alleria got out her own sleeping bag. Laderic spread his out in a soft patch of grass, setting his bag down on top of it. Odie tried to lie down on Laderic's things, but he was promptly shooed away. Dejected, he went over beside the rock wall to lie down where the grass was a bit shorter so he could still see everyone. Emery was content to sleep in the branches of the canopy around them.

"We should collect materials for a fire," Laderic said, peering through the trees. "After that, we can get some rest."

"I think we have enough food to make it through the next couple of days, but we will be completely out by the time we reach Strita," remarked Midiga, digging through her things and retrieving several strips of salted meat. She passed them around to the others, even offering some to Mavark and Prysmi, who respectfully declined.

"Dragons don't need to eat often, another trait I have gained

194

through my bond," Mavark explained. He thumped his tail on the ground, and Midiga flinched and not without him noticing. He held his arms out, palms up and open. "Believe me... I know the stigma that comes with being a drake alamorph better than most. I don't expect you to trust me right away, but I do hope you give me a chance." His dark eyes searched hers, reading her body language like an open book.

Midiga was slightly embarrassed, as she was hoping her demeanor toward Mavark had gone unnoticed. She nodded stiffly, turning her back to him and sitting cross-legged on her blanket. She inhaled a shaky breath, trying to calm herself into a state of meditation. It was hard, though, with a dragon so near.

Prysmi was lying on the ground, her position surprisingly cat-like. She folded her claws in front of her, basking in the sun. Her scales glistened as she moved, each breath scattering light in new directions. Alleria was fascinated, admiring the dragon, obvious and unashamed. "Your scales... I've never seen anything like them," she said as she set Reia down on the ground and reached her arm out toward Prysmi's side. "Can I—"

"Of course," hummed the dragon, lifting her wing slightly to give Alleria a better view. The elf gently rested her palm on the scales, which were surprisingly cold. They felt like metal; smooth and perfectly molded to her skin. They were also thin, reminding Alleria of feathers. Her wings also spoke to this. They looked just like giant bird wings, though with scales instead of feathers.

Prysmi was elegant and lean, agile and small. At her shoulders, she was just eight feet tall, her wingspan just over twenty-six feet in length. Her tail was nearly double the length of her body, ending in the razor-sharp halberd that was her main weapon.

"Can you breathe fire?" asked Reia, curious. "Maybe you could help me control my magic better?" But Prysmi was shaking her head.

"I am a silverback dragon," she explained.

"What does that mean?" asked Alleria. "You can't breathe fire?" The dragon shook her head. "Can you breathe... anything?" Again, Prysmi shook her head no.

"I guess I have forgotten how little the citizens of the Far Land know of my kind," she lamented, a deeper sadness beneath the surface. "I should reiterate—I am the last silverback dragon."

The clearing became quiet, everyone now listening to the majestic and sad creature before them. Even Midiga, back turned to the rest of them, had an ear cocked in her direction. "We silverbacks were hunted to extinction for our scales, which are thin and sharp, light, and hard as a diamond. We are the smallest of dragons—I am full grown, even considered large for my kind. We cannot breathe fire or use any kind of magic. Our tails are our weapons, some ending in spearheads, some in spikes. Mine, of course, is a blade.

"The last time I saw another silverback was over ten years ago... The poachers got to him before I could. I tried to stop the attackers, but they knew exactly how to take us down. They were professional silverback hunters, after all, and knew all of our weaknesses. They went right for his wings... Without mobility, we are extremely vulnerable. If I had gone back to rescue him... they would have killed me, as well. I escaped, saving my species from total annihilation. Alas, it was all for nothing. I am the end of the line...

"I encountered Mavark soon after. I never expected to bond with a human. Perhaps it was my isolation that drove me to his company. But, nevertheless, we've been together ever since." Her azure eyes were wet, and Alleria was stunned, shocked that such a powerful creature was shedding tears right in front of her.

"I'm sorry," she said, feeling dreadful and empathetic.

Prysmi turned her head toward the elf, her eyes portals to an entire universe. "Each day, I celebrate life—you should do the same. Do not dwell on the past. That will get you nowhere. We must all look ahead." Mavark had come up to her side, placing his forehead on the dragon's shoulder. Her chest hummed in what would be the equivalent of a cat's purr. Midiga's ear twitched.

The story had sobered the mood, with everyone falling into silence for a while. Alleria and Reia went into the woods to fetch firewood, as they preferred to do each time they made camp. Alleria knew she was good at making fires, and she enjoyed doing it. She liked the feeling of being useful, and this was a way she knew she could be. She and Reia would spread out, never farther than they could hear each other's thoughts, and would collect only the most perfect tinder.

Emery perched high in the boughs of a tulip tree, the tallest tree she could find in the area. She felt more comfortable high above everything where she could see what was coming and monitor each of her friends. *Friends.* She savored the thought, having been without those she considered friends for so long. Even Laderic, though he got on her nerves more than anyone had in years. She was ever thankful she had continued to travel with them even for a few more days, if anything just to extend this feeling of—dare she say—happiness, for a while longer.

Midiga could not focus. She had stopped even trying to meditate after a while and was only trying to relax, but even that was not working. She was tired, but in an irritating way, more mentally exhausted than physically. She couldn't stop her mind from turning and working, and if she didn't get some of this energy out, she was going to explode. "I'm going for a walk," she announced, a little louder than she had intended, standing from her spot on the ground, and turning toward Laderic.

"I'll come with you," he said immediately, standing to follow her. As he stood, he became lightheaded, stumbling backward a few feet.

"No, stay here," Midiga chided. "You're exhausted."

"You shouldn't go alone though," he pleaded, walking

197

toward her. "Please don't." His eyes were wide, fearful. Though it seemed like a lifetime ago, he remembered all too clearly the incident with the bear.

The felid sighed, frustrated. She was about to change her mind and sit back down when Prysmi spoke up. "I'll go with you," she said, taking a few steps toward Midiga, who took an instinctual step back. "I'll need to get out of this saddle first."

Midiga narrowed her eyes, confused, but watched curiously, as Mavark removed the leather saddle from her back, and Elwyse along with it. The necromancer was still unconscious, sleeping peacefully, his hands tied tightly with rope. Mavark placed him beside Odie, who whined and curled up by his side.

The drake alamorph leaned his back against the cliff-face, crossing his arms. "Don't be gone too long. I might need you if our friend here wakes up," he told Prysmi.

"I'll be here—" started Laderic, before breaking into another huge yawn.

Mavark tilted his head, eying Laderic incredulously. "And you'll be asleep if anything goes down. No offense, but you're useless until you've had some rest."

Laderic opened his mouth to argue and, instead, yawned yet another time. "You're probably right." He groaned, sitting back down on his bedroll. "Fine."

Prysmi shook her body back and forth, stretching after getting out of the saddle. "That thing is so stiff," she mumbled, extending her wings in another stretch. They were huge, covering most of the clearing in shade.

Without warning, her scales began to glow. The light coming from her body was so bright that Midiga had to look away. *What is happening?* Midiga wondered feeling panicked once again. Instinctually, she reached behind her back for an arrow, though remembered after a moment that her bow had been shattered. She cursed, with nothing to do now but wait until the light died down. Her heart was pumping wildly, and she braced herself for whatever was to come.

As the light faded, Prysmi was nowhere to be found. In her place was another drake alamorph, a woman this time with silver hair. Her wings were large and feathery, and her tail took the shape of a halberd at its end. *Wait—Prysmi?*

The dragon had taken the shape of a human before their very eyes. She had snake-like features, an angled face, and scales dusting her skin. She wore silver armor that looked to be made of her own scales and similar in structure to Mavark's heavy armor. At her side, she carried a long, thin sword in a silver scabbard. She held an unnatural beauty similar to the elves.

She extended the wings on her back to steady herself, appearing angelic for a moment. "Oh, it has been a while since I've taken this form," she said sheepishly, blushing. She made eye contact with Midiga, who quickly looked away after realizing she had been staring. Prysmi inspected her new body, checking everywhere to make sure she had morphed correctly.

"I got firewo—*Prysmi?*" Alleria came out of the woods and nearly dropped the armful of firewood she had collected. "You can change into a human? You are so gorgeous!"

"Why, thank you," hummed the dragon-woman. She folded her wings behind her, the tips so long that they brushed the blades of grass beneath her feet. She noticed Midiga's shock and took a few slow steps toward her, hoping this form was less intimidating than the other. "All dragons have the ability to take human form, I included. I am just around Mavark so much that I forget that most normal people have not interacted with a dragon before."

"N–no, it's fine," Midiga stuttered. "It was just surprising, is all." She quickly whirled around, facing the trees and steadying herself. She took deep breaths to slow her heartbeat.

"Wonderful. We shall be off then," Prysmi confirmed, sounding a bit nervous, nodding toward Mavark as she and Midiga headed out into the forest together.

Laderic watched them go. "It makes me feel so much better that she went with Midiga," he sighed. He leaned back on his palms, relaxing. He closed his eyes. "Man, I am *exhausted.*"

Alleria was busy building a fire, Reia fetching her sticks from their pile of wood. "Me too," she said, fighting another yawn. "After I build this, I'm going right to sleep."

It didn't take her long at all, and once she was finished, she and Reia curled up in her sleeping bag. Sleep took her easily. Laderic had already fallen asleep, snoring quietly with his mouth open. Mavark watched over them, stoic, glancing toward Elwyse every few minutes in case the necromancer were to show any signs of waking.

MIDIGA AND PRYSMI walked in silence for a long while, Midiga in front with Prysmi following quietly behind. Together, they enjoyed the ambience of the forest in their own way. Midiga relished in the refreshing feeling of soft moss and dirt between her paws as she walked. Birds sang high above them, flitting between branches in a colorful dance. Ahead, she could hear the gurgle of a small body of water. She headed that way, albeit subconsciously, as she was lost in her own thoughts. Occasionally, she glanced back at the dragon-woman who followed her, though unsure if she was making certain she was still there or hoping she had disappeared.

Prysmi was hyperaware of how nervous Midiga was around her, but she tried her best to pretend she hadn't noticed. Most people, in general, were fearful of dragons, hearing naught but terrifying stories of their wrath. So she couldn't blame the felid for her demeanor. She was going to try her best to prove her wrong, which was why she volunteered to accompany her in the first place. Laderic knew Prysmi and had encountered other dragons in the past, and so was unfazed by her presence. The elf was naïve and curious, and those feelings overtook whatever natural wariness she might have had. The fae woman, if she was to be true to her species, was not afraid of any of the natural beasts of the Far Land, for the fae were the most connected with nature of all.

But the felid… Knowing their already suspicious and nervous natures, she knew Midiga would be a tough one to win over. She knew of the cat-woman from Laderic's brief mentions when they had traveled together years ago, and she was determined to make a good impression, especially if they were to be staying in Strita for a few days before moving on.

Plus… there was something about her. Prysmi couldn't

shake it. The dragon hadn't encountered many felidae in the past. Strita was nearly exclusively humans, though was inclusive of all races. Since it was such a small town without any major trade routes going through, having visitors beyond the usual suppliers was a rarity.

It was strange, watching this woman who was so different from her, and yet so similar. Felidae, like dragons, were extremely close to the beasts of the natural world. They were created by the gods not long after the dragons, after all. To be sentient, but also feral, it was a combination unique to the animalistic races of the Far Land. And Prysmi was drawn to that, to someone else that shared that same experience. She hadn't spent time with anyone like her for so long… so long…

"Oof!" Prysmi walked face first into a tree branch. Midiga turned to watch as the dragon ducked under the branch, careful that her wings did not get caught, either. "Sorry," Prysmi mumbled, apologetic. "Lost in thought."

"That makes two of us," Midiga said, turning back around and continuing to the creek. They came upon it shortly after, the water having carved a path through the trees, heading southwest. It was clear as glass, with fish darting up and down the stream, swimming up the miniature waterfalls that cascaded over small rocks. They scattered when Midiga and Prysmi approached, but then slowly went back to their normal business.

Midiga began to scan the area, searching the ground. For what, Prysmi had no idea. The dragon sat down on the edge of the creek, fanning her wings slightly to catch some of the sunlight that was beaming down at them. The water had cut a natural hole in the green ceiling of trees, warming the water and giving light to the flora around them. Flowers that normally could not grow this deep in the forest were flourishing near the water's edge. Prysmi caressed the petals of a yellow blossom, enjoying the way they felt on her fingertips. In her human form, many of her senses dulled, but not the sense of touch. This—

along with taste—was greatly intensified. She enjoyed feeling different textures with her hands while in human form and definitely preferred to eat this way.

Midiga eventually found what she was looking for, picking up a long, thin branch that was still green in the middle. With a small dagger, she cut off the smaller branches attached to it until it was just a straight pole. She then began to dig through the brush, looping her claws under some thick, green vines, and stripping them from the bark they were attached to. Prysmi was fascinated, watching as the felid delicately split the vine down the middle with her dagger, slicing it down its length in the center with her knife. Then, she carefully peeled a hair-thin sliver of sinew from its center, separating this single strand from the rest of the vine. She expertly tied this elastic line to the tip of the pole she had made. Only after this did Prysmi recognize the tool she was creating.

"A fishing rod," she stated. Midiga nodded, wordless, as she plucked a barbed thorn from the trunk of a different type of tree, fastening it to the other end of the line. She pulled on the line, testing the tautness of her knots and the flexibility of the rod before sitting down on the edge of the water, several meters away from Prysmi. She cast her line into the water, staring at the thorn at its end intently.

The two sat in silence for a few minutes, the dragon having a million questions on her mind but unable to bring herself to ask them. Fish darted back and forth, some curiously swimming up to the thorn but not taking a bite. The tension was building, and Prysmi could not hold her tongue any longer.

"Don't you need something on the thorn as bait?" she asked innocently.

Midiga shook her head. "The thorns of the ralai tree secrete a sap that is tempting for fish. It's the easiest way to make a functional fishing rod, especially if you don't have anything to bait your own hook with." She recited all of this as if she had memorized the exact words from a textbook. She smiled to herself, still keeping her eyes trained on the thorn in the water. "Give it time—they'll come around."

And she was right. Within another couple of minutes, one fish became too curious and decided to go for the sap. The line grew taut, and Midiga jerked up hard on the rod, standing and pulling with her whole body. The fish pulled back, and a tiny struggle ensued. Unfortunately, the rod could not handle the tension, and the pole snapped in half after only a few seconds.

Midiga stood, frozen with only half of the rod clutched between her paws. Prysmi flinched as the rod broke, watching Midiga, tense. After a moment, the felid flung the other half of the pole into the woods across the creek, yowling, and cursing in her own language. She sat back down on the banks of the creek, putting her face in her hands, defeated.

Prysmi didn't know what to say. "Hey... it's all right," she attempted. Midiga was silent, ignoring her. "Why... don't you use your weapons to catch one?"

"I don't *have* a weapon. My bow is in pieces," Midiga snapped, jerking her head up and staring daggers at the dragon-woman. "Obviously, I would have done that first if I *had* one and not gone through the trouble of making a stupid fishing pole." She put her head back in her paws, exhaling harshly.

Prysmi was a bit taken aback but was still concerned for the felid. "I didn't mean a weapon like *that*," she clarified. Midiga glanced over at her, slowly lowering her hands. "I don't even really use this thing. It's just for show," Prysmi said, gesturing toward her own sword in its scabbard with a look of disgust. "I meant your weapons—those." She slowly reached out, taking Midiga by the paw. Midiga watched, a bit shocked, as the dragon turned her hand over and pushed on her pads, unsheathing her claws.

"Even in my human form, I prefer my natural weapons to any *tool*," she stated. She let go of Midiga's hand, holding her own hands up before their eyes. They, too, ended in claws. "These," she started, then gesturing back toward her bladed tail, which she lifted slightly into the air, "and that."

Midiga's first reaction was doubt—how could she hunt with just her claws? But... a memory was surfacing in the back of her mind. A memory from the battle, of her shattering the seals on the skeletons' chests with nothing but her claws. A memory of adrenaline, of passion, of desire... Suddenly, she realized she was staring at Prysmi and quickly looked away. "Okay," she conceded hastily, standing and heading down toward the water. Prysmi smiled, following her down the banks into the creek.

They spent the next few hours fishing with nothing but their natural weapons. Prysmi's hands appeared as human hands but were crowned with thick, sharp claws instead of fingernails. Midiga, claws unsheathed, eventually got the hang of things. They stalked their prey, plunging their hands into the crisp water and snatching them out of the creek. Soon, they were catching fish left and right, pulling them from the water quite reliably, breaking their necks, tossing them into a pile behind them.

They had started out working in silence, but soon, got to small talk about the task of fishing. This led to a more friendly conversation until the two were actually making jokes and laughing aloud. Midiga could feel herself growing slightly feral but was able to keep it under control. Fish never did it for her quite the way the large game did. Besides, this work was fun, and she didn't feel nearly as serious as she did when she was pursuing a deer. She actually felt quite alive, unsure as to why she hadn't been fishing this way all along. *Oh, well,* she thought, *this is definitely how I'm going to do it in the future.*

The sun was making its descent when they finally took a break. The tension between them had been broken, and Midiga felt much more relaxed than she had since they started their walk. "I'm so glad we did this," she said genuinely. Her stomach rumbled, and she laughed. "Guess we should eat some of our prey, huh?" Prysmi grinned, nodding excitedly. Midiga reached into the pile and grabbed a fish, bringing it up to her mouth, raw. She stopped though, looking up at Prysmi. "I guess we should cook some for you, huh?"

The dragon shook her head, also reaching into the pile for a fish. "I know I've taken a different form, but I don't know how you keep forgetting that I am a dragon." She brought the fish up to her mouth, taking a bite right out of its side.

Midiga watched for a moment, mouth agape, before smiling and taking a bite of her own fish. It was delicious, though a bit too mild for her taste. She was used to the strong tasting fish back in Ulandyl. "We should do this in my hometown some time," she suggested. "The fish there are phenomenal." Prysmi's face lit up, and she nodded enthusiastically.

They ate their fill, stealing glances at each other occasionally and smiling to themselves. Midiga found herself feeling a different kind of nervous around the dragon now, though she didn't know why. Something about her smile, and her voice, and her eyes… She blinked hard, shaking her head back and forth, as though she were trying to make those thoughts fall out.

"It's nice to eat and be like this, you know, with someone else," Prysmi mused after a while. "I don't have other dragons to spend time with, and nearly all of the people in Strita are human, not as close to nature as we are."

Midiga nodded, leaping at the distraction. "I haven't shared a meal like this since my dad was alive," she mused. A quick pain gripped her heart, but she quickly pushed it down, gathering herself. "I'm sorry for earlier," she admitted after a moment, looking down at the forest floor. "About being afraid of you. I heard your story earlier, but I didn't listen." Prysmi was silent, watching her with crystal blue eyes. Midiga continued. "I can't say I know how you feel… My species is far from extinct, but I know what it feels like to lose someone you're close to since I-I

206

lost my dad, and—" Midiga's throat felt tight, and the words stopped themselves from leaving her mouth. *Not now.*

Prysmi placed her clawed hand on Midiga's shoulder, peering at her face closely. Midiga flinched, turning to look at her, fighting tears but to no avail. Prysmi gently reached up to her cheek, wiping a single tear from her silver-gray fur. "There's no need to apologize," she said firmly. "I know my species has not done a lot to gain trust from the others in the Far Land. It's only natural to be suspicious. Don't worry about it." The felid nodded, wordless. Prysmi sat back, eyes turning misty as she absentmindedly stroked her wings. "And I'm sorry about your father. That must have been hard."

Midiga said nothing as she stared off into space, fighting the dark thoughts that were clawing their way out of the trenches she had buried them in. "It's nothing," she assured, mostly to herself. *I've gotta move, gotta do something*—"Come on," she said suddenly, smiling and getting to her feet. "Let's get back to camp and share the rest of these fish."

Prysmi grinned, standing as well and helping gather the fish in a cloth. They chatted all the way back, Midiga careful to keep herself talking, drowning out the creeping grips of depression threatening to strangle her all over again. *It was seven years ago,* she kept telling herself while Prysmi was speaking.

Why can't I let this go? She smiled, nodding without actually hearing anything the dragon was saying, pretending to listen as she battled the demons of her subconscious.

CHAPTER 17

ELWYSE'S BODY FELT heavy, and he couldn't figure out why. He was lying down on something soft. And he was so... hot. Why was it so hot? It never got hot in the cave. He groaned, moving to take his jacket off, but his hands were immobilized. Tied up by... something. A rope?

Suddenly, he remembered, eyes snapping open, setting first on Odie, who was back in his unaltered form, lying against a stone wall in front of him. He yipped happily, bouncing through the grass over to his face. *Grass.* Elwyse's eyes grew wide with fear. "No..." he whispered. He wriggled, rolling himself onto his left side and freezing with fear.

He was outside.

"No!" he cried, struggling and writhing on the ground to no avail. "Do you realize what you've done?" He scanned the area around him frantically, locking onto the drake alamorph, who was leaned up against the cliff wall, eying him coolly.

"And what exactly would that be?" asked the half-dragon. "Capturing you and shutting down your little operation?"

"It's wasn't *my* operation," Elwyse sneered, struggling for a moment to sit up. He saw his legs were also bound together, and he groaned. "Take me back, I'm begging you!" His voice panicked. This intrigued Mavark, but he kept silent.

"What's—oh, he's awake." Laderic yawned, sitting up and rubbing his eyes. The sun was behind the trees now, almost completely set. He glanced around, scanning the treeline. "Midiga and Prysmi back yet?"

Mavark closed his eyes, silent for a moment, then opened them and nodded. "They're headed this way now. Couldn't have been better timing." He nodded down toward Elwyse, who was pulling at his bindings to no avail, ignoring Odie who was bouncing around him and yipping happily.

"Please... you have to take me back," he pleaded, shimmying himself around to look at Laderic. "I promise, I won't kidnap anyone else. I-I'll keep to myself." There were now tears in his wide eyes.

Laderic smiled, slowly. Something about watching Elwyse struggle and beg was enticing. "I would *love* to hear this," he started, getting to his feet and walking toward Elwyse, deliberately.

Alleria had woken up, as well, and was watching the commotion, clutching Reia in her arms as she sat cross-legged on her sleeping bag.

Laderic knelt down until he was eye level with Elwyse, face nearly touching his. "Tell me why I shouldn't kill you right now," he threatened, so quietly that Alleria could barely hear.

Elwyse's mouth gaped open and then shut like a fish, not sure now if he was more scared of Laderic than—"Because they'll kill me. They'll kill *you* and all of your friends."

"You mean like you tried to do?" Laderic's voice was colder than ice. Without warning, he shoved Elwyse to the ground, standing up straight and towering over the necromancer. He stuck his boot into Elwyse's chest, pressing down, hard. Alleria flinched but said nothing. It was as if Laderic wasn't even the same person. "Right now, this is how I see it," he hissed, a sinister look in his eyes. Mavark, as well, remained silent, watching carefully. "You tried to kill me, you tried to kill my friends, you *imprisoned* us underground, and now, we have you in custody, and you're trying to scare us with some looming made-up threat?"

He drew his sword, and Alleria squeezed Reia tighter. Mavark's hand drifted to his own sword, but he remained where he was. Laderic pointed his sword at Elwyse, resting the blade on his neck. Odie growled, yapping but staying out of range. "You had better start talking, right now," he whispered, deathly serious.

Elwyse swallowed, opening his mouth to speak when Prysmi and Midiga came out of the woods. They were jogging, Midiga carrying a sack of something wet. When they saw Laderic standing over Elwyse, they ran faster.

"Prysmi said something was wrong." Midiga panted as they approached. She observed the situation, Laderic threatening Elwyse as he lay tied up on the floor. "I thought so," she confirmed, staring daggers at Elwyse. "Can we kill him now?"

"We aren't killing him," said Mavark, quietly but firmly. "He is my prisoner, after all. He'll go to the jail in Strita until I can figure out what the Ambassadors want me to do with him."

Laderic ignored Mavark, still staring coldly at Elwyse, pressing the metal of his sword against his neck. "Talk."

Elwyse's eyes darted between them, and he took a deep breath. "You made a mistake dragging me out of Ewa'faita," he began, voice trembling slightly. "I was just there *guarding* it—"

"Well, there's nothing left to guard now," Mavark said. "The spring was plugged up with rubble. It's just normal water now."

"Who were you guarding it for?" demanded Laderic. "You keep saying 'they this,' 'they that.' Who is 'they?'"

Elwyse closed his eyes, squinting them shut. He opened his mouth and said something, but it was too quiet for anyone to hear.

"Speak up!" Laderic barked, impatiently, pushing his sword into his neck a bit further until a thin line of blood appeared.

"Laderic..." warned Mavark, drawing his sword a bit more. But Laderic ignored him once again, holding his weapon steady.

Elwyse swallowed, licked his lips, and spoke again. "The nightwalkers," he whispered, and a tense silence overtook them.

Laderic nearly dropped his sword, removing it from the necromancer's neck, feeling his heart rate double. *No...* he thought, turning away from Elwyse and scanning the woods frantically, but there was nothing. He felt a rage growing in his chest, and he threw his sword on the ground, kneeling and grasping Elwyse by the shoulders, shaking him like a rag doll. "So you're working with *them,* huh?" he roared.

"Laderic!" Alleria cried. She set Reia down and stood, rushing over to pull him off Elwyse, who was still tied up and completely helpless as he was thrown around. "Stop! Let him talk. He's clearly not on their side if he's so scared!"

Midiga rushed over as well, and the two of them wrenched Laderic off the necromancer, who struggled to remain sitting up after becoming so disoriented.

Laderic was panting, still seeing red. "Explain yourself," he said darkly, murder threaded through his words. He noted his sword on the ground but didn't reach for it yet, as Midiga and Alleria continued to hold him back.

Elwyse took a shaky breath, calming his nerves. "F–Four years ago, I was traveling through this area of the Brushdeep," he began, voice shaky. "I found the fort, something called me to it. I can't explain it... I think it was just the presence of the magic power, but when I found the magical spring, I also found trouble.

"The nightwalkers were already there, using the water for...

211

experiments, I guess you could call them. These nightwalkers were different from ones I had met in the past... They were sinister, evil. Working together, claiming to serve some higher power. Instead of killing me, they told me I could live if I stayed in the fort and guarded the spring, scaring outsiders away with my magic. They told me I could use the spring's power to fuel my necromancy, as long as I never left...

"Whatever they had been using the spring for wasn't working out, and they soon abandoned their project, leaving me there alone. They told me they would come to check on me every now and again, and if they found out that I even so much as *visited* the surface, they promised me a fate crueler than death." He paused, eyes turning glassy as if he had seen some kind of unmentionable horror. After a moment, he blinked, returning to his story.

"Since then, I remained underground. For four years, I've stayed there, with no one but Odie by my side. I did my best to keep outsiders away, and they or their servants would come every few weeks or so to check on the status of the spring. They usually sent their canid followers to sniff around upstairs and make sure I hadn't left my post. Their visits have been more infrequent as of late, but they were supposed to be here just two days from now." He looked up at Laderic, pleading once again. "You have to take me back there, or we'll all be dead! Or worse—"

"Not happening," Mavark spoke, shutting that idea down instantly.

Alleria was frozen, mind racing, connecting the dots. "You said they were looking for me... Did you say they had canidae working for them?" Elwyse nodded, avoiding her gaze. Terrified, she locked eyes with Laderic, sharing the same thoughts.

"If you don't let me leave, they'll find us," the necromancer whispered. "The canidae are bloodhungry. They have hunters for every single race in the Far Land. They have pieces of my clothes. They'll track me down, and I'm sure once they catch the scent of your elf friend here, they'll make finding us and killing us a priority." His voice was monotonous now, accepting his grim fate.

Alleria was shaking. "M–Midiga? Laderic?" she asked, panicked. She let go of Laderic's arm, taking a few steps back. Her friends were silent, shocked as she was. She shook her head. "But nightwalkers have never came for me," she rationalized quickly. "Only canidae."

Elwyse frowned. "They rarely do their own dirty work. After they abandoned the spring, they hardly ever came to check on me themselves. But this time, a few of them were supposed to come and test something in the water, but now that it's gone... they're going to kill all of us." The last phrase he said as a matter-of-fact statement. He stared blankly at the grass in front of him, a tear leaking from his right eye and dripping down his cheek.

Laderic looked at Mavark, who was still stoic. "We should kill him," he said. "Then we can take Alleria to safety."

The drake alamorph shook his head. "No, he comes with me, alive. I don't like killing if I can help it. You know that."

"Mavark!" Laderic yelled, taking a few steps toward his friend and gesturing wildly with his hands. "Did you *not* hear what he said? Nightwalkers, who knows how many. Midiga and I saw black fog on our way to Strita just a few days ago. I feel it in my bones. He's telling the truth. We will all be killed!" Alleria, hearing for the first time the news about the fog, began to cry softly.

Mavark shook his head, sheathing his sword and walking over to Elwyse. They all grew silent, watching as he took a spot behind the necromancer. "No, we won't," he declared, planting his feet behind their prisoner. "We have bait, and we'll have an advantage." He gestured toward Elwyse, taking a motivational tone. "We know they're coming. We take Elwyse to Strita. We'll have at least a day to prepare. I'll get the people in town ready, and we set up an ambush." He grinned at Laderic, who was unconvinced. "They think they have the element of surprise... but now the tables have turned. Laderic, we'll take them down. All of them. We'll end this once and for all!"

Alleria stood, shocked, feeling a tiny glimmer of hope spark in the back of her mind. *End it, finally...* For a brief moment, she imagined what it would be like not to have to run anymore. Emery suddenly whizzed down from the trees, hovering beside Mavark with her hands on her hips. "I like what he has to say," she mused, having been listening from up on her perch. "If we're doing this, though, we need to get moving soon. We have a lot of ground to cover."

"Emery, you don't have to come, this isn't your fight," Laderic said, but she shook her head.

"Who's gonna carry my bag all the way there?" she said, gesturing over to Laderic's pile of things where the fae's bag had been strapped together with his own. "Besides, I can't let you guys handle this on your own! All of us combined, we can finally end this thing! At least for Alleria's sake."

Prysmi and Midiga were nodding in agreement as well, but Laderic was still unsure. "Mavark, I've seen this first hand. I don't think this is going to go like you think." He pointed accusingly at Elwyse. "He got us into this mess, and killing him is the first step out of it!"

Mavark's gaze turned serious. "Laderic," he said with voice dark, "I don't want to have to fight you about this." Midiga's tail began to twitch. "The necromancer is my prisoner, and I'm not going to let anything happen to him until justice is served. If you do not want to come with us to Strita, I cannot force you, but you aren't going to lay a hand on him." They stared at each other, each refusing to look away first.

Laderic was stunned, gritting his teeth and holding his

tongue. He was at an impasse, knowing he would not be able to convince Mavark that he was wrong. He ran the options through his head, reluctantly admitting to himself that, if it came down to a fight, he would lose that too. *But... what if he's right,* he thought suddenly. *Maybe we can take them on with all of us together.*

He broke eye contact finally, inhaling deeply. "Fine," he huffed, breaking the tension. "We'll plan an ambush." He glared at Elwyse. "You'll tell us everything you know—and I wouldn't try anything if I were you. I know you think he's protecting you right now, but don't get it confused—he's *not* on your side."

Mavark nodded, coming around and kneeling in front of Elwyse, looking into his eyes. His sapphire wings flared behind him, blocking out the sun, casting the necromancer in darkness. "Just in case there's still any confusion," he began, and before anyone could react, he drew back his fist, punching the necromancer square in the face and knocking him out cold. Everyone was stunned. "*That's* for trying to kill my friends," he concluded, standing back up and walking over to Prysmi's saddle.

In silence, they gathered their things. There was no more time for rest—not until they reached Strita. "You know, we still could have gotten more information out of him," Prysmi told Mavark as they retrieved her saddle.

Mavark nodded, unhooking some of the straps. "Yes, but solidarity with the rest of them is more important than that right now. We know what we need to know. In two to three days, we are likely going to have some unwanted visitors. He'll wake up by tonight, and we can question him further. Right now, we need to get to Strita."

Prysmi nodded, accepting her soul partner's judgment. She closed her eyes, enveloping her body in blinding light once again as she shifted back into her beast form. Mavark hitched the saddle on her back as the rest of them finished packing.

"Did anyone *not* get any sleep?" Mavark asked, taking charge. Midiga raised her arm meekly. "I know you're likely exhausted, but do you think you could make it a few more hours until we absolutely have to stop for the night?"

"You can ride in the saddle," Prysmi suggested, padding over to the felid and kneeling down.

Mavark nodded in agreement. "I can carry the prisoner for now." He lifted Elwyse with ease, slinging him over his shoulder like a sack of potatoes. Everyone else was ready, bags packed, and on edge. "If we cover some ground tonight, we should reach Strita before tomorrow night, and there's room at my place for everyone to sleep in a bed."

Alleria smiled at Reia, for a moment forgetting the situation they were getting themselves into. Prysmi took the lead, and, anxiously, they began to make their way to Strita once more.

CHAPTER 18

THEY DIDN'T RUN into much trouble at all the rest of the way to the village. Maybe it was because the rumors about this path through the Brushdeep were exaggerated and unfounded, or maybe it had something to do with a dragon traveling with them. Nevertheless, they made it to Strita before the sun had set on the following day.

The woods opened up to a valley, the mountains seeming to appear out of nowhere as they came out from under the thick canopy of leaves. Flanked on its eastern side by mountains, with a small river flowing from a cave at the base of the nearest mountain, Strita spread itself throughout the valley along the mountain's face. It provided those who lived there with a strategic natural wall in case of an attack, though the town had been generally peaceful for over a hundred years.

A small, rocky path led up into the mountains, and a dock on the river harbored several large sailboats, which could be taken out to sea using the river's path under the mountain. This was the main reason a town had even formed this far away from civilization, as food and other goods were easily transported out to sea and back again.

So, although Strita was an inland village, it had the feel of a coastal town. The single market in town saturated with fish, delicate shells, and other exotic ocean goods. Many of its residents were seafaring folk, making their living on ocean expeditions, sometimes lasting for months at a time. Their peak fishing season was in the summer months as the fish explored further and further north in the warm water.

Mavark's house was on the outskirts of town—a small, quaint cottage with a decent sized farm spread out behind it. He raised horses, having five adults and two foals at the time. Normally, horses are skittish around dragons, but these had grown up with Prysmi by their side and treated her as a sibling. They nickered as the travelers approached, trotting up to the fence, and dangling their heads over the side. Prysmi hurried over to them, bumping foreheads with each of them in turn, spending a bit more time with the little ones.

Elwyse had woken up as they traveled but had kept to himself. Once awake, Mavark untied his foot bindings, allowing him to walk instead of being carried. He didn't try anything, but rather picked up Odie carefully from the ground and held him tightly the entire time. He spent most of his time staring, his mouth gaping at the forest around them, admiring individual blades of grass and leaves each time they stopped for a break. Emery, of course, delighted in this, and quietly educated Elwyse on the different types of foliage in the Brushdeep Forest. He drank it in, wordless and entranced.

They reached Mavark's house on the hill with daylight to spare. Elwyse was to remain outside with Prysmi for the time being. Before Mavark could even knock, the door flew open and a woman nearly tackled him to the ground. "Thank the gods!" she cried, tearful, squeezing around his neck tightly. Mavark hugged her back, a tender moment. After a long embrace, she released him and pulled back.

"It is so good to see you, my love," Mavark said warmly. He gestured toward her. "Everyone, this is my wife, Ysmira." The elf woman did a half-courtesy, giggly and clearly overjoyed that Mavark was back. She was quite tall and thick in her hips and thighs. Her skin was dark for an elf, a caramel color that complimented her dark hair beautifully. Her eyes were golden, as Alleria's were. She carried with her the unnatural beauty that accompanied all elves.

Ysmira clasped her hands in front of her, scanning the crowd behind him. "Oh, you brought guests! Please, come in!" She held the door open and ushered them inside, observing each of them in turn. Laderic entered last, and she grinned mischievously. "I should have *known* Laderic was involved with all of this!" She slapped him on the arm, joking. "What kind of trouble did you get yourself into this time?" she asked.

Midiga bared her teeth in a smile. "I'm glad she already knows the drill," she chided. Laderic groaned.

Ysmira whipped up a quick meal for them, the travelers not realizing how ravenous they had become until they started to eat. They ate happily, starting in on their conversation with warm bellies. Mavark quietly took some food out to Elwyse and Prysmi, even giving some scraps to Odie, though the zombie dog did not need to eat.

They spent the next hour or so filling Ysmira in on what had happened. They explained to her about Elwyse and the warning he had given them. They mentioned how the nightwalkers were working with the canidae when they finally came to Alleria. She slowly removed her hood and watched as Ysmira's face went from confusion to awe. "Oh my," she said, tears instantly filling her eyes. "I–I have not seen another of my kind for quite a while." She reached out, clasping Alleria's hands between her own. "You have no idea how welcome a sight you are."

Alleria smiled, eyes turning a lavender color with the

compliment. "Oh, th–thank you," she stuttered, feeling modest.

Ysmira noticed her eyes change color, and she furrowed her brow. "Your eyes," she said, peering closer. "Did they change?"

"Yeah, they do that sometimes," Alleria admitted.

Ysmira was silent for a moment. "Strange," she muttered but said no more on the topic.

Midiga and Emery introduced themselves as well, going into a bit more detail than they had with Mavark. This was unintentional but likely had to do with Mavark's intimidating appearance versus the motherly aura that Ysmira projected with her every move.

"That's wonderful that Laderic has another close friend that can keep him out of trouble," Ysmira told Midiga after she finished introducing herself. Laderic rolled his eyes, already having accepted that the two of them would bond over roasting him like a hog.

"So, how long have you known Mavark?" asked Alleria, curious about the history of the only other elf she'd ever met.

"Oh, my manners," Ysmira said. "Of course, let me give you the short version. Mavark and I met over a decade ago when I was still on my own—a renegade elf is welcome nowhere in the Far Land. His kindness got the better of him, and he decided to aid me in my search for a permanent home. As we traveled, we fell in love... and we decided to make our home here in Strita. We got engaged, and then he encountered Prysmi, and our whole life was turned upside down." She smiled as fond memories of the past bubbled up to the surface. "Of course, it was quite strange when he started growing wings and a tail, but this didn't change my love for him." She looked at Mavark, who took her hand. "We married shortly after, with Prysmi as our witness. We have been together ever since."

"So, do you travel with Mavark when he takes jobs?" Midiga asked.

Ysmira nodded. "Occasionally, but recently, I haven't. My

real passion is collecting knowledge about elves and their—our—mysteries." She sighed heavily. "I hope one day to see the last elvish city in the north—Nara'jainita."

Laderic, Midiga, and Alleria exchanged glances. "That's funny you say that," began Laderic slowly. The three of them, in turn, relayed to her the reason they had come to Strita in the first place. Her eyes seemed to get wider and wider as they spoke, and so did her smile.

"We were hoping you could help us find it," Alleria finished.

Ysmira stood from her seat, pacing back and forth for a moment, muttering to herself. She paused, opened her mouth as if she were going to speak, then shook her head, and kept pacing. Finally, she sat back down. "Of course, I'll help you," she confirmed. Alleria breathed a sigh of relief. "However, as of now, I know nothing of the lost stronghold's location other than what you know."

The table grew silent, the travelers feeling dejected. Alleria frowned, feeling her cheeks get hot, but before she could get too upset, Ysmira continued. "However, all hope is not lost. I'm sure you have all heard of Ewa'jainito?" They nodded, recalling the story Emery had told them of the mountain city. "My next excursion was going to be there, though the city is infested with all kinds of mythical creatures that don't take kindly to intruders. However, you say you can use magic, and your eyes change color... and you are an alamorph."

Alleria nodded, confused about what those things had to do with anything.

Ysmira smiled, folding her hands on the table. She took a deep breath, launching into a lecture. "The major elvish cities are spread out across the Far Land," she began. "Ewa'jainito, the mountain city; Kaina'jainito, the ocean city; Oru'jainito, the desert city; and of course, Nara'jainita, the ice capital. Hundreds of other cities used to dot the Far Land, but their names have been lost.

"Each of these major cities has many things in common, the most important being the treasure rooms, only accessible to other elves. In fact, they require elvish *blood* to open their doors. Most artifacts found in these rooms have been pillaged and stolen, since any old thief could come across an elf, take some blood, and use it as the key.

"My previous explorations and research have led me to believe that, inside of Ewa'jainito, there are quite a few of these containers only accessible to royalty, requiring the blood of a member of the royal family to open. I believe there may be an ancient map of the Far Land located there, as well. Each major city had their war plans locked up tight so only a select few could view them, and I am positive there is a strategy map located *somewhere* in that city. That map would be our key to finding Nara'jainita."

They sat in silence for a moment, comprehending. Reia actually spoke up first. "But... wouldn't that require someone in the royal family to open the boxes?" she asked.

Ysmira's eyes shone with excitement. "This is why I have put off my expedition. But now, I feel preparations may be in order." Her eyes drifted toward Alleria.

There was a long pause before the pieces fell into place. The young elf was shocked, as everyone in the room had turned to stare at her. "*Me?*" she asked, balking. "No... No way! No, you're definitely wrong," she sputtered. "How could you think that?"

Ysmira shrugged, her eyes still twinkling. "I have studied elvish history significantly. One of the most notable traits of female elvish royalty is their color-changing eyes and that they are alamorphs." Her eyes glanced over at Reia. "The fact that you may have royal blood in your veins may be one of the reasons you are able to use magic and others are not, but that's just a guess. All of this is a guess, really, but it's the best we have to go on—and I think it's our only chance of finding Nara'jainita."

Alleria stared, mouth gaping, trying to process this new piece of information.

I just found out I'm an elf last week, and now I might be royalty?

Mavark interjected into their conversation. "This is wonderful news and will be good information to go from—*if* we survive the next few days," he said darkly. "We need to spend the next day and a half preparing the town for the imminent attack. We don't know how long we have until they strike, but we need to act now. If what Elwyse said is correct, a mix of canidae and nightwalkers could be here in three days or less." He stood from the table, kissing Ysmira on the head as he passed her, heading out the door. "I'm going to take the necromancer to the jail for more questioning. You should all get some rest. Tomorrow we start our preparations. We need you at your best."

After Mavark left, Ysmira showed the tired travelers to their beds. It had been over a week since their stay in Acrosa, and so much had happened in a short amount of time that it was hard to comprehend, but this night was not for comprehension. It was for rest. Even Emery slept in a bed, sharing it with Alleria and Reia. Midiga and Laderic passed out in the same bed in another room, too exhausted to even talk. Midiga swore she was asleep before her head even hit the pillow.

It was a good night's rest for the group, and they were welcomed with a hot meal the next morning, cooked by Mavark and Ysmira before they woke up.

Each of them slowly rose with the decadent smell of eggs, roasted tomatoes, and glazed ham. Breakfast began jovially, but as the food disappeared from the table, so did their sense of humor. The shadow of the events to come had settled over them until they were practically silent as they cleaned up their plates.

"ELWYSE IS IN the jail to the east, there"—he pointed—"nearly touching the foot of the mountain," Mavark explained. They had left the house and had gathered in his front yard, overlooking the village for the first time in broad daylight. "If any of you wish to speak to him again before this all goes down, you are welcome to. I will ask that you do not lay a hand on him." That last part was directed at Laderic, who continued to stare down at the jail without making eye contact with Mavark.

"I also ask that you each, please do your best to spread the word and warn the citizens. We will be encouraging the elderly and children to evacuate on the boats out to sea for a few days. All that can fight will be encouraged to prepare. This isn't the first time a threat like this has arrived at Strita's doors, and it won't be the last." He paused, pondering for a moment, before speaking again. "I will say, though... please refrain from telling them exactly *why* we will be attacked. I don't know how they might react knowing that the nightwalkers and canidae are only after a prisoner and a renegade elf. I worry that they would sooner turn you over than stand and fight. Simply tell them that the word has come from Mavark, and you don't know many details, only that they must flee or fight."

Everyone else nodded except for Alleria, who looked conflicted. She crossed her arms over her chest. "Would it... not be better for me to head off on my own again?" she asked quietly. "I mean, I don't want anyone dying because of me..." She frowned, looking down at her feet.

Mavark was shaking his head. "Absolutely not," he assured. He thumped his tail on the ground adamantly. "These nightwalkers and bloodhungry are dangerous and would hurt people, regardless. You being here gives us a fighting chance to stop them *now*, before they can do any more damage. Look at it as a tactical advantage. This is by far our best chance."

With those words of encouragement, they split up into groups, each heading in different directions to take care of different orders of business. They weren't expecting the attack to come for at least two more nights.

Little did they know, they were wrong.

CHAPTER 19

MIDIGA AND PRYSMI headed north, directly down the hill from Mavark's house toward the town. Prysmi was in her human form—large, angelic wings relaxed on her back, their feather-like tips brushing the ground behind her as she walked. "I figure this would be a good time to show you around, as we have to go and warn everyone anyway."

Midiga nodded, taking in the impressive landscape. The mountains to the east at their right were quite imposing. At the moment, the sun—though it was on the rise—was still blocked behind the giant walls of rock. It wouldn't be peeking over the peaks until near midday. For now, beams of light shone over the mountaintops, framing them in a glittering halo.

Prysmi wrung her hands, a bit nervous as they walked. "I also wanted to introduce you to our fletcher," she began, and Midiga's ears perked up. "I know him personally—he and I get along much better than most other people in town. He doesn't seem too afraid of dragons."

"Would he... have a bow that I could use?" Midiga asked.

She had been worrying nonstop about having to fight this battle without her weapon. Prysmi nodded, and her heart soared, picking up her pace with new energy. "Let's go then!" she whooped, breaking into a run.

Prysmi smiled broadly, pointed teeth glinting in the sunlight, picking up her pace, as well, until they were racing each other to reach the outskirts of the town.

ALLERIA AND REIA hung back at the house, watching as their friends headed down into town. Midiga and Prysmi were laughing and teasing each other, which made Alleria smile. *I'm glad Midiga got over her fear of dragons.* She watched them, almost jealous of how close they had become in such a short amount of time.

Mavark headed off on his own, taking flight on his own wings, soaring down the hill quite majestically. Alleria watched him, *definitely* jealous this time. *I wish I could fly... Maybe Prysmi would let me ride in her saddle one time. Wait, is that rude to ask?*

Surprisingly, Laderic and Emery had paired up, talking seriously about something as they made a beeline toward the jail. *Of course, Laderic wants to talk to Elwyse again.* She was pleasantly surprised that he was going with Emery, though, and this made her heart happy. *Everyone is getting along so well.*

Nevertheless, something was keeping her from heading down with them. Reia, by her side, looked up at her, confused. "Is everything okay?" asked the kitsune.

Alleria frowned, looking back toward the house where Ysmira had gone back inside. "I–I'm not sure. I think I'm just a bit overwhelmed from yesterday. I–I think we should stay and talk with her for a while."

Reia nodded in agreement. "I think that would be good for

you. I'll come with you. I'm interested in learning more about elves, too!"

That was the only confirmation she needed. Alleria turned and walked back toward the house, wrapped up in her own mind. *Now that I'm finding out so much about my people... all I want to do is learn more.* She turned the handle, opening the wooden door to find the other elf handwashing dishes in a sink.

When Ysmira heard the door open, she turned, and her golden eyes lit up at the sight of Alleria. "Please, come in!" she said warmly, her voice as welcoming as the cozy house. She turned back to the sink, continuing to scrub the dishes from breakfast. Alleria quietly shut the door behind her. Reia ran over and jumped on a kitchen chair, sitting up straight with her face barely reaching over its surface.

Alleria sat down at the table as well, debating on what she wanted to ask, realizing suddenly that she had a million questions. It was overwhelming, and she couldn't decide where to start. *Just say something—*

"Could you... tell me about elves?" she blurted, instantly feeling embarrassed, and annoyed with herself that she couldn't have come up with a better question. For some reason, she felt tears brimming in her eyes.

Ysmira whirled around, like a child being tempted with some candy. "*Could I?*" she repeated, voice rising in pitch with excitement. "Why, young girl, you've come to the right place."

LADERIC INSTANTLY BEGAN marching down the hill, heading directly toward where Elwyse was being kept. He didn't expect Emery to join him, but he didn't argue.

"What are you gonna ask him about?" Laderic asked Emery as they walked together—well, he walked—Emery zipped along, flying at shoulder level, animated as ever.

"I'm just coming along for, you know, information," she said unconvincingly. Laderic eyed her incredulously, and she sighed. "Okay, okay, I'm curious about the bloodhungry canidae, and their connection to the nightwalkers, and why they're after Alleria. I'm worried about her." She mumbled that last part, as though she were admitting something private.

Laderic raised his eyebrows. "Funny, that's what I was going to ask him about. For the same reason..." They continued in silence, each feeling embarrassed but for different reasons. They made a silent agreement not to pry into each other's reasoning.

It was a bit of a walk to the jail, so they were able to see some of the town before getting there. They passed a section of the market where it seemed nearly every vendor was selling fish of some kind. Surprisingly, there were no fae vendors.

"There's not a lot of foot traffic through Strita," Emery explained. "Fae usually set up their booths in major trade hubs with a lot of commercial activity, like Acrosa, Ulandyl, and Starpoint."

"Where have you worked?" asked Laderic, keeping an intense focus on their conversation so he could avoid the beckoning of the salespeople. He avoided any eye contact with them, not wanting to be sucked into their grasp.

Emery shrugged, hovering close to Laderic in the crowd. "Everywhere, really, though Acrosa is my favorite. Mostly because it's closest to Charandall." She smiled faintly. "Not like it matters. I can hardly carry my own things back and forth as it is."

"Why do you take so much with you?" Laderic asked. "Like, what is so heavy in there, for you, I mean. Bricks? Er... pebbles?"

Emery scowled, punching him in the arm playfully. "No," she began, sighing. "I carry around a lot of my sister's things... too many, really." She frowned, mood darkening slightly. "I just can't seem to let go, even physically."

Laderic felt bad for asking. "There's nothing wrong with taking your time to get over something like that," he assured, dodging the verbal bullets from another salesman. "It seems like all of us have things we can't let go of... echoes of a past that won't release us."

They finally made it out of the market. The mountain face was directly in front of them now, an intimidating presence. The jail was situated at the foot of the mountain before the incline started. It was absolutely dwarfed by the rock formation.

Emery inhaled deeply, holding her breath for a moment. "It's helped a lot though, traveling with you guys," she admitted. "I haven't really had friends since Wyndi died, and I think this has been good for me. And, well, something about Alleria too. She reminds me of my sister so much... something about her is just, *healing*, you know?" She felt her cheeks get red, glad though to see Laderic nodding in agreement as they approached the outside of the jailhouse.

"Yeah, I know exactly what you mean."

MIDIGA AND PRYSMI took their time in town before heading to the fletcher. They went house to house, knocking on doors and warning people about the attack. They took Prysmi seriously, recognizing her with equal amounts of respect and fear. Most people said few words but did not seem as panicked as Midiga expected.

"I'm surprised how well they are handling this," she remarked after they left their tenth house. All of the residents they had seen so far had been humans, and to Midiga, they seemed quite independent and sure of themselves.

Prysmi confirmed this. "Most of the people who live here are outcasts in one way or another. The sense of community in this village is stronger than anywhere else I've been." She fanned her wings a bit, catching sunlight as it began to filter over the mountaintops. "Strita is quite a strategic location and Mavark—over the years—has organized evacuation drills for exactly these kinds of situations. There's a very loose local government here, but I guess you could say he has become their unofficial leader, though he's frequently gone. It probably has to do with him being a drake alamorph—people fear him—but they also respect him, and they listen to him, so they know exactly what to do in this case. They've all done it before."

Midiga noticed later that she was right. Though they had given hardly any instructions, soon, dozens of children and elderly began to file out of the houses in an orderly fashion, heading toward the dock and loading themselves and their belongings onto the larger boats. They were to remain on the ocean for a week unless they heard otherwise. Everyone cooperated so well, it surprised the felid and made her respect Mavark that much more.

Finally, they reached the fletcher, as the sun was starting its descent. Outside, arrows in quills were displayed on a wooden porch, the arrows fletched with feathers of every size and color of the rainbow. Midiga was overwhelmed with excitement.

"These arrows are amazing," she said, resisting the urge to pick up and feel each one of them. Some were tipped with silver, others with steel. She itched to test their sharpness but kept her paws firmly by her side.

Through the windows, she spotted a wall of bows, each hung precariously on a nail to display their perfect balance. Some were long, engraved meticulously with patterns and runes in a language she didn't understand. Others were short and simple, carved from all different types of wood. Unable to wait any longer, she threw open the door, eager to begin testing them out.

The store was quite small and more than a little cluttered. It was square with a long counter along the back wall. Another door was behind the counter, covered with a black cloth, likely separating the fletcher's work area from the rest of the shop.

Prysmi followed behind, finding it adorable how ecstatic Midiga was about getting her new bow. Though she preferred her natural weapons herself, she understood the bond a warrior has to their weapon of choice. *It must have been difficult for Midiga to lose her bow,* she thought. *I'm glad I can do this for her now.*

Midiga was marveling at the bows on the wall, eying a few of the longbows in particular. Prysmi watched her, quiet, but taking notes in her head. They were there for a few minutes, admiring the fletcher's work, but there was no sign of him.

"Hello? Burlo?" called the dragon after a while, scanning the store. She heard some clamoring from the back of the shop, and she smiled. Midiga couldn't wait, her tail whipping back and forth from the energy building in her core. This energy vanished, however, when she saw the fletcher come through the door.

Without a word, Midiga turned and stormed out of the shop.

"Midiga?" called Prysmi after her, confused, and turning to follow. "Just a second, Burlo," she told him, exiting the shop behind the felid. Before she could even get a word out, however, Midiga rounded on her.

"A *canid?*" she exploded, jabbing her clawed finger toward the dragon.

Prysmi was confused. "What? He—yes... Is there a problem?"

"What do you *mean* 'is there a problem,'" Midiga hissed. "You expect me to buy a weapon from *him*? Canidae can't make bows—everyone in the Far Land knows at least *that* much. I should have known from that shoddy craftsmanship I saw outside—"

"You said the arrows were amazing," interrupted Prysmi, narrowing her eyes. "I'm not sure what Burlo being a canid has to do with anything. You need a weapon, and—"

"I wouldn't be caught *dead* with a bow made by a canid," Midiga sneered. "And I can't believe you would try to get me to buy one from him! To give him my money? Don't you know what canidae are capable of? I mean, they're the ones trying to kill us!"

Prysmi was taken aback. "Those are bloodhungry... Not all canidae are killers," she countered. "How can you think that?"

Midiga whirled around once again, stalking back toward Mavark's house. "You know nothing," she said darkly, shaking with anger. All she could see was red. She began to run, leaving Prysmi behind her.

Prysmi was absolutely stunned. And, beneath that, she felt quite hurt. Tears sprung to her eyes, both of sadness and anger, and she dashed them away with the back of her hand. *How... What just happened?* She couldn't believe how instantly racist Midiga had turned after Prysmi thought she had gotten to know her so well. *Something terrible must have happened to her... but that's not an excuse.*

With a heavy heart, she turned around, heading back to Burlo's shop to apologize.

ALLERIA AND YSMIRA had done nothing but chat the entire day about everything from elvish cuisine, culture, language, and history. The young elf soon felt as though she should have been taking notes, as it was almost too much information to take in.

They sat on the front porch now, relaxing in handmade rocking chairs (courtesy of Mavark) and drinking homemade tea. The sun was setting, and Alleria could distantly make out quite a few large boats leaving the harbor and heading under the mountain, out to sea.

"I have another question, and I don't want to sound stupid,"

Alleria began. Ysmira waved her hand as she took another sip of tea.

"What did I say earlier? There are no stupid questions." She smiled, reaching out and touching Alleria's shoulder.

Alleria took a deep breath. "Okay, why is your skin so dark?" Ysmira was quiet, and Alleria hurriedly continued. "I mean to say, I've just always heard—at least from Midiga—that elves are fair skinned, light hair… You know, like me."

Ysmira thought for a moment before responding. "That is a common misconception about the appearance of elves. Yes, we are beautiful, but what does that entail?" She frowned, eyes unfocused as if she were watching something unseen. "Somehow, in the last thousand years, the definition of beauty has translated to be only fair skin and light hair, which is where that stereotype comes from…" She turned then to look at Alleria, eyes filled with fire. "But they are dead wrong.

"Elves have lived on this continent for thousands and thousands of years. We once had cities all over the Far Land, including far to the south, below the equator. And the people of some of our *greatest* kingdoms had skin black as night. In fact, in many paintings in the ruins that I've explored, just as many dark-skinned elves are present as fair-skinned elves. They were powerful, influential leaders who did amazing things for the Far Land. And then, as you know, they disappeared into the north, along with the rest of our kind."

Alleria was confused. "So… if there are just as many dark-skinned elves in the north as fair skinned elves, why do people think elves are *only* fair skinned?" She frowned, stroking Reia in her lap, who was fast asleep. "I mean, wouldn't there be dark-skinned renegade elves like us? You're the only other elf I've seen before, but I feel like there can't be many renegade elves out there with olive skin like yours or darker if this stereotype is so prevalent."

Ysmira was nodding as Alleria spoke. "I know what you're

saying. In fact, I've traveled all around the Far Land—this was years ago—and encountered many renegades. You are correct in your assumption. I was by far the darkest skinned elf I met." She sighed, looking up at the sky. "I just wish I knew what happened to all of them! My memory was wiped, as yours was too. I don't know if we'll ever know the truth until we reach Nara'jainita."

They were quiet for a while, listening to the peaceful ambience of the farm. The wind gusted down the mountainside, bringing with it the smell of the sea just over their ridges. The horses behind the house whinnied as they socialized with each other. Birds in the surrounding forest sang their hopeful songs.

Alleria had finally gathered the courage to ask the question she was most curious about. "Why do you think I'm royalty?" she asked, feeling scared all of a sudden. "That doesn't seem like me at all... How can you seem so sure? I mean, I'm sure other elves are alamorphs. And I know my eyes change color, but how can you be sure other elves don't have that too?"

Ysmira's eyes drifted to Alleria's eyes and then down to her hands. "Isn't it obvious?" she asked slowly. "Your magic."

Alleria frowned. "So, elves can't use magic normally, right? Like, you can't?" Ysmira shook her head. "So, only royalty could use magic?" But Ysmira shook her head once again. She sat up straighter, leaning forward on her knees, staring down toward Strita, her eyes misty and unfocused.

"Over the years, I've collected a variety of texts from elvish ruins across the Far Land. They are written in elvish, of course, a language I've had to teach myself, yet has come naturally to me. Perhaps it is in our blood. In any case, my research has led me to believe that *all* elves could use magic before their disappearance. How they lost that ability is still unknown to me." She took a long sip of her tea, which was starting to grow cold. "It's not the fact that you *can* use magic that has brought me to my conclusion, but it is the *way* your magic manifests.

"Elvish magic was unique back then, as it was almost

identical to modern-day light-bringer spectrals in that it is energy-based. However, in elves, the magic would take on a color representative of that elf's aura. So, there was a *rainbow* of spellcasters once upon a time, and not only were the colors different, but the way the magic manifested itself was different, as well. You had magic coming out like a wave, magic flowing like water in tendrils, and even magic taking the shapes of animals as it presented itself.

"*Your* magic intrigues me for two reasons—one, its color is white, a combination of all spectrums of light. This coloration was well recognized and documented by elves to be indicative of royal magic. The monarchy of the elves was heavily rooted in religion, with elvish queens and kings believed to be the living incarnate of Dietha and Bathur, the elvish gods themselves. The two were often depicted in paintings and murals as collecting the colors of magic from all elves and distributing it back to the people as bright, white light.

"The second reason for my assumptions is that your magic manifests itself as *orbs* of light. I'm a little less certain about this part, but in all of my research, the only elves using spherical magic were royalty, specifically the ancient queens.

"This, along with the fact that your eyes change color—a trait possessed by the last known elvish queen, Ophelina—has made me almost completely sure that, while you may not be directly related to the king himself, somehow, someway, you are connected to the elvish royal family."

She paused, allowing this to sink in for a moment. Alleria appeared a bit overwhelmed but now less skeptical about the situation. "I know this is a lot," Ysmira admitted, "but you may be the key to both of us discovering the truth about our heritage."

She frowned then, turning away, her eyes darkening. "However, I will say, the more I've looked into things, the less sense it makes. Why did the elves suddenly abandon their cities for Nara'jainita? What happened to Ophelina? Why did elves suddenly lose their ability to use magic? Where are the elves from the southern kingdoms? There are too many questions... and I fear we may not like the answers."

ELWYSE HAD SPENT most of his time staring out the single, tiny window in his cell, memorizing how the sky looked so he would never forget again.

The color had started to come back into his face—slowly, but surely—since he had come back to the surface. Surprisingly, the drake alamorph and the rest of his captors had made sure he was eating well... *after* punching him in the face. He already felt healthier, his shape beginning to fill out once again. He could still see his ribs, but they didn't protrude from his skin as they had when all he was eating was whatever he could catch using his undead army.

I will never *go underground again,* he promised himself. He sat on his cot, stroking Odie, who was, for once, calm. As the day passed, he noticed Laderic and the fae woman through the window approaching the jail. He sighed, preparing himself to answer more questions, as they had promised before to interrogate him further.

Laderic spoke to the guards, informing them that he was there with Mavark's permission, and they allowed them in. Elwyse was being kept in a separate room from the rest of the prisoners. Laderic was informed that he was wearing bracelets and anklets laced with *levinium,* or ward stone—a rare mineral used to weaken magic power.

Elwyse knew this but didn't care, as he had no interest in using his magic. He had relied on the energy from the spring for so long, he wasn't sure he would be able to cast spells at all anymore. He sighed, dejected, resigned to simply wait for death to take him as he knew it would in these next few days, once the nightwalkers and their dogs came for him.

"Hello, Elwyse." It was Laderic standing outside of his cell.

"Just ask me what you want to know and leave me be," he muttered, completely uncharacteristic.

Laderic and Emery made eye contact. "We just had a few follow-up questions for you," Laderic began, "about Alleria, the elf." Elwyse had no reaction. Laderic continued. "You said the nightwalkers were looking for her, and we know the canidae were as well. We know they must be working together now… I guess all we want to know is why do they want to kill her?"

A memory flashed before Elwyse's eyes, of that bottomless pit, the black fire, those cold, soul-void eyes—"Caine…" he whispered, barely audible.

"Who?" asked Laderic. "What did you say?" Emery had frozen, hoping and praying she had heard wrong.

Elwyse cleared his throat, turning for the first time to look at Emery and Laderic through the cell bars. "The canidae serve the nightwalkers. I believe they are more like mercenaries. However, the nightwalkers themselves… they serve Caine, the celestial of chaos."

The room seemed to take on an immediate chill. The silence was crippling. Emery's wings stopped beating, and she landed roughly on the ground, holding her hand over her heart. Shocked, Laderic knelt beside her. He put his hand on her shoulder. "Are you okay?" he asked, concerned. She was breathing hard. When she looked up, her eyes were filled with terror.

"That's not possible," she stated, trying to convince herself more than anyone else. Her lungs felt shallow, as though she could not take a full breath.

"What? What does that mean? What's the big deal?" Laderic was genuinely confused.

Emery stared at him. "If you took *any* stock in the gods and what they represent, you would not take this news so lightly."

She looked at Elwyse, pleading. "How do you know this? How can you know for sure?"

The vision overcame Elwyse again, and he had to blink it away. "They... showed him to me," he whispered, voice shaking. Tears gathered in his eyes but did not fall.

Paralyzing fear gripped the fae woman. "But Alleria! Why does he want Alleria dead? Please! You must tell us," Emery begged, but Elwyse could only shrug.

"I don't know that. I only know it has something to do with his own well-being. Apparently, Alleria is the key to his demise in some way, shape, or form." He took a deep breath, exhaling shakily. "These nightwalkers have seen this... *demon*. They've been in his very presence. I tried to warn you before, their powers are not normal. Nightwalkers should not be able to use this kind of magic. They were using their powers to try to... *breed* more nightwalkers from the magic spring beneath Ewa'faita. But they had no success. They can shape the earth with their darkness and even conjure this consuming, black fire just by—"

"What did you say?" Laderic said, feeling a cold chill trickle down his spine.

"I said they were using their power to clone more nightwalkers, but it—"

"No," Laderic said. "That last part."

Elwyse frowned. "They can conjure black fire, something that only fire-dancers should be able to do."

Black fire. Laderic's head was spinning. He felt sick, holding a hand out to steady himself against the wall. *That can't be right. It can't be.* But logic told him otherwise. He had only thought, at first, that these nightwalkers were simply another group of spectrals causing trouble. Not that they were the very same ones, the same ones who—

"Emery, we should get back," he said, monotonous, interrupting his own train of thought. He turned away, heading

239

out of the cell as if he were fleeing a monster's presence.

"But, Laderic, I still have more questions! You can't leave now!" she called, pleading with him to no avail. "Laderic!"

But he was already gone.

MIDIGA HAD LOCKED herself in the room she shared with Laderic. She couldn't bear to face anyone after her outburst. An internal conversation thrashing in her mind was ripping her apart:

What is wrong with me?

Nothing, you did the right thing.

But Prysmi is right, it didn't matter that it was a canid.

Yes, it does! They're all murders. They can't be trusted—

There is no possible, logical way that all canidae are untrustworthy!

Yes... They killed Dad...

That doesn't mean all canidae are bad!

They tried to kill you before... They're coming for you now... You can't trust any of them!

Suddenly, there was a brisk knock at the door. Midiga's train of thought paused, and she snapped her head toward the door, heart pounding in her chest. But there was no voice, no follow-up knock. Slowly, she stood, unlocking the door and peeking outside.

On the ground, tied together with a thin piece of cloth, was a glistening new longbow and quiver filled with arrows. The bow was black, etched with beautiful carvings of soaring birds and leaping deer. Its polish shone even in the darkness of the house. Lying on top of the bow was a letter, written in beautiful cursive handwriting:

Midiga,

Though I am upset with you, I also want you to be safe. Take this bow and use it well. Though it was fashioned by a canid, I can assure you, on my life, it is of the highest quality.

I have not known you long, but I am still very upset by what happened today. My soul is aching. I know that this is not who you are, deep down. Something must have happened to you to make you feel this way, and I hope that one day, you'll talk to me about it.

Your friend,

Prysmi

The tears came then, as she finished reading the letter, stroking the bow in her lap with tender love and admiration. She sat on the bed, holding her face in her paws. Tears slid off her whiskers, wetting the letter with her sobs.

"I will," she whispered into the darkness.

"I will."

ALLERIA LAY IN bed that night, unable to sleep a wink. Reia was fast asleep beside her, twitching ever so slightly in her dreams. Emery hadn't returned from Strita.

Royalty... It was hard to comprehend. And she still couldn't shake the ominous tone of Ysmira's voice at the end of their conversation as she had spoken about the elvish kingdom of Nara'jainita. *Why can I use magic if the others can't?*

And the gods, was she somehow connected to them? It was all too much to think about, though she was unclear about her own fate, one thing was certain—she *had* to help Ysmira uncover the mysteries of their people. To uncover the truth. Too many things just weren't adding up.

I guess now after all this is over, we'll head to Ewa'jainito and try to find that map. She wondered for a moment what would happen if Ysmira was wrong. What if she didn't have royal blood? What if they couldn't find the map? Where would they go? What other leads would they have? She sighed, rolling on her side in bed and clutching Reia to her chest. The fox was warm, helping to soothe her thoughts. She kissed Reia's soft head, closing her eyes.

Whatever happens, I will *discover who I am,* she decided, feeling sleep beginning to overtake her.

I will.

EMERY FOUND LADERIC behind Mavark's house, sharpening his daggers on a whetstone beside the barn. The horses were skittish, shying away from him as he did so as if they could sense something was wrong. He was deep in thought, jumping with surprise when Emery touched his arm. He grabbed his dagger, aiming it at her, before sighing with relief. "Emery, please don't do that when I have a weapon in my hand. I almost killed you."

"What was *that* back there!" the fae exploded, jabbing her finger into his chest. Laderic stood and took a few steps back, putting his hands in the air.

"There wasn't anything else to talk about. Those nightwalkers are delusional, thinking they serve some mystical entity of *chaos*." He spat the last word out sarcastically.

Emery glared at him. "I should have known you of all people would take this lightly, what, with your disdain for the gods." She spun around, starting toward the house. "I"m going to tell Alleria. She needs to know what she's getting into."

Laderic leapt forward, grabbing Emery's arm and holding her back. She jerked herself out of his grasp. "Get *off* me! Who do you think you are?"

"You can't tell Alleria," he said, pleading. He lowered his hand away from her.

"Why shouldn't I?" Emery demanded.

"She doesn't need the extra stress," he tried to explain. "I mean, *I* don't think this Caine guy is that big of a deal, but I don't know everything." It was as if the words were poisonous coming out of his mouth. They tasted bad on his tongue. "If he does turn out to be a problem, we can tell her then. But, for now, that's just going to make her panic more. I mean, she just found out she's possibly elvish royalty and all that. She's got a lot on her plate at the moment."

Emery froze, debating. *He has a point.* "She has to find out eventually," she started. Laderic nodded quickly in agreement.

"And *that's* when she'll need to know. But, right now, I think it would be counterproductive to give her something else to worry about. Besides, if we stop these nightwalkers in a couple of nights, she might not have to worry about the celestial at all."

"I don't know about that..." Emery warned—but she conceded. "Okay, I won't tell her, *if* you promise to tell her *before* she eventually gets to Nara'jainita."

Laderic nodded vigorously. "Of course," he lied, breathing a sigh of relief.

Emery turned back around, glancing over her shoulder before she started flying away. "I hope this is what's best for her," she warned ominously. Then, she turned and flew off toward Mavark's house. The wind gusted, droning with an unsettling howl. When it stopped, it left naught behind but silence.

Laderic sat back down on the log, sharpening his dagger again. "I know it is," he assured himself. He pulled his blade across the stone, the metallic sound calming his nerves.

He had been fantasizing about killing the nightwalkers since Elwyse told them days ago that they would be coming. But now, knowing they were the very same nightwalkers that killed his family...

I will kill all of them, he thought, gritting his teeth and pulling his blade across the stone once more. *All of them.*

The horses balked, sensing his mood, shying away from him

once again. They pressed themselves against the far side of the fence, the whites of their eyes showing as they rolled their eyes with fear.

Laderic didn't notice. His grim thoughts continued. He pulled his blade across the stone again.

Then, I will find the pale-cloaked spectral, and I will shove my blade through his heart. He had better pray to his celestial god that I don't find him—but it won't do him any good.

I will.

CHAPTER 20

THE REPORT WAS not good. It was not good at all. And Karkos was terrified of having to be the one to deliver it. As he ascended from the depths of Ewa'faita, he made grim eye contact with the other canidae in his squadron. They whined with tails between their legs, watching him exit the fort into the twilight followed by two other canidae on his left and right.

Standing outside, facing the darkening forest, stood the nightwalker captain flanked by a dozen or so nightwalkers in their usual black garb. Their cloaks were made partially from cloth and partially from darkness, making them appear to meld into the encroaching night. The captain's own white cloak shone in the fading sunlight, nearly blinding to look at.

Karkos cleared his throat. "M-my lady, Lucia," he began, addressing the pale-cloaked nightwalker. No response. "The necromancer has escaped... The spring has been completely destroyed." His voice trembled, and an involuntary whine escaped his lips.

The captain turned, deliberate and slow. The other

nightwalkers took a step back, glancing at each other in fear. She faced Karkos, holding her large, curved staff in her left hand. At the top of her staff rested her pitch-black spectral stone, glistening and sinister. "Did *he* dessstroy it? Or sssomeone elssse." Her voice was like a snake, lulling and soft, resting long consonant sounds on each *S*.

Karkos swallowed hard. "There was a human, a cat, and a fairy. A drake alamorph and his pet too. And, well, you see, we caught the elf girl's scent, as well—" He heard the captain's sharp inhale, and his voice got caught in his throat.

Lucia stood frozen for a moment. Karkos's tail was between his legs, his knees shaking. Slowly, she reached up, pulling her hood down from her head. Her ash colored skin seemed to blend perfectly with her dark hair, which seemed to be made of the shadows itself. Her eyes were pale blue, icy and piercing.

"Sso," she began, "you mean to tell me the elf you were ssuppossed to take care of monthss ago has now compromissed *our* objective."

Karkos opened his mouth, closed it, and then opened it once more to speak, but no words came out, just a small whine. His ears pulled back against his skull, he suppressed the canid urge to lie down in submission.

Without warning, Lucia raised her hand. Beneath the feet of the two canidae beside Karkos, the shadows seemed to come alive. They spiraled up from the ground, wrapping tendrils around the legs of each of his comrades. Karkos watched in blank horror as the shadows began pulling them into the ground. The canidae were screaming, their barks unintelligible as they sank into the shadows, like quicksand. It was over in a few moments, and Karkos felt a bubble of fury form in his chest—but he dared not move lest he suffer same fate.

It was over in a matter of seconds. Karkos bowed his head reluctantly, visibly vibrating with fear. "My l–lady," he whimpered, "we will get her, I swear it."

"I *know* you will," snapped Lucia, "or you will not show your face to me again." She scoffed at him, glaring at his bowed head, daring him to make eye contact. "Thiss time, I'll be ssending a few of my men with you. I can't trust you *dogss* to do anything right."

Karkos held his tongue, hard as it was. He glanced up for a moment before quickly looking back down at the ground. "You would... not accompany us yourself, ma'am?" he asked.

Lucia laughed—an eerie, chilling sound. It hung in the air, seeming to have its own weight. "You should hope I never need to do that, dear Karkoss," she spat. "Bessidess, I musst now travel north and inform Caine of the losss of this power ssource... Luckily, for you, he wass nearly done with it anyway." Karkos remained silent, and she scrunched her nose up in disgust.

"Go now, to Sstrita," she ordered, pointing at the canidae who were filing out of Ewa'faita. She gestured toward four of her nightwalker followers, who fell out of formation and joined the canidae beside the fort. "They are likely to expect our arrival if they have the necromancer. You musst travel through the night tonight. The necromancer should be taken care of, but remember, the elf iss the priority. The dark king needss her eliminated."

After another moment, she spun back around, her white cloak splaying out behind her. She raised her staff, signaling to the rest of the nightwalkers to follow her. A thick, black fog began to creep in from the trees, enveloping their cloaks and melding with their bodies. Karkos watched her leave, red eyes narrowed, but still remaining silent.

Lucia gave one last order before she disappeared.

"You attack at dawn."

247

COMING SOON

Echoes of Ashes: Pyre
Echoes of Ashes: Inferno

LEAVE A REVIEW

The best way to support an indie author is to buy their books. The second best way is to leave a review. Go to amazon.com to leave a review for Echoes of Ashes: Ember and show your support for Schmidt's work!

ACKNOWLEDGMENTS

Thanks to my friends for always pushing me and believing in me: Houston, Abby, Sarah, and Kane.

And thanks to my parents who told me I couldn't, and in doing so made sure I would.

ABOUT THE AUTHOR

JESSICA SCHMIDT was born and raised in Louisville, Kentucky. Always a passionate reader, she began writing at the age of fourteen and hasn't stopped! She is currently a senior at the University of Louisville and is working toward her bachelor's degree in marketing.

Schmidt began writing her debut young-adult fantasy novel, Echoes of Ashes: Ember, at the age of nineteen and has been exploring it and refining it ever since. Schmidt credits her mother with being her biggest inspiration and supporter. After her mother's death, Schmidt decided to publish Echoes of Ashes: Ember in her honor.

Want to follow Jessica's work?

Visit her website: jeschmidtauthor.com

Made in the USA
Lexington, KY
17 February 2018